MW00675404

FINDING THE WAY HOME

*A Collection of Chicago-
Themed Stories*

WILLIAM GEUSS

Copyright 2014 William Geuss United States

Revised 2nd Edition
Published by Backcourt Press, USA
November 2014

Cover image: Chicago skyline © Russiangal |
DreamsTime.com
Cover design by Rita Toews

ISBN-13:
978-0989914703 (Backcourt Press)
ISBN-10:
0989914704

Acknowledgements

My thanks to my wife and muse Joan Geuss, to my editor Judith Everard, to Matthew Buttsworth who formatted the Ebook editions, and to the many beta readers who provided valuable feedback and encouragement.

I am grateful to Jos van Geffen and Yura Spiridonov and to Emily Ezust for permission to use their translations of a song text by Galina Adol'fovna Galina in slightly modified form in *It Happened in Warsaw*.

This book is for my mother whose curiosity and creativity hopefully rubbed off on me.

Visit the author's website at
http://www.williamgeuss.net.

The Stories:

- Death Along the Main (a couple retires on the same day and finds that the distance in their marriage can no longer be ignored);
- *Stray Dog in New Buffalo* (an adolescent girl faces conflicting expectations in her immigrant family in Chicago);
- *Flying the Coop* (a couple resigned to the consequences of choosing careers over children gets a surprising second chance);
- *It Happened in Warsaw* (the mysterious discovery of a battered cello in Warsaw proves fateful for a musicologist of Polish descent);
- *Neapolitan Nights* (the death of her parents frees a never-married teacher to pursue her dream of traveling to Italy);
- *Distant Thunder* (a handsome Australian resurfaces in Chicago and focuses on the wealth of a vulnerable female);
- *Death Along the Des Plaines* (the claims of career and family clash as a recently widowed police officer copes with raising his young son near Chicago);
- *Beyond Buenos Aires* (budget cuts in Chicago schools and the resulting marital turmoil prompt a couple to escape to Buenos Aires over Easter break);
- And in *Dumpster Days*, a novella, a young translator chooses Chicago to find his place in the world in this coming-of-age story.

TABLE OF CONTENTS

Death Along the Main

Spring daffodils in Chicago cope with rollercoaster temperatures by simply waiting, sometimes well into April. For the past fifteen years, this unpredictability had tested Harriet Hahnemann's ingrained need to anticipate and plan in detail, qualities which accounted for her success as a meeting planner for a national medical society on Chicago's north side. Nevertheless, today would be her last work day; then retirement—and what to wear and what to pack for business trips a thing of the past.

As she walked to her office through intermittent drizzle past beds of daffodils with cautious hints of blossoms to come, she thought: after all, this is Chicago. Silly to expect a tiger to change its stripes—or Robert either, for that matter, and she wondered if during their summer ahead in Germany she would miss the press of planning and her husband would miss his newspaper deadlines. This was his last day too—that much they had agreed upon after twenty-five years of marriage.

But when had they last gone to the same place at the same time? Robert's assignments for the Sun Times had taken him to Europe while Harriet's work took her to domestic destinations. It must have been back when they were raising Libbie. Since her death sixteen years ago, they had frequented the same airports more often than the same apartment—lives somehow in sync, but parallel.

Harriet finished her final day at the stroke of five and went down to the conference room, briefcase in hand. It contained the few personal effects she kept in her office—foremost, the photo of Libbie on her eighth and last birthday that each of them had on their desks at work. She entered and saw the staff of six gathered for wine and cheese and the obligatory send-off cake.

Stella spotted her first and said, "Hey, how does it feel to be heading some place besides a madhouse meeting?"

Harriet raised her eyebrows. "I haven't had a chance to think about it yet. I just finished documenting every detail for the next two years' of meeting so the next person can hit the ground running." Looking around at the familiar faces, she admitted, "Frankly, I am ready for a break."

Noting the signs of fatigue around her eyes, Stella said, "Hate to say it, girl, but you look it," and handed her a glass of white wine.

Harriet took a cold sip and felt the tension in her shoulders ease.

"I am so sorry we haven't talked lately," Stella continued. "I don't even know what's on your calendar after this." Glancing over Harriet's shoulder to the door, she said, "Oh, here comes that globe-trotting husband of yours!"

"Today was his last day, too, and tomorrow it's off to Frankfurt—together, for a change." Getting on that plane, she thought, will be like walking the plank; but at least we'll be holding hands when we jump ... maybe we'll still remember how to swim.

"Hello, dear," Robert said, as he shook his umbrella and put it in the stand.

Turning to Stella, he said, "Hi Stella, how is she holding up?"

"Just this last meeting to get through but she didn't have to plan it."

"That's right, Robert, if I'd had to do it, this party would have been a sorry affair."

"Well, the sendoff I got at the paper wasn't much different from the usual drinks after a deadline. This looks more like the real thing."

As her colleagues approached to wish them well, Harriet felt the tension return to her shoulders as she realized how unsure she was of what came next.

She looked at their faces. Stella was the one she knew best and her hug the most heartfelt. Would she remember what they all looked like in six months? During her fifteen years at the medical society, contact had been limited mostly to planning sessions in the office between her visits to venues and meetings. She sometimes regretted that it was not easier for her to escape her head and open her heart. And now it was too late.

"Well," Stella said, "This is special. In real life you don't often get to see a couple ride off into the sunset together."

Like Harriet, Robert had reservations. If we hadn't accompanied each other a time or two after Libbie died, he thought, I wouldn't have a glimmer of hope it's possible to find our way back. Once, he had gone along to Miami to explore its Cuban culture while Harriet managed a meeting. On her free night, they happened onto a Latin dance contest at the hotel next door and snuck in to watch. The exciting marimba and drum rhythms together with Cuban rum drinks soon melted away the rough edges of their estrangement, and it was late, after rare, highly charged lovemaking, that sleep finally claimed them.

Stella's voice brought him back: "Do you think you'll miss the paper, Robert?"

"One thing is for sure," he said, smiling at Harriet. "I haven't covered a story like ours before—but I will have help on this one."

"Time to go," Harriet said. "Everything at home is ready and tomorrow we fly." She took him by the arm and, amid 'goodbyes,' they walked out together.

Several days later and seven time zones east of Chicago, Robert and Harriet Hahnemann sat on a bench along the Main River in Frankfurt and watched a little girl on a two-wheel bike pedal past. Spring was late again in Germany as well but further along than when they had boarded the plane after their retirement parties. Traveling to an apartment near Frankfurt for the summer and reaching this bench along the river had exhausted their ability to plan. If the message across the cake they cut had read *What's Next?* instead of *Congratulations—Well Earned* it would have spoken directly to what each of them wondered.

To their relief, the sun shone on the fresh green pastels of new leaves and grass with enough force to bring Germans outdoors and provide the couple with distractions. Beyond the walkway used by pedestrians and cyclists, boats on the Main River, still gray with swift spring run-off, moved past. Both Robert and Harriet hoped the sun reflecting off the water would restore their depleted batteries enough for them to embark on this unfamiliar phase of marriage.

Noting the rapid tempo of the child as she pedaled away, Harriet said, "Robert, look how steady the little one is already without training wheels. Do you remember how you had to run along and guide our Libbie that spring until she could ride alone?"

"I do," he remarked absently as he watched a tour boat moving downstream. He wondered where the boat's passengers were bound and envied them the certainty of their destination. He refocused on the tyke speeding along the walkway and said, "It took Libbie forever to get that steady."

A sharp blast of the boat horn warned a crew sculling away from the boat club across the river and reminded him how quickly unexpected events could change things. Libbie had been struck by a car as she walked her bike on a crosswalk.

Fifteen yards behind the German girl, her parents trailed with a stroller holding a younger brother. Both Robert and Harriet had wanted only one child but when she died, they did not have the heart to try again. Each still wondered if the other had similar regrets about that decision.

Just then, their attention was drawn to an emaciated, shabbily-dressed man with head shaven. He carried a blue backpack and limped slightly as he made his way in the opposite direction. He was ranting something with an East European accent that sounded like: "roust you around, just like the rotten bulls." The tails of his open shirt flapping in the wind from upstream lent a comic air to his ominous figure.

The little girl steered around him, wheeled to one side, and pulled up to gaze across the lawn where a police car had stopped. Two officers got out and bent over a prone figure in the shade.

"*Aufwachen!*" said one and, noticing a salmon-colored *Financial Times* newspaper next to him, the officer bent down and tried English: "Hey buddy, we want to see if you are OK."

"Yes, and we need to see your papers too," his partner said. "*Ihren Ausweis, bitte!*"

When the body did not stir, the first one said, "*Moment*, Fritz, ich glaube nicht, dass er aufwachen wird."

"*Oh, Mann*, you mean we have another stiff here?"

„*Ja—wahrscheinlich Drogen oder Selbstmord.*"

"I'm betting suicide—it was drugs the last time."

"You take a look around, and I'll call it in."

Robert and Harriet noticed the little girl point at the blue police car when her parents caught up with her. Two matronly women strolling in the opposite direction also paused and craned their necks to see what was happening as the warning wail of a Martin-Horn approached in the distance. Soon, the ambulance threaded its way through traffic and silenced its siren as it descended to the roadway along the Main quay and was met by the taller police officer.

The second officer walked over to Harriet and Robert and heard her say, "Well Robert, it looks like excitement follows you, even when you try to get away from it."

Spotting a *Herald Tribune* on Robert's lap, the officer addressed them in English. "Excuse me, sir. We found someone in trouble over there under that tree and want to know if you noticed anything going on while you were sitting here and how long you have been here."

Robert glanced at his watch. "I'd say about a half hour; we were just on our way back to the station to get a 12:30 train." He turned and said, "Nothing in particular struck me. Did you notice anything, Harriet?"

"No, Robert, just the people walking by—maybe that disheveled man who sounded so disgruntled?"

After the officer took a description of the man, Robert as a retired reporter knew what came next. "I need to ask your names in case any other questions come up," the officer said, and wrote: "Robert and Harriet Hahnemann" along with their address in Idstein, a small town about twenty-five miles distant, and their contact number. Then he moved off to question others seated along the river on benches or lying on blankets farther downstream.

While Robert was relieved not to be on assignment, he couldn't resist a glance towards the small group of police and emergency personnel who had lifted a still figure onto a stretcher and begun loading it into the ambulance. He wondered if he and Harriet might have missed anything because of jet lag from the flight over. Perhaps something would occur to them in the night, like it sometimes did with day and night so topsy-turvy the first week or so.

As they walked back to the Hauptbahnhof for the train to their summer rental in Idstein, Harriet said, "Oh, Robert, I really am relishing the prospect of doing everything we never had time for—music festivals, museums, wine festivals, outdoor cafés, and, like today, simply strolling along the river."

"Me too," he said. "Today was a good start ... I just hope we don't over program ourselves—that would spoil it for me."

"We'll have to work on not working too hard at it," she agreed.

Later, in their apartment, he lay on the raised stone bench of the hearth to soak up warmth from the fire place and doze.

Seemingly in her sleep, she called, "Don't forget to write to Libbie," from the couch where she had snipped off the reading lamp and succumbed to another wave of jet lag, a knit afghan drawn around her.

Addled, he wondered, was this still today or was it yesterday? In a way, we are time-traveling, back and forth somewhere between our future and our past, he thought, before dozing off.

In bed that night, he woke once to the steady plop-plop of water as heavy mist blew against the building, condensed and dripped onto the window sill. In the morning Harriet stirred next to him and cleared her throat. He heard a door close with a click-clack and guessed it was early, around six, and struggled to place the noise in the catalog of morning sounds other tenants made as they left the building. Judging from footfalls on the stairs and the steps heard through the open window receding along the sidewalk, he settled on the neighbor across the hall. "Must be Herr Frank. I don't see what he does in the morning—going, then coming and going again."

"He has to have his *Broetchen*," she said drowsily, "... and they have to be fresh."

"I wonder what that makes us? We buy day-old bread and eat it for a week ... we even eat left-overs." He glanced at the weather station next to the bed which registered Teutonic conditions and read: "Fifteen degrees Celsius or sixty Fahrenheit in here. I think opening the window at night may be overdoing it."

With a rustling sound, she turned under the down comforter to face him. Seeing the fluffy cover shift and rise with her hip sent an expectant shiver down his stomach. "I've been thinking of how I want to live my life in retirement, Robert," she said, dashing his hopes. "Changes I would like to make."

He knew what would follow. She was a planner and most comfortable with a concept that took her far into the future. He wondered if he was deficient in some important way with his approach to life, waiting to see and making choices as things came along. Not that he was completely *laissez-faire*. He often thought of things they might do. Most often related to reaching out to others—like inviting the young German-speaking couple over they had met at church once. But it never happened, and he realized his erratic attendance on Sunday mornings made him equally at fault that they seldom found opportunities to socialize since fatigue or travel trumped entertaining.

He suspected that the closest thing to insurance against their small number of friends dying off and stranding them in old age was to have younger friends. Hearing about young people's aspirations and dreams somehow compensated for the void left by losing Libbie and it flattered him to think that the lives he and Harriet led might interest them, perhaps even give younger people the stuff of dreams.

He was half listening when she began to outline her new routine. Though it sounded a lot like the old one, better not to interrupt and to show interest with simple questions. Sharing with each other about their separate worlds had helped bridge crises more than once during the course of their marriage. In any case, he was glad that her long-term plans included him.

They heard his phone ring through the bedroom door and he rolled out to answer. When he returned she said, "That's pretty early for anyone over here. Was it telemarketing or a late call from back in Chicago?"

His eyes told her it was more than that.

"No. It was Ulrike Hempel in Wiesbaden, my old choral buddy Dieter's daughter-in-law. Dieter was found dead along the Main River yesterday... right about the time we were sitting on that bench."

"How awful ... didn't her husband Franz die of a heart attack and her child inherit some kind of rare condition?"

"Yes, it killed Franz. You remember all that? You're handling jetlag better than I am," he said and slid back under the duvet.

"What did she say?"

"The police contacted her this morning. They want to establish the cause of death before they release his body. They said 'it could have been suicide.' Ulrike's parents moved to South Africa and she doesn't have any family here, so she called me as a last resort."

"How terrible to be alone at a time like this."

"Ulli heard Dieter say we would be here in Idstein this month and knows that I have ways of finding things out. She doesn't buy suicide and wants me to see if I can learn anything."

Harriet was silent.

"That's not exactly what we came over for, is it?" he said. "Perhaps I should stay out of it and encourage her to wait for the police report."

"Robert, he was important to you. I think you have to help her."

He realized it was something he was better prepared for than finding a way to reconnect as a couple and moved over to encircle her with his arms. Resting his cheek on her shoulder, he said, "Thank you. I said I could meet her in town today for lunch."

The road to Wiesbaden and to his appointment with Ulrike wound through hills covered in beech forest and passed pasture and cropland vibrant with spring planting; then it crested and sloped steeply down through woods and along the city cemetery.

Fully concentrated on the traffic, Robert hoped to spare himself the disapproving honks of edgy German drivers. His foreign assignments had taught him that traffic behavior revealed something deeper about a society. Here it seemed rule-bound, unforgiving, and inspired by one ideal of how an auto should be driven—as fast as possible to the next impeding vehicle which was to be followed as closely as possible—all to show that you and your car were up to the task.

After negotiating the descent into Wiesbaden, he found his way to the garage below the Marktplatz. After the automat spit out the ticket, he pulled into an empty space on the second level down.

He sat for a moment before climbing into the sunshine. They had agreed to meet at the Schlossplatz during Ulrike's lunch break. He had met her when she was fifteen when he visited Dieter the first time after their student days.

She was convinced that her father-in-law had not killed himself. But why? Families are sometimes the last to accept that brutal fact, but Robert wanted to keep an open mind about this and look at all the possibilities—murder, suicide, accident, and natural death. Yet he knew that a reporter's first hunch was often the best motivation to keep him going and he did not think Dieter's death was of his own choosing either. Sometimes his hunch was dead wrong but eliminating it got him to examine the other possibilities.

The brightness blinded him when he stepped onto the square and glanced up at the clock on the Marktkirche tower to get his bearings. Once his eyes adjusted, it told him that the wrong turn he made when searching for the parking garage entrance had made him late, so he quickened his pace through lunchtime foot traffic and entered a street that led gradually uphill.

Ulrike worked at Wiesbaden's city archives, and he was glad she had suggested they meet at the Andechs Restaurant under the Rathaus. It was on his list of places to revisit when he came, but it saddened him to remember an earlier visit with Dieter to the original Kloster Andechs perched on a hilltop west of Munich.

He stepped out of the sunshine and followed the cool, dark stairwell down to a vaulted space echoing with the clatter of china where good, honest fare and monastery beer awaited him.

A tall blonde woman in a gray wool jacket stood and waved at him from a table near the wall.

He waved back and approached. "Hallo, Ulli," he said and kissed her cheek, noting the addition of fine wrinkles around her eyes on a pleasant face otherwise largely unaltered.

"Mein Gott, Robert, wie lange ist dass her!"

He realized it had been four years since he had seen her and her daughter Katia at Dieter's sixtieth birthday party. *"Du hast recht.* It's been awhile. *Und wie geht es Katia?"* he asked.

Her face brightened. *"Gut."* Then, finishing in English, "considering"—and the strained look returned. "Katia's condition hangs over my head like a cloud. A treatment has been found in the US, but the drugs are so expensive and have to be taken for years.

We never know how much time she will have and the chances of affording treatment are just as uncertain. Our insurance is good here, Robert, but it does not cover everything everywhere."

He recalled that Dieter's Christmas card several years ago had brought news of son Franz's death; some disorder that could cause extremely high cholesterol levels and a heart attack by age thirty. "You've had a lot to deal with, Ulli," he said.

For a moment, she looked as though she would lose her composure and he quickly added, "We are so glad you called us. As I told you, we were at the river when they found Dieter, but we had no idea it was him." The waitress returned and they placed their orders for the least damaging items on the menu before moving on to the reason for meeting.

"Robert, I can't believe this was suicide because Dieter never would have abandoned us. He loved Katia more than anything, and he told me last week he expected to arrange for the money for treatment soon."

"I see what you mean. But what about natural death? Wasn't he on heart medication, like Franz?"

"Yes, Franz inherited Dieter's condition and passed it on to Katia. But Dieter was in good spirits, Robert. His doctors told him his condition was stable."

"First Franz, and now this…"

"At least with Franz," she said, "we knew what could happen—just not when." She touched his sleeve and said, "I hoped you might be able to find out more about what really happened to Dieter."

"Of course I will try. I think I still have some contacts. And, you're right. Things don't seem to add up."

"It's hard to imagine Katia without her Opa. And now I don't know how we will be able to afford the drug. It shuts off the gene that causes the problem and was just approved in the US, but it hasn't been approved here."

He knew how much he missed his own daughter, Libbie, and imagined it must be far more devastating from the child's perspective. "Ulli, have you been to Dieter's apartment?"

"No, I haven't had time yet. Once the police complete an autopsy, they promise to give me anything they found on his body. Do you think there might be something there that would tell us more?"

"It's possible. Would you like me to take a look?"

She nodded and reached in her purse and handed him a set of keys. "In case of an emergency, he had keys to our place too."

Before they left, Robert asked her about her work and how Katia liked school, and he saw the tension begin to drain from Ulli's face and realized she must manage to keep her life together only by dint of great determination.

Then, they climbed back into the sunshine and hugged briefly. When she pulled back, her eyes glistened and she said, "*Danke*, Robert."

"*Aber, natuerlich, Tschuess, Ulli. I'll call you soon ... und Gruss an Katia!*"

As he drove out of Wiesbaden and passed the shaded corridors of ornate tombs among the trees of the town's North Cemetery, Robert wondered how long it would take for the autopsy that would tell them what caused Dieter's death and determine when the burial could be arranged.

Farther along, where the road wound back down towards Idstein, he passed a sign indicating a section of the Roman *limes* or frontier wall that checked the Teutons to the north from the encroaching Roman Empire to the south, and it brought back the days spent as Dieter's seatmate on a bus years ago when they met as students on a choral tour. A friendship had developed as Dieter shared his knowledge of the European history evoked by regions they traveled through and sowed a seed that had sprouted in Robert—and inspired all of his subsequent striving. After that, Robert's life was spent waiting for opportunities to return to Europe and explore the continent his great-grandparents had left behind.

It moved him to realize how profound an effect Dieter had had on him, and he knew it would be hard to turn away at this point. Even if they found nothing in the autopsy, he would dig further … and risk telling Harriet he had another assignment.

She had walked into the town center and found that their favorite pastries were as tempting as ever and returned with one each of them. It was close to 4 p.m. when they sat at coffee in their small apartment and Harriet exchanged the remaining portion of her *Kaese-Sahne Torte* for the uneaten half of his strudel in their unspoken ritual developed as an illusory strategy to hold the line against rich foods when traveling. Alone, neither could bring themselves to leave such delicacies uneaten, so they would forgo ordering them.

"Tell me how Ulli is," Harriet asked. "And little Katia."

"I didn't see Katia. She was at school. But Ulli looks careworn. Katia needs expensive medication and Dieter expected to have the rest of the money soon."

"That sounds like a lot of money. Where was he going to get it?"

"I wondered that too. Do you suppose he got himself into something risky that backfired?"

"Then it becomes a police matter … shouldn't you leave it to them, Robert?"

"I don't know," he said and drank the rest of his coffee in silence.

When evening came and his brooding was unbroken except for monosyllabic responses to direct questions, Harriet said quietly, "Look, Robert, it's always like this when we have time together, and I really think I've had enough."

She's right, he thought. Whenever he got back from an assignment or she returned from a conference, it took time to find their way back together. But soon, he got the itch again to go after another story and left her behind before he even stepped out the door.

"If we can't talk or make plans together, I just don't see the point of being married to each other," she said.

He couldn't imagine a life without her as his safe harbor and anchor, yet something prevented him from saying so. Perhaps it was basic truthfulness. Perhaps the opposite was true—that he was more frightened of being shipwrecked together and confined to close quarters. But he knew that such flabby reasoning would set her off, send her down the path she was nosing into that led away, with the risk that there would be no holding her.

He grasped for a line to cast across and tether them together for a while longer. "You are right about a lot of that, Harriet. I see that. And I agree: We need to find a new way of going about things. Or try to find our way back to where we were ... before Libbie died."

She received this information in silence. Her shoulders drooped and her eyes glistened, but he was helpless to ease her pain, with his own now buried so deep.

"It's just that Dieter meant a lot to me, and I feel bound to help Ulli, if I can. To find out what really happened to him." He looked at her and waited for her to say something.

She struggled to regain control and said, "OK, Robert. That's more than you've told me before. Look, maybe I can help you with this. That might be a place for us to start."

"I'd like that."

She sensed his relief and continued. "For a change, we are both in the same place. We might as well be on assignment together."

"But aren't you scheduled to meet your sisters in Barcelona?"

She looked surprised. "That's right. I forgot! It's tomorrow I have to fly out."

"We still don't have a police report, but Ulli gave me keys to Dieter's apartment. Why don't you come with me to see what we can learn before I drop you at the airport?"

After a subdued breakfast together the next morning, they drove into Frankfurt and crossed over to the ancient Sachsenhausen district south of the river and found street parking near a half-timbered restaurant, the Zum Stern. They climbed to the third floor of the building next door and found Dieter's apartment. When they unlocked it, the smell of spoiled food met them. Books and papers lay strewn about, shelves were overturned and drawers opened.

"Wait here," Robert said and pushed the door fully open. He listened for a moment, and stepped inside. Without focusing on any one thing, he let his gaze slowly roam. Hearing nothing, he walked from room to room and, finding no one, called to Harriet, "It's OK. Come in and walk through the apartment. Then come into the living room."

She did as asked and joined him to sit on one of the two chairs he had righted. "I don't like this, Robert. Shouldn't we call the police?"

"Yes, of course, but what does this tell us?"

"That someone wanted something Dieter had."

"Exactly. And that they didn't get it directly from him—or he wasn't willing to give it to them. The question is: did they find it here?" he said.

"We can't tell," she said. "At least it wasn't easy to find. I'm guessing they didn't and it wasn't on his laptop. They smashed the screen and left that. They even searched the fridge and threw everything on the floor. This looks like the result of frustration."

"Let's take a look around before we call Ulli. It's up to her to make the report."

"What are we looking for—I have another hour before we need to leave for the airport."

"I would say any diary or documents or letters. And I think we need to handle everything with cloth or move things around with a pencil, so we don't destroy any finger prints the police might look for."

The next forty minutes were spent poking through the disorder, but nothing in particular turned up. Just as they finished in Dieter's office, Harriet found a letter from a bank in Luxembourg dismissing him for "a grave breach of contract."

"I wonder how this squares with Dieter saying he would have money soon for Katia's operation," Robert said.

"I don't know, but there must be some connection," she said and laid a hand on his arm. "I am sorry Robert, but I think we need to go to the airport."

"You're right." And after a moment, he added, "I wish you didn't have to."

Harriet gave him a hug. Would he miss her or was he reluctant to leave so soon? Best not to press him on it, she thought and headed for the door.

Twenty minutes later, they exited the autobahn for the airport, parked, and entered the terminal. For the first time she could remember, they were together as one of them departed and looked like any normal couple taking leave of each other.

"*Gute Reise, Liebchen,*" Robert said. "And give my love to Sophie and Maggie."

"I will. Take good care, Robert."

The two-hour flight to Catalonia was uneventful, but her cab ride from El Prat airport to the harbor-front hotel her sister had booked took almost as long. In a fever of excitement, FC Barcelona soccer fans snarled traffic with banners flying and horns blaring as they headed for a regular match in the stadium west of the waterfront. She herself did not follow any sports but envied them the sense of purpose and direction such devotion gave to their lives.

Harriet welcomed the time to decompress and called up pictures of her sisters: Sophie, younger by five years, and Maggie, older by four. Sophie, the most dashing of the three, designed women's clothing and lived with a painter in Atlanta. Maggie had worked in Philadelphia as an accountant and married late, to a surgeon.

The three of them always began their stay with some relaxation and then moved on to strolling and shopping. The first day was reserved for sessions in the hotel spa for a sauna, a cold plunge, and a massage.

As they lay back wrapped in thick, monogrammed towels, Harriet listened to Maggie tell about her decision to separate from her husband, George.

"We were arguing about something trivial when I found a funny charge on his credit card. After I pressed him, he finally admitted that he had paid a call girl during his last medical convention. I read him the riot act, and he accused me of always thinking of myself first. He said he did it to experience oral sex just once before he died."

Their younger sister Sophie propped herself up on an elbow and said, "Are you sure he doesn't have a point, Maggie? I mean everybody tries things out nowadays and maybe it's an opportunity for you two to change directions—loosen up and experiment together. By the way, did you ask him if it was really so great?"

"Of course not! If our sex life was OK for fifteen years, why do things have to change now?"

Harriet remained silent. She and Robert had reached a crossroads too but from different directions. After Libbie died, their careers insulated them from the risks of intimacy and set the parameters of their marriage. There really was no turning back for either of them, and she couldn't predict what lay ahead.

Their sex life, when they managed to find time, had become routine as well. Both of them had opportunities down through the years to experiment. She wasn't sure about Robert, but she had found that an affair returned less than it demanded. Twice in the last ten years she had indulged at conventions with interesting men, but the guilt and added pressure of fitting in a fling during her work life more than offset the excitement. It wasn't worth the trouble. Was there some other route open, if they were to continue together?

After dropping Harriet at the airport, Robert called Ulli to tell her what they found and asked her to report the break-in to the police.

"I will," she said. "Now they'll have to see that Dieter didn't kill himself."

"Did you notice any change in him lately?"

"It's strange. He seemed anxious but still confident Katia could begin her treatment. I had pretty much given up hope after that foundation for children with rare diseases, Take Heart, turned down our application. A month ago, Dieter said Take Heart was a client of his at the bank in Luxemburg and we should apply for help again."

When asked about the termination letter they found from the bank, she said, "He never mentioned it. I forgot to tell you that the police said his wallet was missing. But I do have the cell phone the police found on his body."

"That's a break. I'd like to look at that with you," he said.

He met her in Wiesbaden at Maldaner's, a coffee house centrally located and frequented by long-time Wiesbadeners drawn by the dark velvet curtains and brass-trimmed display cases crammed with pastry and cakes. The few tables outside were already full, so they went inside. He had missed lunch and ordered a piece of cheese cake without any qualms of conscience and a small pot of coffee.

"Thank you for helping me with this, Robert. It's too much for me to bear alone."

"Ulli, Dieter was important to me," he said, "and I want to do what I can."

She gave him a grateful smile and took Dieter's phone out and opened it. To their relief, it was not password-protected.

"Let's check the logs of calls made and received," Robert suggested.

Two names repeated: Friedrich Leichthand and Ernst Auerbach, the latter a German journalist familiar to Robert. "Do these names mean anything to you, Ulli?"

"Dr. Friedrich Leichthand is the director of Take Heart, the foundation we applied to. But I don't know an Ernst Auerbach."

"This is interesting. I do. He's a reporter for *Der Spiegel*," a magazine known for investigative reporting which Robert read whenever he could find it. He made note of the time of the calls and the numbers and returned the phone to Ulli.

"You better hang on to this in case the police want to look at it again. I'll see what I can learn about what Dieter was up to."

While driving home, Robert decided to start with Ernst. He hadn't seen him since they met in Switzerland covering a story about the dormant bank accounts of Holocaust victims that held millions in unclaimed funds. Traffic was heavy. It was after five p.m., always the most perilous time to be on the road with everyone rushing to get home, and it was nearly six before Robert reached Idstein.

He couldn't believe it when he got Ernst on the first try. "Hello, Ernst. This is Robert Hahnemann. The last time we talked was in Berne in 1996."

"Yes, I remember. Every so often I see one of your pieces in the *Financial Times* and some English editions of our papers here."

"Well, I've noticed you keep pretty busy too. I see yours in *Der Spiegel*."

"I'm flattered. What brings you to Germany?"

"My wife and I both just retired and came over for the summer to figure out what comes next. But the reason I called … an old friend of mine, Dieter Hempel, was found dead along the Main and his daughter-in-law asked me to look into it."

"That's a coincidence. I got a phone call from him four days ago."

"I know. She showed me his cell phone. She doesn't think it was suicide, but the police seem to."

"The papers don't print names, but when I read about it, I had a hunch it might be him, so I made a phone call and found out who it was. Sorry to hear you lost a friend. Knowing you, you'd like to know what we talked about."

"Yes. But what say we work this one together. After all he did call you first."

"OK. But I don't have much. He told me he had a big story too sensitive to talk about on the phone, so we agreed to meet. He never showed up, and he didn't answer his phone. I wasn't completely surprised to learn about his death."

"That is interesting."

"He said he worked for a bank in Luxembourg and had information he would be willing to sell."

"Well that fits somehow with something I've learned. I found a letter of dismissal from the bank for breach of contract. And his daughter-in-law tells me he expected to have money for an expensive treatment for his granddaughter soon—she has a congenital heart disorder that killed her father and maybe Dieter as well."

"He sounded pretty confident I would do business," Ernst said.

"The other person Dieter was in phone contact with is the director of Take Heart, a charitable foundation for children with rare diseases. Do you have anything on them?"

"They've been extremely successful at fundraising. It's rumored they don't score well on their mission to help applicants. And their officers live very well, but no action has been taken against them."

Robert then told him about the break-in and Dieter's ransacked apartment and the smashed laptop.

"OK. Well that gives us more. Let's dig in and check back when anything else comes up."

"Good to be working together," they agreed and hung up.

His third day in Germany had proved exhausting and Robert had reached a threshold. Crossing it would require more energy and drive than he could muster. Depleted, he was incapable of formulating any plan beyond getting some rest. While he had doubts about his ability to stay the course in pursuit of this story for Ulrike, he felt equally unprepared to mount a retirement program that would satisfy Harriet and fill his own void. He poured himself a glass of brandy and waited for the heaviness he hoped would bring sleep.

The next morning, he opened his eyes to church bells calling to early mass and it came back to him: She had left him. It was her annual get-together with her sisters. Sometimes they met on the West Coast or Hawaii for a week, but this year, since Harriet was already in Europe, they had chosen Barcelona.

The bed was cold without her. He would have to get another blanket. Pulling on a shirt against the chill, he propped up the pillows and lay back, surveying the room as though seeing it for the first time. The absence of the one person who had inhabited the same space as he for decades, whose body had warmed the same bed, somehow sharpened senses blunted by brandy the night before and his surroundings came into focus: A sewing machine on the desk, a quilted wall hanging, a bookcase with knickknacks interspersed between the pastiche of colored spines of the few books along the shelves—all seemed to take on a heightened presence.

He imagined that the perspectival lines stretching away from these objects must come together at a distant point somewhere beyond the wall he faced and he hoped that, although he had been distracted over the years by a persistent yearning to reconnect with his immigrant family's origins, he and Harriet would reconnect somewhere out there too.

He got up and raised the blinds to sunshine and swung open the window. Brisk air awakened a sense of possibilities, of new people, of new connections to fill the void. Was that what drew him again and again on these assignments?

He showered, and then organized his thoughts about the case. What happened to Dieter's wallet? Why wasn't his cell phone taken? The police would have mentioned a suicide note. If Harriet was right, the laptop didn't satisfy the burglars but frustrated them.

When Robert got back from walking into the village for groceries and a paper, he found a message on his machine inviting him to Ernst's apartment that evening to talk about things and meet friends he was having in. Robert welcomed the chance to sound out Ernst about possible bank connections to Dieter's death and to avoid a second evening in an empty apartment.

As Harriet strolled Las Ramblas the next day with her sisters, the flamboyant color and vibrant energy along the avenue failed to capture her attention. Their conversation of the day before preoccupied her. Sophie's candor was appealing, but the idea of groping to find new patterns in her marriage with Robert was as unsettling as the other extreme, throwing in the towel. While she was closer to her younger sister in many ways, was she really that different from Maggie, the eldest?

The next morning, Robert again woke slowly, unsure of his surroundings. He tried to remember who had talked him into this. A face swam up out of the foggy recesses of his brain ... but the name wouldn't pop. A voice ... he recalled her voice, low and a bit hoarse, teasing and compelling—probably easy work given the advanced state of meltdown he was in by one a.m. Next came a kaleidoscope of images, close-ups of body parts, textures, smells, motion and pressure accompanied by an unintelligible stream of groans, sighs and yelps audible over music streaming from a stereo in the background and overlaid by a pungent mix of patchouli and weed.

How had he gotten from Ernst's apartment to the one containing the bed he woke up in fully clothed? A moan and a giggle sounded nearby, and he reached out his left arm to explore the bed next to him. Empty. Again. Finding only a tangled sheet, he rolled over onto his right side and peered down blearily. Several bodies lay intertwined in a sprawl beyond deciphering by the pale light from a shadeless window. Although he had the impression that shapes were shifting in some coherent pattern of movement, it hurt his eyes to focus more than a few seconds. Since no faces emerged from this cursory scan, he collapsed back into a stupor and conceded that he might never really decipher what transpired during the previous night.

After returning home, Robert filled the day as best he could with cleaning the apartment and shopping for food to prepare a welcome for Harriet the next day. A long walk in the forested hills above town calmed him and led him to believe there were forces within and without to draw upon to redirect his life.

At breakfast the next morning, Harriet told her sisters she was flying back earlier than planned to get on with putting her own life on a new footing. To her relief, they didn't try to talk her out of it and, when her cab came, they parted in the lobby with the familiar vows to stay in closer touch the coming year.

As Robert walked to the station and caught the train into Frankfurt, Harriet's words, *I don't want to spend the rest of my days in the marriage we've had* resonated with his own thoughts. He realized that, for once, he could take the initiative rather than waiting for an assignment. In fact, the regional paper had mentioned that an exhibition of Dutch painting was opening at the Staedel Museum just across the Main River from the bench where he and Harriet had sat that morning five days earlier. When he reached the *Hauptbahnhof*, he transferred to an *S-Bahn* for the airport.

Harriet looked amazed when she saw him wave as she exited the baggage area. Her face was somehow softer and lightly tanned. When he hugged her, she felt relaxed.

"What a nice surprise," she said. "We should meet like this more often."

Robert was pleased and glad she had not needed to settle for a cab ride home. "You look so relaxed. I hope it means you're up for the rest of the surprise."

"And what is that?"

"I'm taking you to see a special exhibit of Flemish and Dutch painting that just opened at the Staedel.

Then we can lunch at Holbein's next door. Do you remember, Harriet, when we first did that fifteen years ago?"

"I do. It was your birthday, wasn't it?"

"Yes. And as I remember, you fell in love." He smiled mischievously.

"What do you mean?"

"You said, the colors made you feel alive—and you wanted to learn to draw."

"That's right. I do remember. I even took a drawing class at the Art Institute when we got home. Then I started the job at the medical society and that was the end of that."

Robert remembered her disappointment. They had often visited art museums together before Libbie was born, but it had been a long time since they had managed to be in the same city at the same time long enough to do that.

On the train back into Frankfurt from the airport, she asked him, "How is our case coming along?"

His recall of the time spent with Ernst was clear but what transpired afterwards was still a loss. "Ernst has sources with the police. He learned that they questioned the fellow we saw with the shaved head. He had Dieter's cell phone and wallet. He told them that some rough looking people showed up while he was searching what he thought was a drunk and they scared him off."

"That's something anyway," Harriet said. "I thought about it a lot but couldn't come up with anything. I think it stopped me from really getting into the sister thing. I felt like I was letting you down. And I guess I let them down too. I see what your assignments do to you."

She took his arm as they walked from the station to the museum. When they arrived, they joined the queue that wound along to the ticket booth and on into the building. Once inside, they began their visit together but soon moved through the gallery at different speeds. Harriet came back to get him to show him something she particularly liked in the next room but only after Robert pointed out details in one painting or another she had overlooked and already passed by.

It was on one such mission that she found Robert as he stood before a canvas by Breughel of a crowded sixteenth-century market place, a study of peasant humor amid tumult, shown in a riot of color.

"I would love to be able to paint like that," she said. "Do you like it?"

"Normally I enjoy his paintings but, for some reason, it bothers me." It showed a woman looking out an upper window across the square and a thief stealing from a blind man and two men dragging a young woman around the corner of a tavern.

The next morning they slept late and made love for the first time since arriving. In the middle of the afternoon, the buzzer sounded and Robert called from the living room, "Harriet, can you get the door while I pick up the newspapers? It must be Ulli dropping Katia off. Remember, she and her friend Gabriele Hartmann are going to a *Maifest* in Eltville. She'll come by for her tomorrow morning at 8 o'clock."

Harriet buzzed them in the street door below and waited while they climbed to the second floor. She took the child's hand and said, "Hello, Katia. My, haven't you grown. How nice of you to visit!" Turning to her mother, she took her hands and said, "Hello, Ulli. Come in.

After Katia went into the living room to find Robert, Harriet said, "We were shocked to hear about Dieter."

"Thank you, Harriet. This is so nice of you. Gabi said it's good for me to go ahead with the plan, since we are going to this fest every spring."

"Hello, Robert," Ulli said when he joined them. "Katia's things are here in this bag—her favorite bedtime books, a board game, and Dora, her dolly."

"Do you still love to draw, Katia?" Robert asked.

"Ja, I will put you in my pictures too ... with Opa."

"She really misses her Opa. But thanks to Katia, he still is all around us in her pictures."

After filling them in on Katia's routine and leaving a cell phone number, Ulli left to drop her car at Gabi's on their way over to the Rhine valley.

Once they had learned Katia's board game and eaten a light supper, first Harriet, then Robert sat on the edge of the sofa bed in the guest bedroom and read Katia a story.

"*Gute Nacht, Katia. Schlaf' gut, Dora*," he said and rose to leave after tucking them in together.

"I want the light on so I can read Dora to sleep," she said and, when he seemed to hesitate, pleaded, "*Bitte,*" for emphasis.

"*Gut,*" he said, "*aber nicht zu spaet.*" He left the door ajar and went down the hall to join Harriet in the living room.

By then, she had finished in the kitchen and already awaited him on the couch. Candles cast soft light in the room as he slid next to her. They smiled at each other and sat for a time in silence listening to Katia's sing-song voice in the background and remembered bedtimes long ago. Harriet squeezed his hand and said, "We still know how to do this, don't we? Maybe we can work together again after all."

"Yes. And the candles are nice, too."

She leaned against his shoulder and said, "It was so romantic in Barcelona, Robert. All outdoors is like a grand performance—everyone plays a part and is the audience at the same time."

He took her hand and looked at her. "Do you want to go there together some time?"

"That would be nice. But some of the things we talked about got me thinking ... about us: I was having a hard time enjoying Barcelona, so I came back early," and she told him about her conversation with Maggie and Sophie.

Robert didn't believe in meddling in other people's private lives, which included the lives they each had led apart from each other, and he began to think about his promise to help Ulli and what they had learned.

She noticed immediately that his mind was wandering and said, "Robert, this isn't easy. I want to talk about our future, and you aren't helping me. More of the same won't do. You just aren't listening."

Something Harriet said about people watching from balconies along Las Ramblas, while all the many dramas unfolded below them, made Robert recall the Breughel painting of the crowded market place with the woman being dragged away.

He sat up suddenly. "I'm sorry, Harriet, but something you said makes me think Ulli could be in danger. The next stop for whoever tore up Dieter's apartment, when they couldn't find what they wanted on him, would be to go after Ulli."

"We have her cell number. Do you want to call her?"

"I think I better." When several tries proved futile, he said, "I hope this doesn't mean we're too late."

"She probably can't hear the phone in all that noise. They always have loud music and everyone gets pretty happy."

"I don't like this. I would never forgive myself if something happened to Ulli after Dieter. We promised to look after Katia." He stood up. "I have to go find her."

"Maybe you're right. We can talk later."

"I'll call as soon as I know something. I promise," he said and hurried out the door.

Forty minutes later, in Eltville on the Rhine, Robert left his car dubiously parked and hurried down towards the river. The tumult of music and voices drew him like a beacon to a harbor, this one as congested as the traffic he had navigated to get there. He pushed his way into the noisy festival crowd. Young bodies, drawn from the entire region, shifted in swirls and clusters, their hearing dulled by the seductive local wine and foaming pitchers of beer as they struggled to maintain their precarious claim to the small patch of ground on which they stood.

At the smell of onions and sausage grilling, Robert's stomach punished him for eating such a light supper. He decided to penetrate to the center of the square and stand on something to give him an overview of the throngs around him. I've got to get to her before they do, he thought.

With one elbow extended like a prow to indicate his course, he forged through the surge of bodies. If that fails, I'll go to the stage and have the MC page Ulrike to the podium. That, he realized, could also draw her into the clutches of any pursuers.

Peering right and left, he pressed on and reached the center of the square with no sight of her. He paused, and then stepped up onto a table to gain a better view.

Fairgoers close by whistled and shouted, "*Hey, so was macht man nicht. Wir essen auf diesen Tischen. Herunter!*"

Robert ignored the growing chorus long enough to slowly scan 360 degrees, hoping the disturbance and his visibility would draw her attention. Just then, he heard Ulrike's name paged over the PA system and his heart froze. He jumped down, keeping the stage in view, and roughly pushed his way through the crowd in as straight a line as possible.

He reached the stage and, as he looked around, a muffled scream came from behind the platform. He circled around and caught sight of a woman being bundled away by two men; her feet drug on the ground as though she were unconscious or inebriated.

"Ulli, Ulli. Hey! Leave her alone. Help!" He ran towards them as they packed her into a waiting car.

It sped off just as Gabi came around the stage and called, "Ulli! Are you alright?"

Robert caught his breath and asked her, "Are you Ulli's friend from Wiesbaden?"

"Yes," she answered. "We came to the stage when she was called, and I left her for a minute to use the restroom. When I come back, I can't find her, and I hear someone call her name, so I come to look."

"She's been kidnapped," Robert said. "We need to call the police."

Just then, Robert's phone rang.

"Hahnemann," he said.

"Ja, I know that you are. We have the girl and she has what we must have but plays dumb. You must talk to her and convince her to cooperate. Then nothing happens to her and she goes free."

Robert realized they must think Dieter left copies of whatever leverage he had with someone and logically settled on Ulli. "OK, let me talk to her."

He heard a muffled cry in the background; then a voice near hysteria said, "Robert?"

"Yes, are you alright, Ulli?"

"Just scared."

"Have they made threats?"

"Just to keep me until they get what they say belongs to them."

"Tell me what they are looking for."

"They say I have something Dieter gave me to keep for him, but I don't know what they are talking about."

"Did they say it was information or some kind of material?"

"No, but he said they would hurt Katia, if I don't cooperate."

The pain in her voice moved him. "Katia is with us. Didn't you tell me, he gave you a card to open on Katia's birthday?"

"That's right. It's on my closet shelf."

"Well, that could be it. We have to give it to them."

"Robert, you have a key to my apartment. There's one in the set I gave you for Dieter's apartment."

"OK, put them back on."

He heard a rustling as the phone was passed, then the man's voice: "*Ja*, what can you tell me?"

"We think we know what you want and will give it to you. But you must release her then, unharmed."

"That is what our people want, too."

It was 10:30 p.m. and he was a half an hour from Wiesbaden. "I need to drive to Wiesbaden for this. Tell me where to meet you," Robert said.

"Tomorrow at 10 a.m. Send the material up the Neroberg Tram with a red ribbon on it with someone and the second tram down after that will bring what you are looking for. If we see any police, you will not see her again, and the little girl will be next." The line went dead before he could reply.

The Neroberg, the closest of the Taunus Hills stretching away to the north and Wiesbaden's local mountain, was familiar to Robert. Years ago, Dieter's father had been one of the funicular tram operators and brought Dieter and his American pal up the incline through the terraced vineyards to the top of this steep backdrop to the city. He knew that only two trams were involved—one car went up as the other came down—and he saw that the plan gave the kidnappers time to check the authenticity of the material before escaping by car or foot without being seen by him.

Gabi broke into his thoughts. "Herr Hahnemann, what is happening? What should we do? Who are the people?"

Whoever they were and whatever they wanted, they hadn't found it on Dieter or in his apartment, and it was obviously valuable enough to raise the stakes from breaking and entering to kidnapping.

Addressing Gabi, he said, "Some people connected with Ulli's father-in-law are holding her until she gives them something he had. She wants me to find it, so they will release her unharmed. They don't want any police. Can you help us by keeping Katia until Ulli is back? If everything works out, that should be by noon tomorrow, and we can report it to the police."

"OK, Herr Hahnemann. I will do this."

Then Robert phoned Harriet and told her what had happened. "I'm coming home now and, in the morning, I'll take Katia back to Ulli's. Gabi will meet us there at eight and stay there or take her home with her."

Even though he didn't know precisely what was at stake for the people behind this, he took their threats seriously. Once again, he considered calling the police. Even though they were inclined to classify Dieter's death as a suicide or death by overdose and close the case, kidnapping and threats would surely get their attention. But his instinct told him to delay calling them in and instead attempt to supply what the kidnappers were after.

At the Neroberg tram station the next morning, a group of day hikers and a small group of children heading up to an outdoor preschool in the forest kindergarten were waiting for the 10 a.m. funicular when Robert arrived. He asked their young teacher if she would hand the small package with a red bow to whoever came up and asked for it. "It's a surprise gift," he explained, "and I don't have time to take it up myself."

She readily agreed, "*O, wie nett. Das mache ich gerne,*" and herded the boisterous children on board.

Robert watched the dark yellow tram cars rise through emerald vineyards as a flight of starlings swept over on their way to forage. Three and a half minutes later, the cars from the top arrived below as the package with the bow arrived with the cars above.

He paced until the cycle repeated itself, and the tram from above returned once more. As it entered the station to dock, the silence of the hydraulic system was broken only when the doors clacked open. He watched a group of Chinese tourists disembark and chatter with their guide; they were followed by two teenagers, identifiable by their piercings and tattoos as a couple, if not by the fact that they held hands; last to emerge was an elderly woman with an ancient German shepherd dog on a leash. But no Ulli.

Frantic, he stepped up to the old woman. "*Entschuldigung. Haben Sie vielleicht eine junge, blonde Frau gesehen,*" he asked and raised a hand to indicate Ulli's height.

She shook her head, "*Nein, aber ich kann ein bißchen Englisch.*" She looked down and said, "*Setz Dich, Schatzi,*" and fondled the dog's ears when it sat heavily. "I don't see anyone like that. Are you Robert?"

"Yes, that's me," he said.

"A boy has asked me that I give this envelope to the man waiting named Robert." After looking him over, she handed him the envelope.

Robert cursed to himself but thanked her, and stepped back to make way for her and Schatzi. Of course, whoever they are, they're not to be trusted. Or maybe they're just careful. He opened it and read: "Don't play with us. A birthday card is not what we look for. Look again. We hold her until you cooperate. We call you at midday."

Robert realized that the card had been no more than it seemed. What had he missed? He drove back to Ulli's apartment and this time began to search for memory sticks or CDs.

Under a stack of newspapers and mail on the kitchen counter, he found a note Dieter had enclosed with a CD he had mailed: "Ulli, this contains precious material; photos of you and Katia and me. Please put it in a safe place." It was nearly noon.

He moved to Ulli's desk, switched on her laptop, and inserted the CD. He opened the folder named "Fotos" and saw a set of charming photos of Ulli and Katia and her Opa Dieter. It also contained a subfolder entitled "*Verschiedenes - verschluesselt.*" Clicking on it revealed a series of encrypted files and a letter in which Dieter summarized the importance of the files: spreadsheets showing Luxembourg bank transactions from the Take Heart foundation which he had copied and taken with him upon being sacked.

Robert e-mailed a copy of the subfolder to Ernst and waited for the promised phone call with further instructions.

The rapidity of what followed surprised Robert. The phone rang, and he heard the familiar voice ask him if he had the materials. Robert described the files, and they asked him to e-mail them to a nondescript address. First, he erased Dieter's letter and then sent them off. Twenty minutes later, Ulli phoned to tell him she had been dropped at the Wiesbaden *Hauptbahnhof,* unharmed. She asked about Katia, and Robert assured her that she was at Gabi's.

He swung by the imposing red sandstone train station and picked her up. Aside from her gaunt look, she seemed OK, but he asked, "Should we go to the hospital first, Ulli, or straight to the police station?"

"I'm OK," she said. "Most of all, I want to see Katia—but let's talk to the police first. I don't understand what's going on, but these people must be stopped."

The grilling they got about the ordeal during the next two hours seemed meant as much to chastise them for not reporting it sooner as to gather information. Before they left for Gabi's apartment, where Tante Harriet was filling in while Gabi was at work, the police told them the autopsy had not revealed signs of either foul play or of suicide. Dieter had died from his heart condition.

Ulli received this news with consternation, if not disbelief. When they stood at his car again, she looked at Robert and said, "All of this makes even less sense to me now than before, Robert. Will we never know what it was all about?"

He put his arm around her shoulders and said, "I don't know, Ulli, but my promise is still good. I won't give up until something comes of this."

They drove to Gabi's apartment on a steep side street in the crowded neighborhood near the Bergkirche and, after a search, found street parking. Harriet met them at the door and hugged first Ulli, then Robert. "Thank God this madness is over," she said, "and you both are safe. Gabi dropped Katia at her school this morning, and I plan to pick her up in another hour."

"Thank you, Harriet. This has been a nightmare. But knowing Katia was safe with you made it bearable. Won't you come along and pick her up with me?" Then, she called Gabi with the good news, and they decided to celebrate together at Ulli's after work.

At the school, Harriet stood at Robert's side, her right arm entwined through his left, and they watched as Katia was brought to the street door by her teacher, broke free, and ran to them, screaming "Mutti!" and gave Ulli a tearful hug.

Harriet's moist eyes met Robert's and she matched the squeeze he gave her hand. "We didn't do too badly together, did we?"

"No, we didn't," he said. "I just hope we don't get another assignment like this."

Gabi was waiting for them at Ulli's with pizza from Enzo's down the street, and they had an animated celebration.

After seeing Ulli and Katia reunited, Harriet and Robert spent the next three weeks exploring the region—as a couple or, sometimes, the four of them together. Day trips to small towns with castles and churches, often featuring a concert or a festival related to wine, or with trails through vineyards above the Rhine triggered memories each of them had banked but not shared before from their separate lives during the last fifteen years.

On pleasant days, the two of them walked in the soaring beech forests near Idstein, pausing to sit on benches as sunlight filtered down, and let the present sink in and searched their minds for threads that had broken off when Libbie died.

One morning, as they woke and lay next to each other, Harriet confessed, "Robert, I'm exhausted."

Turning, he took her in his arms.

"Maybe we really ought to go back to Chicago and try our luck there," she said.

"I expected this to take time. Why not sign up for a drawing class here? Why wait until we get back to Chicago?"

She thought it over. "You're right ... there really is no good reason to wait."

"Besides, we want to stick around and give Ulli a hand with things after Katia starts treatment." The money Ernst had given her from the *Spiegel* article they had written made it possible for Ulli to schedule the necessary preliminary examinations.

Ten days later, they found a brief phone message from Ernst: "Buy *Der Spiegel*, Robert, and read our article. And do let me know how that little girl is getting along."

They walked into town to find the magazine and sat outdoors to read the piece over coffee. It detailed the investigation into the foundation and the use of secret accounts to sequester money donated in good faith for children with special medical needs which then was hidden from German tax authorities and diverted to support the luxurious lifestyle of Herr Leichthand and his cronies—all documented by Dieter. It concluded with a reference to the ongoing police investigation of the kidnappers.

"This was really Dieter's story," Robert said. "He'd be glad to know that it ended well for Katia."

"And it's not a bad piece for your final by-line, is it Robert?" She searched his face for signs of resignation but saw none.

"You know, I've been thinking about something ever since college," he said and reached for the small pitcher of coffee to refill their cups. "I think it's time to start my career as a novelist."

"I thought you would need to keep writing," she said. "Novels may not be quite as exciting; but then, who knows?"

William Geuss

Stray Dog in New Buffalo

The first thing Ana learned after she stepped down from the bus in New Buffalo three years earlier was that there had never been any buffalo here at the edge of Lake Michigan—the prairie had started farther west, near Chicago, her point of origin. The second thing she learned soon after when she found a job at the Stray Dog Café: dogs, stray or otherwise, are never allowed in the café bearing their name. Both things had been true of every other place she had waitressed. But most important, she learned that the crush of lunchtime tourists made it easier for her to forget the past.

As her shift began on a Wednesday in late August, a light breeze off the lake tempering the heat caressed her cheek as she watched the hostess lead a frazzled-looking family out to her area on the screened-in porch overlooking the harbor and announce, "Ana will be with you shortly. Enjoy your meal."

When Ana approached with an armload of vinyl-clad menus, the family looked grateful for shade, most likely after a bright morning in the nearby sand dunes. From facial resemblances, she gathered that they were grandparents with a grown daughter and pre-teen grandsons.

She brushed her shiny dark hair back and said, "My name is Ana, and I will be your server. How is everybody doing? Have you got enough room here?"

"Yes, we're just fine," the grandfather answered for everyone. "We're on vacation. We got lots of fresh air and sunshine in the dunes this morning, didn't we boys?"

Their groans brought a smile to Ana's face as she moved smoothly around the table to hand out menus. "Where are you from?" she asked.

"Chicago," the boys replied together.

"Really? I grew up there. My mother and grandfather still live there," she said and felt her stomach contract. "But now, I live right next door," she said, pointing out the window to an apartment building facing the harbor.

"You must like it here," the boys' grandmother said with a wave towards the boats silhouetted against glinting sunlight.

Ana looked over at the breeze-ruffled water as masts shifted from side to side and boats tugged at their moorings. The motion reminded her of preparing her first step with a tango partner in her *abuelo's* dance studio. Although it had been three years since she fled the city and left dancing behind, the physical memory calmed her enough to refocus on her order pad.

"Let me tell you about today's specials," she said and launched into a short list featuring spareribs, shrimp salad, and the soup of the day. After taking their orders, she left to get beverages.

When she returned with water and iced tea, she noticed the older dark-haired grandson in his early teens absorbed by his cell phone, and she heard his mother say, "Ben, please put that away while you are at the table."

Ten minutes later, when Ana came back to refresh their drinks and tell them it would be a few more minutes, the boy's head was again bent over.

"No phones at the table, Ben, or I'll collect it," his mother said.

"But, Mom, I just wanted to see if Zach texted me back," he said, half pleading, half complaining, and took his time closing and pocketing it.

He looked up and it startled Ana. *He looks like Harry did around that age*, she thought. *And his voice is full of life, too.* "You have your own cell phone?" she asked. "Aren't you lucky? I didn't have one of those until I was sixteen. And I had to go out and dance on the street for the money."

"Gee," Ben said and gave his mom a surprised smile. "I'm glad I didn't have to do that."

"Where was that?" his grandfather asked her.

"Along Michigan Avenue. My *abuelo* is from Argentina and has a dance studio in Chicago. He was always humming tango songs and he taught me to dance, even though my mom didn't approve. To begin with, I just danced with my cousin and did it for fun."

"Cool," Ben said.

"A few years later, I wanted a cell phone too … and things got complicated," Ana said and broke off with a wistful smile. "I'll just check on your order now."

She managed to finish serving them without elaborating further about Chicago and was pleased to find a handsome tip—but the business card and note left by the boys' grandfather was unexpected. It read:

> *We have several restaurants in Chicago, and I want to develop one with a Latin dance theme. You would be a welcome addition to our staff—so keep us in mind.*

That evening, as she sat in the living room of her apartment with her new roommate, Franny, Ana told her about serving the family from Chicago. Ana's ad in the local paper had caught Franny's eye a month earlier and they liked each other immediately.

"So you've always danced, Ana—I mean since you were little? If only I didn't have two left feet!"

"Yeah, I realized today again how much I miss it … you could say it's in my blood. But when I turned fourteen, I had to get a different partner because my mother said, 'Ana, you don't do that with a cousin—tango gets too personal.'"

Franny pursed her lips as she stroked her neck where pixie-cut hair nearly hid a small red rose tattoo. "I can understand that—especially if the cousin is hot," and they shared an understanding grin.

Ana leaned back. Her eyes defocused and she said, "Well, he wasn't really. But soon, I hooked up with an Anglo who was taking classes at my *abuelo*'s tango studio. And he and I got pretty good." She gazed out at the boat lights in the harbor. "His name was Harry. And this boy today looked and sounded just like him."

"No way!"

Ana glanced back and said, "I mean it! Dark eyes, the nose and eyebrows; the same dark brown hair, cut long. And Harry was into Latin culture. He admired my grandfather … but I guess he sided more with my mother when push came to shove."

Franny waited. The nostrils of her puckish nose flared as if to scent what would come next. When nothing more came, she asked, "Well, what happened?"

Ana got up and closed the window to stem a chill breeze off Lake Michigan. Emotion began to well up like wind-driven waves, but the tightness in her throat yielded when she heard her grandfather's calming voice instruct her: *Ana, collect and prepare your next step.*

She breathed out. "My mother and grandfather were at odds over lots of things. She was carrying me when they left Buenos Aires. But, for some reason she rejected the old ways—at least she wouldn't talk about Argentina. She wanted to blend into Anglo culture and was on my case about it all the time."

"Oh, oh. That sounds familiar," Franny said.

"*Abuelo* was stubborn too—he rejected the culture here as if he'd never left Buenos Aires. And he always spoke to me in Spanish. When I got interested in tango it was like taking sides since the three of us lived together." Ana's hand traveled to her mouth and she began to nibble on the cuticle of her little finger.

Franny's comment, "That sound sticky," was rewarded with an appreciative look.

"After I changed partners, I guess we worked out some sort of truce. Things didn't come to a head until Harry and I decided to move our act up Michigan Avenue to Hancock Plaza."

"Cool idea, I know where that is," Franny said.

"My mom works there. We thought it would be good because people aren't in such a rush, and it's a great space for a dance act. That first day we had our portable sound system all set up ready for the lunch crowd when my mom came out with some coworkers."

Imitating her mother's voice, Ana said: '*What are you doing here! How could you do this to me? You know how I feel about street performers and how that cheapens you—dancing like gypsies! If you choose to stay here, don't come home tonight.*' And she stormed off."

"Oh shit!"

"So Harry and I talked it over—his Spanish is practically as good as mine—and he thought we really should respect her wishes. That was one thing he admired about the family he lived with in Buenos Aires during his high school summer exchange. He said, young people there were careful to respect their elders and sometimes it took time to work things out."

"Wow, that put you in a bind," Franny said and leaned to reach for her diet drink.

Ana continued unevenly and her voice rose: "I told him, 'I can't see that at all. *I* don't live in BA and life is *different* here. You don't always have time to work things out.' So we quarreled and people stared. I said I expected more support from a partner, if I was going to trust him in dancing."

"I don't blame you."

"He said it would be better, if we didn't try to dance today—he'd call me when he knew his next day off."

Franny winced. "What did your mom do?"

"When I got home for supper that night, she didn't say anything since we were gone when she got back after her lunch break—so I let it rest."

"Oooh, that ticks like a time bomb. What happened?"

"When Harry called the next week, I faked a cold and said I couldn't dance. He asked me how things were between me and my mom, and I told him we weren't talking. Then he said I should give her a chance to explain herself. He was clearly taking sides, so I hung up." Ana took a swallow of water and looked across at her roommate. "But here I am, going on about this. Sorry, Franny."

"No, Ana. Honest. I want to hear it. Is that why you left Chicago?" she asked and had to wait a moment before Ana managed to reply.

"When I didn't show up at the studio for the *milango*—that's the advanced tango session —*Abuelo* stopped by the next day at my waitress job to see what was wrong. I told Harry the money was bound to be way better dancing on the Plaza, but he wasn't going to do it while Mami objected. Abuelo said, 'Ana, you are wrong to treat him like this; he understands our ways even better than your mother. I have plans for you. Keep dancing and do not abandon your partner.'"

"Where did that leave you, Ana?"

"My grandfather just laughed at my expression and said, 'You have a lot of your mother in you, Ana—her drive and will. When I brought her and your uncle, Alvaro, here in 1984, I didn't know how they would adjust—in America, you have to be strong-minded. But *my* heart is still in Argentina—and that is the problem.'"

"I just wish I had gotten to know my grandfather," Franny said.

They sat in silence until Franny asked, "That's really complicated. But how did it end?"

"Her brother Alvaro went back to Argentina, and I think my mother was afraid of losing me too. She wants me to stop waitressing and to prepare for a career. That night, my mother and grandfather got into it over me". Ana rose and took a few agitated steps, before continuing. "She yelled that he was interfering, by pretending like I lived in Argentina; and he said he had no choice because she blocked out the past."

"Then he said something I don't understand: He said, 'Ana deserves to know everything', and my mother broke down completely."

She wiped a tear from her eye. "I couldn't stand having them fight over me, so the next day I took money I'd saved, packed a bag, and got on a bus for some place I had never heard of—New Buffalo, Michigan; it sounded like a good place for a new start.

I've been waitressing here ever since. And I guess I'm where I belong—at the Stray Dog Café."

Several days later, as she was clearing tables, she found a Spanish-language paper from Chicago. An article on the first page stopped her: *Tango Institute Founder Gravely Injured.* She grabbed it and scanned the short piece:

> Luis Herrera, who emigrated from Buenos Aires in 1984 and founded the Tango Institute de Chicago, is in critical condition after being mugged as he closed his dance studio Friday night on the Near West Side. He is in intensive care at Rush Medical Center.

The tray she had been balancing fell to the floor and she sat as images of her grandfather flooded her mind. Through eyes squeezed shut, she saw him glide to a tango rhythm and heard him sing its plaintive words. Her first impulse was to go to Chicago, but she realized how much it must have hurt him when she left. And she dreaded facing her mother.

After speaking with Frank, the owner of the Stray Dog, Ana ran home to leave a note for Franny: *My grandfather needs me and I don't know just when I'll be back.* Then, she hurriedly filled the same bag she had arrived with and walked to the Greyhound stop. When the bus pulled up, she hesitated.

"Well lady, let's make up our mind," the driver said. "Are you going to stay or go?" She gave him a blank look as the voices of the two people she loved most clashed in her mind.

"Well," he said in a gentler voice, "I'm leaving now, but you have time to think it over. There's another bus for Chicago through here in an hour."

The industrial landscape reeling past gave her occasional vistas of Lake Michigan as the bus sped Ana towards the city she had left three years earlier. When she first arrived in New Buffalo, she had been haunted by self-doubt and longed for her life in Chicago, a life informed by the rhythms and sounds of tango. Whenever her yearning became more intense, her only shield had been to forget, but the encounter with the family in the restaurant brought the turmoil flooding back. She had abandoned them all. Could they forgive her now?

When she reached the hospital not far from her grandfather's tango studio, it was close to 4 p.m. Her voice quavered as she told the nurse on his ward, "I would like to visit my grandfather, Luis Herrera."

Upon learning that she was family, the nurse answered, "He is still in serious condition. You can go in for a brief visit, but he may not respond because of heavy sedation. He lost a lot of blood from a knife wound and we had to repair organ damage."

Ana entered and sat by her grandfather's bedside. The near hand she took in hers sprouted tubing. Its frailty was jarring and the tangle of equipment mirrored her feelings about how uncertain the future was. In an unsteady voice, she told him in Spanish how sorry she was to disappoint him—that it would not happen again.

As Ana prepared to leave the ward, the nurse stopped her and asked, "Are you Ana? I think there is something here your grandfather wants you to have. He had this in his coat pocket when the ambulance brought him in."

Ana took the wrinkled envelope and saw that it was stamped and addressed to her with a question mark for both the street and the city. Blinking back tears, she left the hospital and crossed to a small park to a bench. The envelope shook as she opened it and read:

> *Querida Ana, si algún dia tuviera la oportunidad de te enviar esta carta, ...*

> *Dear Ana,*

>   *If ever I have the opportunity to send this letter, I want you to know that losing you weighs heavy on my heart. Not a day goes by since we last talked that I haven't asked myself what I might have said differently to keep you with us. I think your mother secretly does the same, even though she shows a hard exterior.*

>   *We have never talked with you about why we left Argentina and came to America. I hope it is*

not too late to reach you with that story. It may help you understand and make it possible to become part of our lives again.

All we told you was that we left after your father, Edgardo, died. It was just as the military regime that brought so much agony and shame to our country was starting to collapse. Edgardo was a journalist and made it his job to find out who was behind the kidnappings, the death squads, and the abduction of children.

While my own way of expressing opposition was to promote tango and give people a physical way to express freedom and positive forces, I was proud of what he did.

Your father began to dig into the disappearance of the child of a fellow journalist when Gabriela was pregnant with you, and I began to get threatening phone calls. They told me to use my influence to stop him if I did not want him to become another statistic. Many families fled Buenos Aires for the security of the countryside, so I told him he should wait until it was safer to dig and then do this job—to think of his unborn child.

One night your father did not come home. After a week with no word, the phone rang and a voice told me I had been warned ... this was what happens to anyone who digs too deep and to those close to them. Immediately, I decided to take your mother and her brother Alvaro far away to keep safe the only ones left to me.

Do not blame your mother for how she has reacted to your father's disappearance—her way has been to forget. It is part of tango culture too, to forget hurt so big that it can be borne in no other way. She has tried to root you in your new culture, to make sure you stay where you will be safe. The fact that Alvaro has returned to Buenos Aires frightens her all the more.

I wanted to name my tango school here after your father, but out of respect for Gabriella, I did not. If you do return to Chicago and take my place, as I have always hoped, I want you to name it after your father. Your Uncle Alvaro writes that tango is coming back among young people in Argentina. Time enough has now passed that Edgardo's story can be told. And he would be as proud of you as I am.

tu Abuelo

Ana sat quietly, slowly digesting this information. It helped explain what she could only guess at while growing up.

She knew her mother would not arrive home from work until later. But if she called her, how would she respond? Ana had abandoned her, was another person who had disappeared—like Edgardo.

While she waited until she could phone her mother, she thought she would try to reconnect with Harry. She still knew the number. When his mother answered,

Ana hesitated before saying, "Hello, Mrs. Stone. It's Ana, a former tango partner of Harry's. I'm back in Chicago for a while and wanted to say hello."

"Yes, I remember you, Ana. How nice of you to call," she responded. "I'll give you his number. He and his wife have moved to an apartment in Berwyn. They just had their first baby. In fact, her middle name is Ana."

Ana wrote down the number and thanked Mrs. Stone. She hung up with a twinge of envy that Harry had gotten on with his life so well. While she was growing up, she had always felt different from others. Either their families had been in America a long time or they were proud of where they had recently come from. Her own family's silence about Argentina had left a void in her that Harry's fascination for Latin culture helped bridge. She now realized he had tried to show her a way to connect both to Anglo culture and her origins. He had been her best friend.

When she reached him a half-hour later, Harry said, "I can't believe it's really you, Ana. My mother said you had called." In a more somber tone, he continued, "You must be here because of Luis. I was shocked to hear what happened."

"I saw it in the paper this morning and came down right away."

"Yesterday, when I went to the hospital, they wouldn't let me see him."

"I had better luck as a relative. But he's still in serious condition." After a pause, she continued. "He left me a letter, Harry. It helps me understand what my mother has been through."

"I am glad to hear that. You were pulled in two different directions. I guess I didn't know how to help."

"No, Harry, you have been a true friend. I'm afraid I let you down. I didn't know what else to do back then either."

"We all worried about you ... and I was angry with you." Then he continued in a softer tone. "I lost a friend and I never did find another partner who worked as well with me. I just hope that we have you back."

"Thank you, Harry. All I can say is I'm sorry."

"The main thing is you're here now. And Luis needs you."

"One thing I'd like to talk to you about is carrying on *Abuelo*'s tango school. I owe it to him—and to my father. Knowing what I do now makes me want this for myself too."

She felt lighter and said, "The tango studio has been *Abuelo's* life work—first in BA and then here. And I may know of an opportunity to somehow combine the dance studio with a new restaurant planned here."

"That sounds great, Ana. Let's talk about it. You must come over and meet Heidi and the baby as soon as you can."

"Thanks, Harry. I will call you. Maybe the baby will learn to tango one day too."

Ana hung up and crossed to a café near the park where she waited over a cup of coffee. It was after six-thirty before her mother answered.

"Hello, Mami, it´s me," she said. As she waited for a response, apprehension and yearning tugged at her in turn.

First, shocked silence—then: "Oh, my God, is it really you Ana?"

"Yes. I'm back. I visited *Abuelo* and he looks bad."

"I know. I was just there. A nurse, who came on duty, told me a young woman had come to visit earlier. I didn't dare hope it was you."

"I want to see you, Mami," Ana managed and wondered, *Am I strong enough to set my own course now? Can things be different for us?*

After a moment's hesitation, Gabriela responded, her voice husky with emotion, "I want you to come, Ana. It has been long enough. We have to talk about things that once were not possible for me."

"Yes. I think so too. When?"

"Can you come now?"

"Yes, it's time," Ana said and sensed that she was ready to come home.

Flying the Coop

After the cab dropped them at O'Hare Airport in Chicago, Willard took his wife's arm and guided her across the sidewalk through the commotion of arriving cars and the thunder of departing planes. It was the year 2020 and they no longer traveled much—not only did their vision fall short of the calendar year, his weight and her arthritis now hampered them as well—however, this trip was too important to miss.

Before they continued into the O'Hare terminal, Willard paused and said, "Helen, I guess this trip actually began eighteen years ago in Seattle ... didn't it?"

"I remember," she nodded. "It was overcast like this. That was in late May, too. And all the flights back to Chicago were full."

His thoughts returned to that moment years earlier in Seattle when he had bent down to put his cap in his bag and looked up to see Helen being swallowed by the automatic doors. Once, inside, he spied her determined figure twenty yards ahead moving towards the check-in kiosks. He caught up and tapped her on the shoulder, wondering if he had been missed. She was busy with the touch screen.

"Remember me?" he said.

She didn't answer or look around and continued her dialogue with the screen: "No, I *don't* want to change seats. No, I *don't* have an extra bag. No, I *don't* want more legroom. *Just give me my boarding passes!*"

After some hesitation, the machine complied. Placated, she said to him, "Here's your pass, Willard," and wheeled around to set off for the security checkpoint line.

He pocketed the pass and called after her, "Why the rush? We don't board for an hour." However, she had again outdistanced him.

By the time he reached the line, Helen was several places ahead of him. Though he hated traveling like this he had to admit he had never told her—and now didn't seem to be the time.

She looked back and said, "Wait until you reach the conveyor tray table, Willard, before you take off your shoes."

He glanced around and pretended she wasn't speaking to him.

Once they had both cleared security, she announced, "Flight 108 leaves from Concourse A, Gate A14," and set off, as if on one of her business trips with only seconds to spare in a race for prime overhead bin space—the prize for the few passengers savvy enough to stand near the entrance to the departure gate and enter the cabin first.

He squeezed into his shoes and followed what he took to be her blue blouse bobbing along the concourse in the stream of passengers ahead. Just as she disappeared, an announcement sounded: "Final boarding for flight 217 to Chicago by way of Salt Lake City at Gate B7." Willard paused. With a shiver of excitement, he veered off and hurried down the B concourse.

Stepping up to the counter at Gate 7, he said, "Excuse me, I'm ticketed to Chicago on another flight. Is there any chance I can get on this one?"

"You just made it, sir. We have one no-show, one empty seat, and no standbys. May I see me your ticket?"

He hesitated, and then handed it over.

After energetic tapping on her keyboard, she handed it back and waved him through.

The thump of my heart must be audible, he thought, as he tromped down the ramp to board and squeeze past protruding elbows and knees until he found his seat. He smiled at his good fortune. He found bin space for his bag nearby. Then he settled into the seat next to a young woman in stylish workout clothes who sat next to the window and was contemplating her phone.

The rising whine of engines brought home what he was doing. He thought, *I can't* and pulled out his phone and dialed. Minutes later, the cabin door thumped shut followed by the announcement to switch off all electronic devices until after takeoff—but not before he had managed to complete the call.

Helen's phone was off so he left a message: "I'm flying on my own, Helen. Being on the same plane doesn't really seem to matter since we're not together anyway. I'm on the 2:15 to Chicago with a layover in Salt Lake. You go on ahead and maybe we'll have something to talk about when I get there. Goodbye, dear."

As he finished his call, he heard his seatmate say, "We can't leave it like that. We'll have to finish this when I get back," and he imagined recalcitrant children at the other end, wheedling permission for a sleepover; but something about her face told him it was bigger than that.

She shut her phone and huddled against the window as the plane began to accelerate. Creaking like a gate hinge under load, its tires thumped against surface irregularities until, with a final shift in sound and an upward tilt, it lifted off the SeaTac runway.

Lulled by the drone of engines, Willard tried to imagine a conversation with Helen that might change things but could think of nothing. Could his action merely have closed the door on an empty room? Soon he gave up wondering and succumbed to sleep as the faces of young people he had counseled over the years drifted by; their expressions ranging from worry to relief as they floated away and left him feeling satisfaction or concern until the next face appeared.

A subtle change in cabin pressure signaled the beginning of the long descent into Salt Lake City and he sat up and glanced at his seatmate. He stretched and asked, "Have you been on the road?"

"You could say that," she answered. "My sister in Seattle had surgery and I was there looking after my three-year-old niece."

"I hope your sister is doing OK," he said.

"Thank you. She is. It was a non-malignant tumor and she should recover completely."

"I figured it must have been something serious. You looked pretty concerned."

"Oh, did you mean my phone call?"

"Sorry, I don't mean to pry."

"It seems unfair that troubles come along just when we're away tending to other troubles," she said.

"That's true. My wife Helen and I have been visiting her brother in Seattle. Henry's the only family either of us has. His wife of thirty-two years just left him."

Her brow furrowed slightly but she said nothing.

"It broadsided him," he continued, "and when he called to ask us to come, we dropped everything and took the next available flight."

"How is he holding up?" she asked.

"He told us about returning to the house and finding her closet and dresser empty and blank spots on the walls where her artwork and photos had hung." A flicker of worry, like he had seen in Henry's eye's as they sat with him in the kitchen, showed in his seatmate's eyes.

"Sorry. I think I'm talking too much," he said but took her unbroken gaze and the slight shake of her head as permission to continue. This time it was Willard, twenty-five years a school counselor, who found himself glad to tell a stranger about his own marriage, the distance which had grown between them and leaving a nagging sense of incompleteness.

Like Henry and his wife, he and Helen remained childless. It had taken them years to learn that both of them were to blame, if that was the right word. But by that time, the damage had been done, and they decided against adoption. It only remained to convince themselves that this freed them to seek fulfillment in their careers: He gravitated towards work with young people, she applied her talent for managing to develop a consultancy for agencies in crisis.

The announcement to return tray tables and seats to the upright position braked him and again he apologized. She had said very little but seemed to be thinking about what she had heard.

In an effort to lighten his own mood, and perhaps hers, he said, "Well, I guess I just left my wife too—for a few hours anyway. We were both booked on the direct flight to Chicago, but I changed to this one at the last minute."

"Maybe getting away is what it takes to straighten things out," she said. Then, in a steady voice that masked any deeper emotion, she shared her own dilemma: She had just learned she was pregnant but could not see investing herself in having children with a partner not fully committed to her—that was the conversation that remained unfinished.

Willard listened as she quietly sketched out the contours of her situation. Her name was Laura. She and Michael had been together three years. They could not agree on the shape of the future, and she had her doubts about solo parenthood. By the time the plane began its downward rush and appeared to hover an instant before landing with a jolt, his own problem seemed puny in comparison. However, he no longer felt exposed for having disclosed so much.

Flying the Coop

As they pulled their bags up the jet way in Salt Lake, the pressure in Willard's left ear suddenly equalized and the whir and clatter of his suitcase wheels jumped a notch in volume. Just then, an idea occurred to him, but he did not mention it until they reached the main concourse. "This may sound totally crazy, but I just might shake things up and give Helen a bigger taste of AWOL … just to see if it makes a difference." A few steps farther, he added: "I've always wanted to see the Great Salt Lake and hear the Tabernacle Choir."

Laura smiled. "It's something to think about." After a few yards more, she added, "Come to think of it, I have a girlfriend here I haven't seen in a while. Maybe I should look her up."

Her words brought home to him that he already had embarked on a new path and he pulled up, as though nearing a precipice. Since marrying, he had never conceived of a life completely on his own and said, "Well, we do have a three-hour layover to think it over."

Halfway along the concourse they turned into a restaurant and took seats at the bar. After an awkward silence, both of them glanced up into the mirror at the same instant. He smiled and shrugged, and she began to laugh, shaking her head. Then she put her head down in her arms and her laughter changed to quiet sobs.

He waited a few moments before he ventured a hand upon her shoulder. That seemed to calm her, and she raised up to wipe her face with the back of her hand and managed a smile.

"Thanks. Michael is right. It wasn't working out. I need time to think of something different."

A server came up and asked, "Can I get you folks something?"

"Hungry?" he asked. Somehow, he felt responsible for this break out and it seemed the natural thing to say.

She scanned the menu. "I guess I am. I'll have the chicken salad and iced tea."

"Make mine the pulled-pork sandwich and the amber draft," he said. He usually heeded Helen's warning that he 'must be trying to kill himself eating food like that' and only indulged when he was with his bowling buddies. Then he said, "On second thought, change that to split pea soup and garlic bread. And I guess iced tea sounds good after all."

They ate and talked about nothing in particular—their work, where they had grown up, and places they would like to travel—but not about their predicaments.

When he next glanced at his watch, it was five o'clock. Helen must be unlocking the door just now. He remembered he had not turned his phone on and Laura's hadn't rung.

"Well, I guess it's time for me to take a break or go home," he said.

Flying the Coop

"I don't know," she said. "I feel so childish. Running away won't change anything. Maybe I'll call."

He nodded and realized he needed to call as well. Excusing himself, he walked out into the concourse and phoned. No one picked up. *That's odd. Her direct flight should have gotten in before this.* He let it ring until he saw that Laura had finished her call and then he stepped back into the restaurant.

She was staring at the TV behind the bar. The sound was off and words streamed across below images of plane wreckage in a field.

He read: *Flight 108 from Seattle to Chicago crashed this afternoon after the pilot radioed that a bird strike had disabled both engines. Rescue operations are underway.*

She turned slowly to look at him. "My God, Willard, was that your wife's plane?"

He sat heavily with his phone still in hand. "Helen," he said. "She doesn't answer."

Laura put her hand on his arm.

Then, his phone rang. "Willard, did you just try to call me? Where are you? Did you know our plane crashed? Are you all right? Tell me you're OK and coming back."

He couldn't speak at first. "I was afraid you were gone, Helen. We haven't really been together for some time, but this gives us another chance. Yes, I'm coming back. Where are you?"

"When you didn't show up," she said, "I didn't board. I checked my phone and found your message, but it was too late to change anything, so I went back to Henry's. How awful. Those poor people."

"I know. See if you can get on a flight tomorrow, and I'll meet your plane."

Laura heard both ends of the conversation and looked relieved as he hung up.

He turned to her. "How do things stand with you?"

"Michael says it's over. He will be gone by the time I get back."

Willard let this sink in and then asked, "Did you tell him?"

"No."

After a minute, he said, "I hope we can keep in touch. You really have to meet Helen."

"OK. I'm going to stay over a few days with my girlfriend, but when I get back to Chicago, we can get together. Here's my card."

Over the next eighteen years, Willard and Helen grew into their new roles as "surrogate grandparents" and now were preparing to fly to Seattle where Laura's job had taken her several years earlier with their "granddaughter," Hope.

Tomorrow was an important milestone for them all: Hope would graduate from high school and—sooner than they liked—head off to college after having given them all an opportunity they believed had been irretrievable.

William Geuss

It Happened in Warsaw

The first time was two hundred and fifty years ago ... but it was the second time that matters to me. That was on a chill spring evening during my fifth year as a fledgling faculty member at Newminster University near Chicago. I had come to Warsaw to deliver a paper to the International Musicological Society on Italian musicians who traveled Europe in the eighteenth century. Like them, I was here to seek my fortune and find favor—the outcome would influence my tenure committee to decide whether I could stay or had to move on.

To provide a distraction from what lay ahead the next morning, I set out for the Starowka, Warsaw's restored old town. Normally, a stroll in cool air revives me, but I found the flicker of the latest flat-screen TVs in the windows of centuries-old buildings oddly disconcerting. As I rounded a corner, familiar music from a boom box perched on a bench drew streams of youths to an open area for what one identified as a flash tribute to Michael Jackson as news of his death reverberated around the globe. Though each of them was in their own world, their bodies jerked in collective patterns charged with energy drawn from the iconic figure who had captured their yearning for a common language—much as the Italians had supplied in their own day—a music connecting them to their past and supplying a bridge into the future.

I came to a fountain on the main square and sat on the basin's edge while the waning sunlight played back a pastel symphony from the surrounding half-timbered façades. The monotonous splash of water blunted the feel of the rough sandstone my fingers slid along as travel fatigue descended like a curtain making thoughts unwieldy: What inspiration did the Italians draw from this place in their day? What success did they have? And what really brought me here?

Last night, to the dull roar of engines, I had traced the arc that spanned from my childhood to the present: My first violin lesson from my Polish grandmother (who alone called me by the Polish form of Charles); my instrument nestled under my chin, she would say: "Karol, can you feel them? Can you hear them? The strings sing for you. Always listen to them."

Though she died when I was ten, the strings of the cello I now play still resonate with overtones of her warmth and have provided the compass that guides me. It brought me first to the School of Music at Newminster ... and now to this conference in Warsaw.

When the chill penetrating the hand dangling in the water revived me, I stood and, on a whim, followed a cobblestone street leading toward the Vistula River. Wood smoke adrift on the evening air and the serenade of birds from the rooftops accompanied me as I pushed farther into the narrow streets. When I began to stumble on damp, mossy paving, I realized that it was pointless to continue—my time slot at 9 a.m. tomorrow would come at 2 a.m. Chicago time.

Before I turned to retrace my steps to my hotel, I noticed the window of a small shop on the right where faint gold letters spelling "*lutnik*" or "violin maker" caught the light. Several unfinished instruments were visible through the smudged glass and hung above a work area covered with wood shavings, carving tools, and a glue pot. I closed my eyes and savored the memory of pungent cedar laced with glue from the time I once spent attending to the repair of my own instrument.

When I opened them again, the air was cooler still, and I saw a beam of late sunlight reflecting off windows higher up as it fell upon a battered cello leaned against one wall in the obscure interior. It struck the burnished soundboard at the f-slot and something stirred in my chest. I watched the ray of sunlight flare like a lantern and travel across the instrument to wrap around the worn varnish along its side panel, revealing scrapes that testified of a long career.

The effect was hypnotic and hairs on my neck rose, my ears began to buzz. I imagined a figure hunched over the instrument and deep, rich tones begin to resound. Squeezing my eyes shut changed nothing, and I wondered could that be me, bow in hand? A vivid theme repeated with ornamentation and was followed by another that took up the opening motif, this time further embellished—and intense yearning welled up from the void left by my grandmother's death.

I was ten, when we were called to be with her. That evening I stood in the room adjacent to hers and approached the door. It was ajar and, as I pressed my face to look in, the adults gathered around her bedside parted. I saw grandmother rise up in bed and look around searching for something. Spying me, she reached out her hand and seemed to gesture to come to her. Then she fell back on the bed, motionless. When my parents looked around to follow her gaze, I pulled back out of sight, certain that she would not abandon me.

Suddenly, the beam falling through the shop window flared again and daggers of pain stabbed through my right shoulder. The music stopped, mid-phrase, as the sun dropped into darkness and murky shadows claimed the street and shop.

It was some minutes before I realized that something important had happened—but, whose music was this, what had interrupted it? The dim light from the street lamp revealed nothing about the proprietor, so I returned to my hotel in a quiet street near the old town.

During the night cello music swept through ragged dreams, joined by a woman's voice, until a scream tore me out of my sleep. I lay still trying to place the musical language which was vaguely familiar, but the meaning of the dreams eluded me and I was left to hear bells of a nearby church chime off the remaining hours.

The next morning at the university, the combination of equipment I brought for my presentation worked better than it sometimes did at home. Since the language of discourse throughout Europe now was English, it was unnecessary to cope with other languages on so little sleep. My talk highlighted the importance of the Italian composers and musicians in Dresden, London, Paris and Vienna in the 1700's, a time when their music was much admired and made it the language of culture throughout Europe. Enviably, my Italian predecessors were sought after and generously rewarded. Though my remarks were well received by my international colleagues, I could only hope for as much back at Newminster.

That afternoon, our hosts suggested, to general applause, that we cap off the session with a night on the town, but the music from the battered instrument still haunted me.

Before we met that evening for what could best be described as a vodka pub crawl, I spent the remainder of the afternoon at the university archives in search of clues to the puzzling music. At the reference desk, I found a spare, gray-haired librarian named Wanda

Terleki who was a specialist in the archive's eighteenth-century holdings. When she told me they included compendia of musicians associated with the court in Krakow and Warsaw and guild registries of instrument makers, my pulse jumped. But, as the afternoon wore on and nothing related to the mystery turned up, I wondered: Had it all been only a dream?

After I finished with the final compendium and I looked up at the clock, my bleary eyes told me that it was 6 p.m. I saw Ms. Terleki hurrying over. "Professor Zielinski, I'm sorry I did not have this ready earlier. It is a chronicle from that period and was in tatters but has been restored. I just catalogued it and thought you would like to see it."

"How kind of you," I said as she nodded and set it down next to the other materials.

After she left to return to her desk, I stretched, squeezed my eyes shut and recalled the battered cello. Again, I thought I heard faint music and I opened the book to search for anything that might match up.

The pages were in surprisingly good condition and halfway through, a reference to the eighteenth-century cellist and composer Carlo Graziani caught my eye. He was listed as associated with a music academy in Warsaw in 1765, which was new information: According to this, his peripatetic career had included a stay in Warsaw; his tenure was brief but promising and ended abruptly when he disappeared. A dead end?

Then it occurred to me … if the music also turned out to be linked to Graziani, my chances looked better for a longer run at Newminster than Graziani had had in Warsaw.

Although this remote possibility was intriguing, I needed to return to Chicago the next day for a tenure review meeting with my department chairman. But I would devote tonight to my colleagues, and I could check to see what they might have on the subject of Graziani in Warsaw—in any case, I still had tomorrow morning.

At 8 p.m. we met in another section of the old town to begin an evening which stretched on as Vodka flowed in astonishing variety and quantity stoking the fires of collegiality. I was told that the university was adding another person to the music faculty and that they would value having me consider joining them. I filed it away but wondered who would recall it the next morning?

Despite their stalwart efforts to detain me, I managed to defect while I still could navigate and hope to rise the next morning to return to the instrument shop for any clues I had missed and then head to the airport to ponder my future on the flight back.

Upon my return to Evanston, purple and white crocuses were pushing up around Newminster University's Victorian-era music building which housed the chairman's office and practice rooms. Even late at night, a jarring mix of vocalization and instrumental arpeggios emanated from its upper windows—as though its original donor was in agony over the danger posed by the capital campaign aimed at replacing it: As an alumni newsletter put it, *with an edifice more befitting a university with a music department of its caliber.*

I knocked and entered to find Dr. Frampton seated behind his dark wooden desk, which, in addition to a bust of a brooding Beethoven, held a framed photo of himself with his second wife. He stood, applauding her as she bowed after a performance of *Carmen,* a rose in her jet-black hair.

When he looked up from architectural drawings of the proposed new building, I noticed that his jowls were much fuller than in the photo. "Tell me about your trip, Charles. How are you getting along?" he asked.

I met his gaze and glanced away. Attempting to sound upbeat, I said, "I didn't find a substantial amount of new material in the archives in Warsaw from my period—but my paper went quite well."

Omitting the curious intuition at the instrument shop and my disappointment that nothing concrete had linked it with the mention of Graziani, I added, "I'm afraid too many wars may have handicapped my efforts to come up with much new about these lesser known figures."

"How unfortunate," he said and gave me something probably meant to be a sympathetic smile.

Unconvinced, I recalled, that he had had it better in his day—when editing a newer edition of an established composer's work was enough to make the reputation which he continued to draw upon.

"Please understand that what you've done so far is very positive," he continued, "but I hear from your tenured colleagues that a significant contribution is still lacking—a study or piece of research that contributes, not only to your field but to the renommée of Newminster."

"I think I understand," I said and got the message: Academic fiefdoms differed little today from the eighteenth-century—ever grander palaces were the order of the day then too, and obtaining a post as court *Kapellmeister* depended upon dedicating a work to your benefactor on a special occasion.

In desperation, I ventured, "Something interesting did happen, though ..." and mentioned finding the surprising reference to Carlo Graziani. "It seems he spent some time in Warsaw. That's not mentioned elsewhere."

Just then, the phone rang and Dr. F. gave me a wave as he answered. His eyes lit up as he glanced at his calendar and told the caller he would be glad to meet with the development committee about the campaign for the new music building and then launched into several minutes of ingratiating chitchat.

Half listening, I remembered retracing my steps down to Warsaw's old town the morning after the pub-crawl to find the instrument shop. By daylight things looked different and it was a struggle to recall details from two days earlier. Cool air met me as I neared the river and turned a corner and found myself in front of the building again. To my dismay, I was peering through newly cleaned windows of a shop that was vacant and now for rent.

I stood for a moment, eyes closed, and listened. This time, just as inside the shop, nothing. I opened them and noticed a clockmaker across the street and went in. With my rudimentary Polish, I inquired about the *lutnik* opposite and the battered cello. He nodded and raised his hands in a gesture of sadness and regret. He replied that his neighbor "died two months ago—after a long illness."

When asked about the cello, he said, "Very old. But in deplorable condition. In fact, my neighbor told me: 'It brings bad luck! No one wants it.'"

Then came the final blow: The shop had been cleared by creditors only the day before.

That had left me as dispirited as I felt today as I heard Dr. Frampton finish his call with, "What could be more important than this campaign?" Then, he rose to end our interview. His chair scraped on the splintered wooden floor, and I knew at once why a grander building was an easy sell to Dr. F.

He clasped my hand before we had fully engaged them and shook it quickly. "Well, you still have time before the tenure committee begins reviewing your work. Take heart and get busy!"

Three weeks later I sat in my office, nearly resigned to coming up short next fall. I was not sleeping well, but it wasn't due to music. Subconsciously, I think I knew that failure to gain tenure would let my grandmother down—and I saw no way around it.

My brooding was interrupted by the phone, and I heard a brisk female voice with a Polish accent say, "Hello, Professor Zielinski? This is Magdalena Nowak with the Polish-American Music Society of Chicago. The recent article in the *Chicago Tribune* about your work on eighteenth-century composers and musicians in Poland is quite interesting."

My mood brightened somewhat. "Why thank you. I just returned from the conference mentioned there."

"It's convenient that you are in Evanston. We received a bequest from an elderly widow a month ago that includes a music manuscript, letters, and fragments of a diary that date from the era of your expertise. Is it possible you would be available to research them for possible publication?"

I sat up. It sounded like a long shot but more than routine material from someone's attic. "Once I examine them, I'll be able to tell you more, but this does sound interesting. Shall I come down and have a look?"

"That would be perfect! We have a board meeting scheduled in two weeks, and I would like to be able to give a status report."

I often passed the Music Society's well-kept, two-story red brick on Ashland Avenue on my way south into the city. The snarled traffic through the busy Hispanic neighborhood north of there was trying, but to my surprise, I found street parking within minutes. When I rang to be buzzed in, I was met by Ms. Nowak, a woman with alert eyes and an engaging smile. Blonde hair made it hard to estimate her age, but I took her to be in her late forties.

"Do come in," she said and firmly shook my hand. She led me into a library with file cabinets along one wall and bookshelves on the others. "Won't you sit down, Professor?" she said, and indicated one of the hard chairs at an oak table upon which a gray folder rested. She pushed rimless glasses back against her nose, and then pointed to the materials. "These are the documents. The donor wished to remain anonymous, and copyright to any published versions would remain the property of the Polish-American Music Society. We can supply copies, but we ask that the original materials remain here."

She cocked her head to review a mental checklist and, seemingly satisfied, said: "Tell me, Professor

Zielinski, what sparked your interest in Poland's musical heritage?"

Her face was attentive and I thought for a moment before replying. "I suppose it goes back to my childhood ... hearing my grandmother speak often of her favorites, the mezzo soprano Madame Schumann-Heink and your pianist, Ignacy Jan Paderewski. When grandmother died, she left me her violin. Ever since, I've had a soft spot for old instruments, Polish musicians, and divas—not necessarily in that order."

She nodded and smiled. "Perhaps then you will be rewarded by what you find here. We are not sure what to make of these letters and the diary fragments. They are all in Italian but, together with the music manuscript, we hope it could be of interest to the academic world." Folding her hands, she fixed me with pleasant gray eyes and said, "All we know is that this material has been passed down in this Polish family for generations and, when there were no heirs, it came to us."

I was more than pleased to be facing a task for which I was suited, and I nodded and smiled in turn. She rose. "I'll leave you now, Professor. How fortunate that you are familiar with the languages involved." She added, "Do let me know what you think as soon as you can," and left, closing the door behind her.

Before I opened the folio, I thought back over the last few weeks since my return from Warsaw. Days of scouring reference materials for anything to augment the tantalizing mention of Carlo Graziani I discovered in Warsaw added nothing to what was already common knowledge: *A virtuoso cellist and often-commissioned composer of sonatas and suites, acclaimed in Paris, London, Frankfurt, and Berlin who incorporated musical techniques learned along the way.* Nothing, however, placed him in Warsaw.

Opening the folio, I quickly saw that the yellowed paper in front of me was an aria for cello and soprano voice with keyboard accompaniment and lacked the first two pages—hence no signature, either of a copyist or composer. When I saw that the first system of the surviving manuscript was written in the same key and joined seamlessly with the music I had heard in the dusky Warsaw street, I pushed back my chair and began to pace around the table with one thought: This could change my prospects for next fall!

Regaining my composure, I sat and examined the rest of the score. The hallmark technical virtuosity of a mature composer was unmistakable. The elegant charm of the melody was taken up by soprano voice. And it was in the same style as another of Graziani's arias, "Talor per l'onde", for soprano with violoncello obbligato which I hadn't remembered that night in the streets of Warsaw.

By the time I finished examining it, I was convinced that this discovery, if shown to be his, could make a splash in the musicological pond with ripples large enough to get me and our department noticed.

I quickly moved on to the small stack of fragile letters written in Italian. The first was dated April 5, 1765 and read:

My Darling,

How can you doubt my love? Why would you have me followed? Who else would I want to hold in my arms in ecstasy one day but you? The building I was seen entering that night was the apartment of the mistress of Count R whom he was visiting. He summoned me to play for them, and I can report that a commission for a new work resulted — an aria for soprano with cello obbligato!

For, you see, the lady in question has vocal talent to match her other attributes, all of which Count R first discovered at the theater where she was playing in a new piece. Since her "discovery," he has gone to great lengths to satisfy her vanity. She lives in sumptuous circumstances and is attended to most assiduously by Count R.

Should this composition please them, I am to be made director of the music academy here! Be patient, my darling. I will have a bright future after the Count can showcase his protégée with my music.

I await your next letter with impatience.

Your devoted C.G.

My hands trembled as I turned to the diary that formed the third part of the materials. From the jottings which bracketed the date of this letter, I was able to piece together the probable course of events when raw ambitions collided.

The next letter was dated three weeks later:

My Dearest,

Your tender care has worked wonders in my recovery. My wound is healing, and I am regaining the movement of my bow arm. I can never thank you enough for standing by me, even though my prospects here have dimmed!

You say that your father has begun to question you about the frequency of your visits to my rooms and the slow progress you seem to be making under my tutelage. It is rumored that he can become violent, if vodka is involved. I must know how great a threat you deem him to pose? I would not have you placed in jeopardy! Should we meet less often?

Yours devotedly,

C.

A final letter showed staining, possibly from tears, and concluded:

And so my darling, you must realize that fate decrees we part lest consequences even more dire overtake us. Although my hand trembles as I pen this final letter, I am comforted that you are the sole person to whom I can entrust what remains of the manuscript which brought me such calamity. Your image inspired this music and will remain engraved in my heart. To show you how much you have

*meant to me during my brief sojourn in Warsaw, I
also include my diary from this time—a year I shall
never forget. Your tenderness and devotion will
inspire my every creative impulse henceforth!*

Addio, yours affectionately,

C.G.

Deeply moved, I puzzled over how these disclosures
might relate to what happened in Warsaw? I sat back
and let my mind drift hoping to piece together a
scenario:

*… a grand villa in a wide street. Night has fallen and smoky
flares light the porte-cochère covering the drive that loops past the
entry. A servant stands at the ready. Inside, from a source
further removed from the street, the sound of a cello mingles with
the voice of a soprano to drift along the corridors.*

*The Count approaches a salon that is the source of the music.
He watches from a darkened hallway, riveted to the spot by what
he sees: Two figures bathed in soft candlelight lending liquid
contour to their movements. A theme, rich in rapid cross-string
passages, frequent double stops, and harmonics rises from the
cellist's bow. His mistress turns from her music and inclines her
body towards the cellist as if to embrace him. When she moves to
face him, her dancing, playful voice, and flashing eyes seem meant
only for him. Rage boils up in the Count, and he curses himself
for being such a fool; his hand drops to his dagger … .*

My musing broke off there because the face I gave
this diva was that of Dr. Frampton's second wife,
Carmella.

I remembered the first time I heard her perform. The pressure of my research and preparing lectures had kept me from most faculty recitals in the spring, but I felt obliged to attend when my department chairman accompanied his wife in her soprano voice recital.

I arrived at Lattimer Hall just after the lights dimmed and eased into a seat two-thirds back. She was on stage near the piano at which Dr. Frampton was seated. When she turned to face the audience, the impact of her presence jolted me. Short, raven hair set off the white of her face. Her hands rested on the hips of a simple black sheath and she parted very red lips to begin her program. Her smoldering gaze moved across our upward-directed faces. A hush filled the hall charged with electricity. Through lowered lashes, she seemed to peer at first one face and then another, as a smile played across her lips.

Spellbound, I scarcely moved until forty minutes later, when she announced she would close with Rachmaninoff's setting of songs by Glafira Adol'fovna Galina Op. 21.

When she began … *How fair this spot* … I was certain her gaze met mine and my breath caught. I sat spellbound until her final words

> *There's no one here … here, silence reigns …*
> *There is only God and I,*

> *The flowers and the ancient pine*
>
> *And you, my dream!*

Her white arms reached out, appealing, and I wondered, could this be meant for me?

With a crinkle of her sparkling eyes, she bowed. A satisfied smile and a graceful sweep of her arm signaled Dr. Frampton to stand from the piano for his bow. Then, looking extremely pleased, her husband followed her off the stage.

As the summer advanced and I readied the materials describing the ominous passions of Graziani and the Count R. for publication, I realized I had surrendered to Carmella's spell. Her voice invaded my dreams; her flashing eyes once again sought mine, the words from her recital …

> *Your smile, your fleeting glances,*
>
> *your rich tresses,*
>
> *so obedient to my fingers*

flooded my sleep as in her song …

> *in a frenzy*
>
> *without regard for reason,*

I would awaken calling her name.

The flood of optimism when I discovered this material about passing muster with the tenure committee gave way to my obsession with Carmella. It roiled my soul and made concentrating on any task difficult until one morning, I awoke with an idea. I was certain my yearning could not withstand the reality that proximity and familiarity always bring—and I would be freed.

Once again I found myself in Dr. Frampton's office. And again he proved to be easily distracted, whether from the noise of his window air-conditioner or the blinking light on his office phone. However, to my delight, it was a simple matter to interest him in having his wife premier the newly discovered Graziani aria with me.

"Carmella would never forgive me if I let this opportunity pass," he said and, with a broad smile and gesture, volunteered himself at keyboard to accompany us.

I was delighted and at the same time alarmed. Was I really hoping for release, or did I fear Dr. F's involvement would interfere with realizing my fantasy of having her to myself? My plan involved some risk, yet, how else to stem these currents that ran so deep?

We settled on a program featuring the aria along with music of the Neapolitan context from which it came. The next day, he phoned to say the development committee wished to sponsor the recital to open the Music School's fall programming. "It's a terrific opportunity to publicize the funding campaign for the new building," he enthused. "We'll invite key donors and provide them with a special program that documents the discovery of the manuscript and the

dramatic moment in the composer's life it reveals—
and it certainly won't hurt your chances for tenure."

I quickly agreed. This was one time I could leverage
the traits I found so distasteful in him to my advantage.
His vanity dictated that he take the stage at every
opportunity, and he must hope to have some part of
the new building named after him.

As for my own ambitions, I had to admit I didn't
mind benefiting from the halo his participation lent
and wondered: Am I any less opportunistic?

I thanked him for his support and, before I hung up,
promised to stop by with copies of the music and a
timetable for rehearsals. With foreboding, I realized
that my rehearsal time with Carmella would not always
require his presence.

We agreed to meet in August late at night in Lattimer
Hall, a space resembling the spiked helmet of Kaiser
Wilhelm plunked down on a small plot next to the
Victorian music building containing Dr. F's office.
Diminutive by comparison to its looming, ghostly-gray
brick neighbor, Lattimer might have sprung from the
rabid imagination of a British newspaperman trapped
in clichés about World War I German imperialism.
Inside, however, the acoustics more than compensated
for this oddity.

I sat with my cello midstage, sleeves rolled up, on a
warm summer evening and waited for Carmella and
Dr. Frampton. The fingers of my left hand twined up

and down the black neck as in the dream that night in Warsaw—my right wrist cocked to guide the bow across the strings at the improbable angles required to send Graziani's music out into the darkened hall. A soft touch on my shoulder first signaled Carmella's presence and sent electricity tingling out to my fingertips.

Turning, I froze when I saw her soft contours and the curve of her neck set off by a short-sleeved black top with a generous neckline.

She smiled and said, "Fredric couldn't come. He had another dinner with the development committee and can't get away. He says, 'Just go ahead'."

Through the pulse in my temples, I heard myself say, "Oh, that *is* too bad," certain she must hear the pounding. We began to go through the score which, by now, I could play from memory. When I closed my eyes, the music came from deep within, calming me. Then I made a confusing discovery.

Whenever I opened them and our eyes met, I trembled at the impact: Carmella resembled the young woman with dark, short hair who looked out under long lashes from early photographs of my grandmother. Was this the secret of her hold over me?

If kept my eyes closed, I was alright but I couldn't and each time my breathing and playing became uneven. She met my apologies with an amused smile until she eventually reached out and put a hand on my wrist and I looked up.

She said, "Charles, let's stop and go for a drink—to relax and get to know each other. That always helps artists perform better together."

We walked the few blocks south to the Bar Louie on one corner and found a small table free. Feeling somewhat calmer after the walk, I went to the bar and brought back rum and coke for her and a dry martini for myself. As I sat, our knees brushed and I inched away. Noise washed over us, and we had to lean in to talk. The familiar way her lips came to tight points at the corners of her mouth intrigued me, and I couldn't think of anything to say.

She met my gaze from under long lashes and said, "Well, why don't you start by telling me how you found this music?" Relieved, I shared what drove my enthusiasm for music and for this music in particular. She didn't interrupt and I talked at length, more a sign of my continued nervousness than of ease.

Afterward, as I lay awake in my apartment, all I could remember was that when I told her about the powerful intuition I had in Warsaw about this music and the providential appearance of the rest of Graziani's manuscript and his letters and diary, her eyes grew large and she touched my forearm and said, "Why, Charles, how wonderful for you!" And I had to face the fact that physical proximity and growing familiarity fanned the flames they were meant to extinguish.

Our meetings at Lattimer Hall took on a clandestine aura as they fell late in the evening when all other activity had ceased. When Carmella arrived, I would greet her by playing from one of her spring recital songs: *"How quietly you come to me,"* which she would then take up…

> *Oh, for many a long hour*
> *In silence of mysterious night.*

Afterwards, even though my tenure was at stake, these nights brought dreams of ecstatic fulfillment torn by dread of the consequences. How far would this go, I wondered. I had accompanied ensembles of all sizes before and worked closely with students and faculty individually; I had always remained professional and focused on my career—but never had a woman affected me so strongly.

Her extraordinary ability to build suspense and drama when performing were familiar to me from her recital and, lacking an audience during our rehearsals, Carmella directed it fully at me—even when her husband was present. While it was clear she was playing a part, I also believed that inside this alluring female on stage, a heart beat that was full of the yearning which great music expresses and made her performances so riveting.

Four days before the recital, I suggested that she and Dr. Frampton come to my apartment for a nightcap after rehearsal. Though I was always careful to avoid any public display of anything approaching intimacy towards Carmella, I had recently received a note from Dr. F. couched as a helpful precaution that easily could be read as a veiled threat that his wife 'could sometimes appear to invite more familiarity than was appropriate, which had led to one situation that ended badly for a junior faculty member some years ago.'

A cold rain fell that night and, because of a late dinner with wealthy alumni donors, Dr. Frampton excused himself after the rehearsal. Consequently, after we tried out some minor changes in the program, only Carmella walked with me the several blocks to the frame house where I rented an apartment.

We entered and climbed to the second floor. I had straightened up what must seem to her my Bohemian setting and stocked aged rum for Carmella and a single malt Scotch for Dr. Frampton.

I took her umbrella and, as she turned to slip out of her coat, she said, "Charles, I hate to think that our time together may be coming to an end."

Her nearness in velvety black and musky perfume sent alarms jangling down my spine. *Can I survive this? Do I want to?*

I turned to lead the way through the narrow hall into the living room, but she did not step back to make room. We brushed together, and "Sorry," was all I could manage my throat dry and cinched off. But I could think of nothing to say anyway and, scarcely audible through the drumming of my heart, a distant voice counseled, *Remember, Karol, music is all that matters.*

The next morning, it took me but an hour to carry out my plan. I stopped at Lattimer Hall and collected the scores for the program, then went on to the music building and left an envelope for Dr. Frampton. It contained a copy of the manuscript I had already submitted to both the Polish-American Music Society and the International Musicological Society and my letter. It read:

> *Dear Dr. Frampton,*
>
> *I regret I will not be able to perform the program this Saturday that was to feature the first performance of work by Carlo Graziani due to an accident.*
>
> *In addition to this passionate music, the composer left us with the enclosed manuscript describing a drama in which the actors are driven by raw ambition to seize opportunity for their gain but, instead, suffer calamitous results.*
>
> *Although the fates of the soprano and her benefactor, Count R., remain unknown, we do know that the composer was the victim of a misunderstanding—struck down by the hand of a jealous lover, which cut short a promising phase in his career—Graziani escaped with his life and moved on from Warsaw to Frankfurt to begin anew.*

As for my part, in four days I leave for Warsaw to assume a position on the Faculty of Music at the university where, fittingly, this work will have its premier in the place where it was conceived.

Please accept my resignation.

Sincerely yours,
Karol Zielinski

On the flight to Warsaw, what transpired that night in my apartment played back in my mind. From the beginning, Carmella seemed to sense how captivating I found her. During our evening rehearsals, we were never sure just when Dr. Frampton would appear, and I knew that going beyond the boundaries of our defined roles would entail considerable risk. On evenings when he did not appear, we would adjourn afterwards to Bar Louie for a drink, and I was painfully aware of the risk any public display entailed.

In my apartment, all such considerations fell away. To gain time and regain my composure, I made us drinks and told her I wished to dedicate some music to her. She had never heard Graziani's aria, "Talor per l'onde" for soprano and violoncello. To restore clarity, I took my instrument, sat, and closed my eyes to let it resonate against my body.

When I finished the first movement, I opened my eyes and Carmella's chair was empty. I sensed her behind me and heard her voice, "*in silence of mysterious night*," husky with emotion, and felt her caresses on my neck and chest. When I gently insisted this could only bring unwelcome consequences, her movements became increasingly ardent, then agitated, when I attempted to grip her wrists.

She tried to take the bow from my hand. I resisted and she pulled away abruptly. A second later a sharp pain made me drop it and pivot around on my stool. She had snatched a letter opener from the end table behind us and sunk it into my right shoulder.

I watched in shock as she stepped back and slumped into a chair, her eyes full of scorn. After a moment, her breathing steadied, and she said, "You really don't know what you want, do you, Charles?"

"You are right," I admitted, "I really didn't; at least not until tonight."

"Well, now it's too late. I'll tell Fredric you made a pass at me, and I had to fight you off."

"I think it's enough, Carmella, if I tell him I have to cancel the performance because of an accident."

She looked startled and then, with what may have been a note of sadness, said "Good night, Charles," and let herself out.

Neapolitan Nights

Car horns sounded. Sheila awoke and lay still trying to remember ... yes ... that's how Cousin Douglas surprised me ten days ago when he drove up to the house in Perry, Iowa. No one ever honked for me before ... but now I'm in Rome ... with Douglas.

Noise from the brawling traffic near the hotel swelled as Sheila found her way back. It pleased her that he had come to her mother's funeral all the way from San Francisco to Iowa. For years, the Christmas letters to them from Douglas' mother had featured his travels to London, Paris, or Madrid. Aside from movies and romance novels, he was her most tangible link to these exotic places.

By the time Sheila's mother died in July 1960, the year Sheila turned forty, she had already drafted the funeral notice for the local paper in her mind. It was brief:

> Yesterday at the age of 74, after more than a decade of declining health, Doris Michaels Henry passed away peacefully at home in her sleep and joined her departed husband of 34 years, Herbert Henry, and her departed only sibling Arthur Michaels of San Francisco.

Having Douglas there had revived Sheila and she added Douglas' name so it read:

> Her only child Sheila Henry, *her nephew Douglas Michaels of San Francisco*, and neighbors and members of First Methodist Church will mourn her. A service will be held Tuesday at Ryerson Funeral Parlor.

Life in Perry, Iowa, had been uneventful for Sheila. Her parents, especially her father, had sheltered her and, although Sheila was cautious about change, she went away to a small college after high school. There, in her Italian classes, Professor Celli rhapsodized about *Roma*, *Firenze*, *Venezia* and *Pisa*. He was dapper, aristocratic and playful in turn, and inspired most of the female students in class to apply for a passport.

Upon graduation, Sheila planned to move to a larger town and teach, but three months beforehand, her father died and she returned to Perry to live with her mother and teach second grade. College had changed her, but her life once again became uneventful.

Like her immigrant grandparents in the stories her father used to tell her, Sheila felt stranded, cut off by an ocean from beloved origins—but she had her passport. She would take it from her stocking drawer on Sunday afternoons and, hoping to catch a breeze, hold it in her hands as she sat on the porch swing with her eyes closed and imagine that the oscillations were the shifting of a liner steaming across the Atlantic.

The Sunday before the funeral, her swing had just departed for Venice, when a horn honked and she opened her eyes to see a slightly balding, paunchy man in a sport shirt and light slacks emerge from a black Oldsmobile. "Hello, Cousin," he called, "it was good of you to let me know about Auntie Dorie's death."

It was Douglas. He too had just turned forty, but in her mind, he was still ten, his age when her aunt and uncle had last visited from California.

She stepped down to meet him. "Of course, Douglas—you are my only living relative. It was always a treat for mother and me to hear about your travels at Christmas. She would be thrilled that you came all this way."

He gave her a damp hug and followed her inside to escape the sun. "When I got your news, I was about to leave for Italy and thought I could stop on the way."

"Italy," she said, nearly forgetting to offer the iced tea she always kept in the fridge. "I've dreamed of Italy for years." However, the closest she came were trips to Des Moines, forty miles distant when the rare Italian film showed in the town's one theater. She would imagine that the smoldering glances on the screen were meant for her and, afterwards, treat herself to cold lemon sherbet and pretend it was *gelato*.

"I hope you will tell me all about it, Douglas," she said. "Mother's visitation and burial will be tomorrow. I'll make supper now and then we can sit on the porch and talk."

They sat late into the evening (this time without her passport) and she heard firsthand accounts of places her swing had never reached.

"Do you plan to travel now that Auntie Dorie is gone?" he asked.

Just that morning, Sheila had asked herself the same thing after speaking with the funeral director, and she hated to admit that she was afraid of finding out if what lay across the Atlantic was equal to her dreams.

Douglas answered his own question: "I tell you what, Sheila; I have a few things to attend to in Chicago after this; then I fly on to Italy to visit someone. If you have a passport, why not wrap things up here and fly over with me? I know my way around and could point you in the right direction."

Three days later, passport in her purse, Sheila took the train to Chicago to meet him and they flew to Rome.

With her ears still droning from the engines, it took all of her concentration to descend to the tarmac and follow Douglas through the formalities of arrival. When they finally stood with their bags outside the terminal, elation that she had crossed the Atlantic washed her weariness away. "I can't believe I'm here, Douglas."

"If anyone deserves it, Sheila, it's you," he said. "Now I'm going to take you on your first tour of Rome."

With that, he loaded their bags into the red Alfa Romeo he had rented, said "Hold on, Cousin," and nosed them out into turbulent traffic before plunging into the throng of motor scooters, cars, and diminutive three-wheeled trucks streaming into town.

"Welcome to *Roma*," he said and began to slalom through the harrowing flow of vehicles. To keep her equilibrium, she braced against the seat with her eyes tightly closed and heard him call out the names of prominent sites they were passing.

The monuments he announced brought up images stored in her mind of scenes from her movies, and it was enough to calm her until he pulled up at their hotel.

"*Ti piace, Sheila?*" he asked, as she cautiously reopened her eyes.

Letting out her breath, she answered, "*Sì, Douglas.* I love it … I only wish I had someone to send a postcard to." Then, she followed him inside to get settled.

Over dinner that evening, he said, "Now that you've gotten a start, let me tell you about my plans. This world is full of surprises, Cousin. Last month I met someone from Naples on a cable car in San Francisco, and tomorrow I'll drive south to visit. They have a five-day religious holiday down there, and no one will be working."

She thought for a moment and said, "I hope you won't think me too much of a nuisance, Douglas, but I'm not sure I can do this by myself. Is there any chance I could ride along with you? I promise not to be a pest."

He hesitated and smiled. "Sheila, I wouldn't have it any other way—of course you can. On the way down we can make up for some of those years we didn't see each other. And once we're there, you'll find plenty to do."

Naples shimmered in the heat as they approached towards evening and wound through streets choked with traffic. After some difficulty, they found the road beyond the edge of the central district that branched off and took them to Sheila's hotel. It led them past cramped buildings with shutters open onto the street where residents sat out on their steps, the men in undershirts, the women in dark cotton dresses … *just like my front porch*, Sheila thought and wondered what they dreamed about.

Douglas rounded a corner and braked sharply for a small black dog that had strayed into the road. He sounded the horn and it barked at them in return. Soon, he pulled over to the curb in front of a small fourth-class hotel. Red letters above the door identified it as the *La Regina*. "This must be it," he said, mopping his forehead. "Are you sure you won't change your mind? I can lend you the money if it comes to that."

She knew that he only stayed in better hotels but years ago had read about this one for long-term residents and short-term guests in a travel article, and it was just as she had imagined it.

"No, I was prepared for this, Douglas. I'll be OK."

They went in and, while Sheila managed to register and was given a room *al terzo piano*, Douglas noticed several male guests pass through the lobby and exit, but not before looking her over. When Douglas picked up her bag to take it to her room, the short rotund woman at the desk frowned, waved a stubby finger from side to side, and said, *"Si uomini e donne fanno amicizia liberamente, fanno una brutta figura."*

Feeling thwarted by such determined resistance, he gave up on the idea and told Sheila unnecessarily, "Well, she says it looks bad if men and women mix freely, so I guess you are in good hands here. Shall we meet tomorrow about ten o'clock? I think you can get a bus nearby, and we can meet at Caffe Della Fortuna just across from my hotel."

Ten sounded rather late to Sheila, eager to make the most of the next four days, since Naples wasn't *Roma*, *Firenze*, *Venezia*, or *Pisa*—but she said, "OK, and thank you, Douglas. I'm not sure I would have come to Italy if you hadn't insisted."

"Your Italian seems to be coming back," he said as they walked to the street door. "I think you will do fine, Sheila."

Moments later, she waved after the red Alfa Romeo as it bumped along the cobblestones and rumbled around the corner.

Then she went up to her room on the third floor and opened the shutters to release the oppressive air. From her small balcony, she saw that other balconies opened onto the courtyard but were still shuttered. She stepped back inside and decided to keep her doors open that night and hope for a breeze.

She lay without covers, waiting for air to stir. Once she thought she heard a voice calling, but when she concentrated, only words like *amore*, *sognare* and *una nota* came through as a radio flooded the courtyard with love songs and kept her awake. After she gave up and closed the shutters, she slept fitfully until a soft noise awakened her, and she lay still for a time before dozing off again.

The next morning, Sheila used the pitcher and basin on the wash stand before stepping into the cooler air on the balcony. At her feet lay a yellow paper wrapped around a small object. It was early and no one else was in sight. Bending down, she unfolded it from around a piece of soft chocolate and read the words: *Bella, I want to know you – Giorgio*, which were scrawled on it. Quickly, she stepped back into her room.

It had been years since she had attracted any attention and, in many ways, that was a relief. Waiting for a clear sign that someone was interested was taxing and always fell short of what she had imagined. Her thoughts shifted to the day ahead and she soon left her room.

When the brass elevator had clanked its way down three floors, she pushed the grill aside and stepped into the narrow lobby. The reception was unattended. When she paused to leave her key in the slot with her room number, she noticed the names of residents taped under other slots; three looked like they began with the letter *G*.

Her slot was empty. Since the rooms had no phones, it would not have surprised her to find a message from Douglas or even another message around another chocolate. To her relief, there was neither, and her plans from the previous evening remained unchanged. She glanced around and, seeing no one, stepped out into the bright street and the splutter of careening Vespas and bleating car horns.

At the sheet metal news kiosk on the corner, she waited for traffic to clear and scanned the titles of magazines on display. She felt the eyes of the vendor looking her up and down and shivered at the thought that her legs were still her best feature. *Could he be the chocolate Romeo?* She ventured a glance his way and was greeted by a broad smile.

"You like what you see in *Napoli?*" he asked.

She nodded and said "*Si grazie, signore,*" and, without looking back, crossed to the bus stop opposite. So he could tell she was new … and he certainly could see her enter and leave the hotel from his kiosk. He was older, but he still looked dashing.

When a bus arrived carrying what seemed like half the city, Sheila crowded aboard with several more passengers. Gradually, her ears became attuned to the chatter of Italian and, between the grinding of gears, she thought she heard the name "Giorgio" come from two men behind her.

With each lurch and swerve, bodies thrust against hers, pushing her against still other bodies making it impossible to turn even slightly to identify the speakers. The temperature climbed and the harsh smell of male sweat overlay the thread of lavender that hung in the air. By the time she pushed her way to exit at her stop, she felt giddy.

"Ciao, Sheila," Douglas called and jumped from his seat at the café to kiss her on the cheek. "How do you like *Napoli* so far?"

Steadying herself against a chair, she said, "You are the second man to ask me that since I got up this morning. And I expect someone would have asked me in the middle of the night if I had left my balcony shutters open."

"What do you mean?"

She told him about finding her cupid's soft chocolate missile.

"Well, did you eat it?" he asked.

"I confess, I thought about it—it was wrapped. I certainly would not have done it in plain sight."

"Did you see who it was?" he said, his voice betraying excitement.

"No, but the man at the corner kiosk smiled at me."

"No other candidates?"

"None so far. But I will keep my eyes open," she promised. "And his name is Giorgio."

"What a coincidence."

"What do you mean?"

"Oh, nothing, it's a common name. Well, I'll be spending time with my friend today. But I'll show you the bus station and tourist office so you can tour to your heart's delight. We can meet here again tomorrow at this time." He shook a finger at her and said, "Who knows, your Romeo may appear at any minute."

She laughed, but when she saw she would be on her own, she remembered the hollow feeling familiar from earlier experiences with men.

The bus to Pompeii left close to the scheduled time to be swallowed up in hectic traffic that soon stalled completely. An ambulance, siren wailing, entered from a side street. It, too, became ensnarled in the jam when vehicles showed no inclination to make way, and Sheila sympathized with the person it carried, hemmed in by forces beyond any one's control.

By the time they reached Pompeii, the sun had further blunted her enthusiasm, but she paid admission and walked on to the ancient remains. The many souvenir kiosks and itinerant vendors prowling the area marred her picture of Pompeii, and she was backing away as one of them said, "Show you around, Miss? You want cold drink? I sell you postcard?" When the voice of a guide addressing a group in British English caught her ear. Sheila approached and stood at its fringe, eager to profit from this long-awaited opportunity.

Soon, behind her, she heard several American tourists begin to call to one another:

"Come over here, Harry. This is too good to miss—I want a picture.'

"Alright, hold on. Stand just a little to the left. That's it. Got it."

"OK. Now let me take one of you, dear."

Like the vendors, their familiar, nasal tones seemed out of place, so she struck out on her own.

Eventually, she found herself on a street signposted *Via dei Sepolcri* where tombs stretched along both sides. Farther along, the remains of houses of victims who met a sudden death 2,000 years earlier captured her attention. Might that have been preferable to her mother's years of decline and lingering? It was hard for her to imagine a death no one had time to prepare for. She and her mother both had been ready—and each, in her own way, hoped that something better came afterwards.

As Sheila contemplated scenes of everyday life snuffed out, she became aware of a man watching her. Had she passed him in the lobby or seen him on the bus? After taking a mental picture, she looked away—grateful that the flush in her cheeks from the heat hid what she was feeling.

After three hours under the sun on hard uneven surfaces, she succumbed and followed the street back to the bus stop to wait. Two younger American women she remembered from earlier in the afternoon sat near her. She gathered that they too were schoolteachers and introduced herself. Judy and Gladys were from the East Coast, also here for the first time.

Though Sheila hoped for conversation about the site they had just visited, her new acquaintances quickly passed on from the all-pervasive sense of tragedy at the extinction of so many lives to the red-blooded vitality of the Italian men they encountered everywhere.

"Gladys, I've been pinched four times in two days. Can you top that?"

"Red marks no one can see are one thing, Judy. I'm just thankful they haven't left hand prints for everyone to see."

"Come on. Couldn't we use more of that spirit back in Boston? It would liven up my commute—and my social life."

Sheila joined in their laughter but did not volunteer the incident with Giorgio at her hotel—oddly, it would seem like a betrayal.

When they reached the central terminal, Judy said to her, "Why don't you join us tomorrow? We're taking a bus to Mount Vesuvius for the day."

"Oh, thank you. But I'm here with my cousin from San Francisco, and I really ought to check with him first about his plans."

"Well, if you are free, it leaves here at eight in the morning," Gladys offered before they parted.

As Sheila's local bus jolted back along the route to her hotel, she wondered what the evening would bring. Then she spied them sitting at an outdoor café. *He must be in his twenties*, she thought; they sat quite close and something about the way Douglas leaned in towards him gave her a start. So this is his friend. She had heard things about San Francisco, but it never dawned on her that Douglas was … like that. It's true, he never married, but confirmed bachelors were no more unheard of than … spinsters. And, she thought immediately of herself and her new acquaintances.

They had laughed together about how fitting it was that the three of them had chosen the Feast of the Assumption of the Virgin for their first visit to Italy. Now she would have to revise her notion of confirmed bachelors … and perhaps of spinsters too.

That night promised to be cooler, so Sheila closed her shutters. When she stepped out the next morning, the courtyard balconies again were empty and another yellow paper around another chocolate awaited her. The scrawled message read: *Bella, make the shutters open tonight and the light on – I come to you! Giorgio*

She lingered for a moment, before stepping back inside to put the chocolate next to the melted remains of the first on the small table near her bed. Then, smiling at Giorgio's persistence, she ate the chocolate and left the room to go down to the lobby.

At the reception, Sheila found a phone message from Douglas: His friend had plans for him, so he couldn't get away … she should continue to enjoy Napoli. Though disappointed, she was now free to join her new friends for the day.

At the corner news kiosk that morning, someone different was serving customers, so she passed on and met Gloria and Judy at the bus depot. On the way to Mount Vesuvius, she listened to them describe in lowered voices the mosaics they had seen at Pompeii the previous day. A man had approached them and offered to show them special art not open to the general public. Since there were two of them, they decided to chance it and stepped into a small building off the main pathway. As they walked down the dimly lit hall, they clung to each other and a series of mosaics glorifying the joys of the gods in all their fleshly possibilities unfolded before their eyes.

"I've never seen anything like it," Gloria said. "I was just glad to get out of there without something … happening—but I think Judy liked it."

"Shame on you, Gloria. I was the first one out the door. What took you so long thanking Giuseppe?"

"Well, I didn't want to seem rude. And besides he blocked my path. I was just about to call for you when he said, *gentleman always opens a door for a lady*, and I could just squeeze past him."

Sheila did not press for more details and asked instead about the tour of Vesuvius they booked for the day. When they arrived, her straw hat was all that saved her from the elements. Sun-parched volcanic reaches and warm wind brought physical thirst, both for water and—she had to confess to herself—for the vitality of life.

Upon her return to the hotel that evening, she found a message from her cousin:

> *Sheila, I've decided to leave tomorrow and return to Rome. Things here didn't work out as I had hoped. Don't feel you have to cut short your stay. Your Giorgio could still show up. I'll come by your hotel in the morning at eight to see what you decide.*
>
> *Douglas*

As she puzzled about its meaning, she heard the woman at the reception greet someone who entered— "*Ciao, Giovanni*"—and thought that accounts for one of the mail slots.

In her room once again, she pondered who her Giorgio could be and stepped out to see if the courtyard offered any clues. Stars were showing and a breeze puffed curtains out from the window on the balcony next door, but no one appeared. Across from her, she caught a glimpse of a man, bare from the waist up, as a woman's arms encircled him just before the light switched off.

Back inside her room, she turned her light on and examined herself in the small mirror on the washstand. When she turned around, it showed what appeared to be a dusty handprint on her skirt, and she smiled. It must have happened on the bus back to the hotel. Would there be more to tell by morning? She took Giorgio's promise and sat on the bed holding the yellow paper smudged with chocolate for a long time before she snapped off the light. Then she undressed in the dark—but she left the shutters open.

When Sheila stood before the mirror the next morning, she saw the reflection of the twisted sheets on her bed. They told a tale no one in her small town would ever need to know. She looked carefully and her face showed no trace of remorse.

During the drive back to Rome the next day, Douglas was subdued, so Sheila thought it best not to ask why—since she knew not all adventures turn out like we expect. In her mind, she had already begun to compose a postcard.

After some thought, she said, "Douglas, I'll remember these days, and especially the nights, as long as I live"—and she decided her postcard should go to Professor Celli.

Distant Thunder

Thunder reverberated across the Australian outback as a black-breasted buzzard shadowed the halting progress of a woman and a man along a little-used trail in the Northern Territory. They had been walking since mid-morning and were drenched in perspiration. Oppressive humidity signaled the approach of autumn rains. The cameras around their necks, rescued from their burned-out jeep, grew heavier with each step.

The woman stumbled, steadied herself, and turned to her companion. "We were lucky to escape, Peter—but I don't think I can take much more!"

He didn't answer, so she added, "My head is pounding—shouldn't we wait for dark?"

He heard, but was feverishly calculating. *We're alone out here. Clouds are gathering; her cheeks are flushed—if the rain holds off just a few more hours, the heat could bloody finish her.*

The stump of his severed left little finger reminded him what failure would mean: The two men who came to collect on his casino debt a month ago would return … a momentary piercing agony and it was over—and the plan for this trip had begun to form in his mind.

Jan's voice interrupted his thoughts again as she took in the form circling above. "Peter, is that thing interested in us?"

He brandished his Nikon reflexively with his injured hand and winced, "At least we can document it if one of us gets carried off, Jan. Might even take a prize!"

Her look of incomprehension confirmed his conclusion about her condition and he gave her a tight smile. "I think we have to keep moving, darling. If we pick up the pace, we can reach the main road before our water gives out. There's no chance anyone will find us here in the back and beyond."

Her shoulders slumped as she slowly turned and trudged on. The slosh of water in their canteens, fainter each time, told him this could turn out to be a very good day.

They had met in the late fall a year ago in Chicago in his photography workshop. After moving on from Albany, New York, he had chosen a new identity and a larger town. And his easy smile and Australian accent always served him well—both as a financial advisor and in his workshops. Someone who made the

American dream work inspired trust both in his students and his clients.

He began each workshop by surveying the class as they chatted—this time a young couple, a gray-haired man with his adult daughter, a heavy woman in black with a loud voice and black-dyed hair and Jan, who was about ten years older than he and kept apart from the others. Although she was thin, had light brown hair, and wore little makeup and no ring, she dressed extremely well. And around her neck hung a very heavy Nikon—which told him: *Money.*

Peter straightened his long, trim frame from a casual pose against the front table and flashed a smile. "G'day friends. My name is Peter Hotson. Glad to see you here. My day job is as a financial advisor, but photography has always been my passion." He looked around the room, stopping at Jan before continuing: "My aim is to help you grow as photographers over the next six months. Of course, that means different things for each of you, so let´s start by sharing what you hope to gain from this course."

The gray-haired man smiled at his daughter and volunteered first. "We want to learn how to stop high-energy grandchildren in action."

"Our snapshots are mostly a blur," she agreed.

Next, with a shy glance at his wife, the young husband said, "We want to learn how to use this new camera before the baby comes."

The woman in black, her voice roughened by years of smoking, said, "I've been at this a while. I just want some coaching on working with light in portraits."

Jan spoke last—in a voice so low Peter had to lean forward to catch it—"Animals and flowers are God's most trustworthy creations. I want to learn to capture their essence."

The woman in black smiled. A slight furrow crossed the brow of the older man, and the young couple twisted in their seats to look back discreetly, but Peter nodded gravely.

Finally, someone who understands, she thought. *That hasn't happened before.*

After Peter ended the class with "Cheerio, til next week," he stepped over to Jan's table as the others filed out and asked, "Can I have a gander at your portfolio?"

"Oh, are you sure?" she asked and then handed it to him. With a flutter of her hand, she said "These don't really express what I feel—I hoped for so much more."

He leafed through the photos, mostly lackluster close-ups of flowers and images of domestic and zoo animals.

She shifted uneasily in her seat and heard him comment: "Nice," or "OK, there's a beaut," or "Interesting," and was aware of his occasional glance.

"Nature and animals," he said. "Just what Australia is full of!"

As he handed back her portfolio, the expensive Swiss watch on her left wrist caught the light. "I tell you what, Jan. How would you like to go along on a shoot with me? Say ... this weekend."

"Oh, I'm afraid I couldn't," came her automatic reply and she slowly blushed.

"Well, think it over. I have some ideas about how to go about this," he said and thought: *Better take it easy.*

After returning home, Jan looked in the mirror and saw that the ravages of divorce had nearly faded. Peter's smile and craggy tan features topped by sandy hair floated into mind and her cheeks grew warm. *Was that smile for me? Should I have just said yes?* And she heard a small, inner voice answer: "Be careful!"

During the week, before each class meeting, she struggled with her expensive equipment, aware that Peter would see the results. Fritz, her pet corgi, bore the brunt of most of her attempts but he could not seem to help.

After each class, Peter made a point of encouraging her. "Jan, you have an eye there. You care about nature." He offered pointers but didn't push the idea of meeting between classes again. Each time, her smile came more quickly and each time he noted her expensive jewelry and tasteful wardrobe were carefully chosen.

After the final workshop in March, he decided to approach her again. Light gleamed from his Italian leather loafers as he casually sat on the edge of her table, leg dangling.

"Jan, you've made great progress." When she looked up and smiled, he said, "It's time to get out there and have a go at it. Let's meet Sunday afternoon at Lincoln Park Zoo—say at the entrance, around 3 p.m. The light should be just right. If you are free, we can get an early dinner afterwards and talk cameras."

She was pleased and wondered briefly why a handsome, younger man should be so attentive before nodding, "OK, Peter, I think I'd like that."

He gave her forearm a pat and watched the twinges of nervous excitement play around her mouth and eyes.

More outings followed the meeting at the zoo as spring unfurled with unusual ardor. Jan had no car and would wait at her Gold Coast townhouse on Chicago's north side for Peter to come by and pick her up. When he turned his dark red Lexus into her well-kept, tree-lined street, the stately homes convinced him that the pay off this time could be bigger than in New York.

With their cameras, they followed the April wildflowers northward into rural Wisconsin and Jan grew steadily more comfortable around him. They had ventured beyond 'student and teacher' and she said, "You know, Peter, I haven't been out much since my divorce. When I saw your landscape photographs, I thought you might be a kindred spirit."

He glanced over. "That's why I asked you that first time, Jan. I recognize when someone is ready to blossom."

"Well, it is springtime and flowers are my favorite subject," she laughed and feelings long extinguished colored her voice.

Peter noticed the change and said, "I think you should set your sights on mounting a show, Jan. I can coach you, and I know a gallery that would be spot on." He gave no sign that a losing streak at the casinos weighed on his mind, and the delight in her face told him that he was getting close—he simply needed to learn more about her vulnerabilities.

Buoyed by the vibrant greens of the countryside, Jan felt a prick of hope that she might again find happiness with a man. The story Peter told about his past sounded harmless but, always, that small voice prompted her, "Be careful! Remember."

On their drive home after dinner from a Sunday excursion, she closed her eyes and settled back into the comfortable seat of his Lexus. When they reached the

Outer Drive along the lake front, she opened her eyes to watch the sparkle of lights from the high-rise buildings flow past.

When he asked her to tell him more about herself., she began wistfully: "My parents were both dead when I met my husband Jim. I guess I wanted someone who needed me. I dropped out of college and worked two jobs to put him through school." Weariness crept into her voice as she continued and light played across her plain features. "Then, we relocated for med school and for Jim's endless residency. The years of grinding away sapped us both … the one thing I learned is that I need to look out for myself."

"Any children?" he asked.

Her voice caught. "Children didn't fit. By the time Jim got established at a hospital as a plastic surgeon and began a practice, there really wasn't much left to build on. That's when he told me the time had come for him to move on to … a more suitable partner." She paused and said, "Up until now, the best thing that has happened to me was finding a lawyer who knew how to put it to him."

Peter gave her a glance he hoped looked both sympathetic and masked his excitement at this disclosure.

Soon after, he phoned to say, "Jan, let's take the whole weekend and drive out to Wyalusing State Park where the Wisconsin River meets the Mississippi. It's quite a ways out, but the countryside and wildflowers are spectacular. I think you and your camera are good to go." He waited a moment and added, "To have a fair go, it means we'll have to stay overnight."

Her pulse quickened. For some time, she had been turning over an idea. *Maybe this man isn't just wrapped up in photography. He must feel something for me.*

Afraid that she was shying, he added, "I really hope you'll go."

She took a deep breath and replied, "Yes, Peter. I'd like that."

After reaching the park that weekend, Peter took her hand and guided her across the challenging terrain along the bluffs above the Mississippi amid volleys of birdsong and flashes of color. As they crouched close together in a blind, he noted her growing giddiness as he coached her on stopping bird activity with a telephoto lens and tripod. Moving on to open meadows, he showed her how to capture the subtle tones and textures of the tiny blossoms sprinkled across the hillside using a macro lens. When they had finished, he drove to a bed-and-breakfast he had chosen in nearby Prairie du Chien.

"What a wonderful day, Peter!" she said as they went in. "I insist on paying for this. It's the least I can do— you have given me so much of your time!"

After dinner as they sat sipping wine and gazed into the fire, Jan sighed drowsily, "Honestly, Peter, I'm afraid I see little difference in my work from the time I first came to you. You are so patient."

A shiver went down her spine when he took her hand and squeezed it and heard him say, "Jan, I see subtlety in your work that only needs nurturing."

Feeling secure, she closed her eyes and left it remain in his for several minutes. Sparks snapped in the hearth and she startled. "Oh dear! I think I'd better get some sleep!" she said and stood up.

Peter followed her up the carpeted staircase and along the dim hall. When they came to her room, she paused and turned towards him. He stepped closer and she quivered like a frightened bird as he drew her close.

When he kissed her, warmth spread through her body, and the sound of her own sigh surprised her as she returned his embrace.

That night marked the beginning of intimacy that frightened her by the intensity of her need. He was both patient and insistent as a lover and, the next morning, when she wondered out loud whether she was doing the right thing, he put his finger to her lips and said, "Shh, it had to be this way."

Over the next weeks, Peter began staying over and moved quickly to make her emotionally dependent.

"Darling, I have to go to New York again to meet with my partner," he lied.

"Oh, Peter, must you? I miss you so. Even when I walk on the lakefront with my camera, all I can think of is Wyalusing and our first night together."

After each absence, the sex was intensely bonding and he felt he was nearing a pay off. He got less cautious and his debts mounted. The next time he returned, he dropped a note in a woman's hand from his pocket. Jan picked it up and scanned it. Panic flickered in her eyes.

Folding her in his arms, he said, "Don't worry, dear. It's from my partner's secretary. They're having an affair, and I pocketed it for him so his wife wouldn't find it."

She relaxed into him and buried a tearful face in his neck. *He is here in my arms now*, she thought and heard him say, "Once I'm set financially, Jan, nothing should keep me from settling down."

Releasing her, he drew a prospectus from his pocket and handed it to her. "This is the opportunity I've been waiting for, Jan." It showed prosperous-looking couples lounging on a terrace with a view of mountains and the sea, smiles on their tanned faces.

She opened it and saw that it was in two languages. She read: *Once the first property is sold, the project will be self-financing and early investors will see a quick return on their money.*

"The English and the Germans can't get enough sunshine at home, Jan. If I buy into this group developing real estate in Spain, I can get on with my life."

Her thoughtful look told him he was getting close, and he said, "Two more shares at $150,000 each towards working capital will get me aboard. Then the project can start."

After a moment's hesitation, she went to her desk and took out a checkbook. "Peter, you have been supporting my projects. It's only right that I support yours."

"But Jan, $300,000?"

"Yes, Peter. I don't want anything to stand in our ... in *your* way. I can invest half now and half in a month."

When he felt how tightly she clasped him when he took her into his arms, he knew it would not be long before it was time to move on again.

A month later, he answered a knock at his New York hotel room. Two sturdy men pushed past him. "What's going on?" Peter managed.

"Since you aren't payin' up, Mac, we've come to collect interest." The larger one grabbed Peter in a hammerlock while his partner pulled out a knife and gripped his left hand. When he couldn't comply with their demands and struggling proved useless, Peter held still, hoping for it to be over quickly. Their parting words, 'Don't be late again!' burned into his brain.

During the night after his return, he drew his bandaged hand sharply away from her and sat up, bathed in sweat.

"What is it, Peter?" she asked.

"It was just a silly accident," he said, "changing a tire, Jan. Really my own bloody fault. Don't worry now."

She told herself, *there is nothing wrong. He's come back to me* and the next day she wrote out a check for the second $150,000.

One evening soon after, they settled in at Peter's apartment to watch a documentary he had recorded on Australia. After pouring them each a glass of velvety Australian Cabernet, he said, "See what you think of this, Jan, it's from down under," and began showing the film. He had selected carefully: Lush images of surreal rock formations and barren stretches of reddish soil took them into the heart of the Australian interior.

He said, "After the first rains, wildflowers carpet the desert" and watched for her reaction. "Just imagine what a honeymoon this would make with our cameras!"

"Oh, Peter, do you mean it … you want to marry?"

He answered with his rugged smile and drew her into a tight embrace to quiet any of her fears. Since he had already extracted what he could from her to stave off his pursuers, the idea came to him of not simply ending the affair, but marrying, taking out life insurance, and cashing out spectacularly. "Yes, darling. We'll marry here first to avoid any problems and fly to Darwin. We can honeymoon in the outback with our cameras—in October—exactly a year since we met!"

To allay any suspicions, Peter insisted on insurance policies for them both before they left. Once there, they rented a jeep and headed south. He watched as she drank in the countryside, her face radiant. Eventually, they left the main road and followed a little-used track to a remote point deep into the deserted terrain.

Peter stopped at a brushy stretch and said he wanted to check something in the engine. He climbed out of the jeep, locking the doors behind him. Then he raised the hood and disabled the electronic locking system. Quickly, he loosened the fuel line, pulled a lighter from his pocket, and stepped back. Ducking down, he scrabbled backwards, flicked the lighter and tossed it into the engine compartment. At the yellow flash and whoosh, he sprang back farther and saw Jan's alarmed face through the windscreen. "The engine's on fire, Jan!" he yelled. "Jump!"

He watched as she struggled with the door until smoke and flame flared up and her screams suddenly stopped. He hunched down and scuttled away before the extra fuel on board exploded and waited until the searing flash had washed over him.

Once the flames died down, he got up and approached the smoking vehicle. Shielding his eyes, he squinted into the cab. Only the metal cases holding their photo gear had escaped damage. He circled to the passenger side and saw that the door was part-way open.

A moan came from behind him. Wheeling about he looked for the source. "Jan?"

The moan turned to whimpering, then sobbing. Movement in a depression twenty yards back from the road caught his eye as Jan raised up.

She shook as he held her in his arms and told him about it: "When you got out to check, I cracked the window and left the door ajar to get more air. The fire started and I tried to open the door, but it jammed. So I braced against your seat and kicked with my legs until it snapped open and I tumbled out in time to get away."

Five hours later found them moving along the deserted track seeking help. Lightning swept the scrub-strewn terrain as thunder rumbled close by; the hope beginning to show in her eyes alarmed him. *Rain could save her ... and spoil everything.*

At first, the change in his face didn't make sense. Earlier, after their narrow escape, she hadn't been thinking clearly. But now, a pattern began to emerge: *He wouldn't bring a phone of any kind along. And he insisted we avoid other people.*

The sky had darkened and fat drops splattered the parched dust as the north wind strengthened. Rain soon pelted the sparse vegetation releasing pungent aromas. "Thank heavens, Peter," she cried, "we're saved!"

He cursed silently, then shouted above the storm, "It's starting to hail, Jan. Let's find shelter." His mind raced.

Clay, then sand, stuck to their boots as they followed the track into a dry wash with dark, low bushes along its course. Nearby, a narrow wooden bridge spanned the dry stream bed. They crouched close to a rock outcropping and sheltered against hammering hail and rain.

As water rose along the bottom of the draw, he held her and searched his mind for a way to realize his plan. Soon, water flowed around their ankles. *That's it,* he thought, *this storm will send a torrent through here.*

She felt the change in his body and looked up. Rain streamed down his hard features. At the cruel glint of triumph, she pulled against the tight grip on her wrist.

Her voice nearly failed her as she said, "Peter, you don't love me, do you? All you ever wanted was my money, wasn't it?"

"That took you a long time to figure out, Jan. Why else would anyone notice you? You're as plain as all your photos."

She struggled harder. "You aren't going home from this honeymoon, Jan. We didn't come out here to the back of Bourke just for a lark. Remember those insurance policies we took out on each other? That bet's going to pay off. I owe money—lots of money. Unless I collect on you, I'll lose more than just a finger."

Immobilized by his grip as he leaned in towards her, she heard a voice revive: *"Don't! Don't let this happen!"* With a sideways lurch, she threw him off balance and the sleeve of her wet blouse slipped from his weakened hand.

Before he could recover his footing, she wheeled and swung her camera by its strap, striking him in his left eye socket, stunning him and opening a deep cut. Desperation had lent the blow force, and he gasped at the sting of blood in his eye before slumping into the rapidly rising water.

Sobbing, Jan slipped and stumbled up the streaming slope towards the bridge. She had reached the center of the span when a blinding flash came with a crash of thunder; paralyzed, she peered down at the violent rush of water. Moments passed—then she felt a hand grasp her shoulder. With a scream, she turned and was met by the smile that distorted Peter's blood-streaked features.

"No," she blurted and looked back into the murky torrent for an instant before wrenching herself free. Then she stepped off the bridge.

He squinted through the rain after her as she was swept away. Ignoring his throbbing hand and eye, he imagined *their* faces when they returned for their money and he threw back his head, but his laughter was swallowed up by the churn of the approaching water. He wheeled around just as the flood surged over the bridge to send the tormenter after his victim.

Within an hour, the rain ceased and the front pushed through to the southeast. The sky cleared and a buzzard resumed its solitary patrol over the steaming land, seeking victims of the storm's violence.

On October 28th, Chicago papers carried this report:

Honeymooning Couple Missing in the Outback

Local authorities in Australia continue the search for two Chicagoans who did not return from their honeymoon in a remote area of northern Australia. Their burned-out rental vehicle was found, but there was no trace of them. The first severe storm of the rainy season recently swept the area which is prone to flash flooding. Foul play has not been ruled out.

Two days later, another item announced that the husband's body had been found, an apparent drowning victim, but there was still no trace of his wife.

Another report followed several days later:

Wife Delivered to Ranger Station, Delirious

Aboriginal tribe members found the wife of the American couple missing in remote Australia along a water course and kept her until she could be brought to a hospital in Darwin. A Hollywood studio is said to have contacted her about rights to her story.

At first, Jan declined to speak with reporters, but after again listening to her inner voice, she knew that the decision to jump had changed her. She would tell her story and the insurance and film money would go to those who had rescued her—and one day, she would return, with her camera.

William Geuss

Death Along the Des Plaines

My name is Rick Auberson. I've been with the Cook
County Forest Preserve Police for two years, and my
beat includes a calm stretch of the Des Plaines River
that runs through marsh and woodlands. I grew up
around here and I can tell you: Chicago swelters in
August. At the station house, we place bets on whether
the heat will give us more suicides or more
homicides—and neither outcome surprises me.

On a punishing day two weeks ago, I listened to the
National Weather Service say: "This makes it forty-
three straight 90-degree-plus days to beat the streak set
back in 1955,"—a new personal worst for me.

But, I'm lucky because despite sub-par a/c in my
patrol car, at break time I can ease off Milwaukee
Avenue into a shady lot along the Des Plaines near
Dam One. Most afternoons a breeze comes up, so I go
to the river to rest my eyes and listen to the locusts

buzz and rattle. They reminded me that the Saturday after next, my boy Jake and I could finally head north to the woods for some serious fishing and mosquito wars.

Oh, yeah, another thing: I'm hoping to make sergeant this fall. The night classes in criminal justice at the local college are wearing me down, so making sergeant would mean some desk duty plus a pay increase.

One more week without complications and we'd be on our way. The vacation part was no sweat. Well, weather aside, you know what I mean. But the promotion wasn't such a sure thing—it was coming down to me or Clancy Branaghan. He was hired six months before me.

I wanted that promotion as badly as I needed it. I had to get my kid out of that trailer park and into a better place, but that afternoon, I just wanted a break to be able to finish my patrol for the day.

Ten yards downstream from where I climbed out of the car, the river spilled over the dam loud enough to drown most Friday traffic noise—and it made me feel cooler. Mine was the only car in the lot and the only people around were a small number of regulars gathered downstream.

They sat in the shadows across the river with their bottles and didn't seem bothered by the heat! Their spot near the bushes away from the bank gave them a clear view across to my parking area. One of them with his shirt off and a swath of tattoos wrapping around his left shoulder used binoculars to give me a once over to satisfy himself I wasn't looking for them. Then, he and his buddies continued to swig and share whatever it was that animated them that day.

My twelve-hour shift started at 7 a.m. and I had been patrolling since with only a short lunch stop. I sat in the shade to lean back against the sloping bank and listen to the locusts singing their welcome chorus. The last three years hadn't been easy.

When Sally, my wife, died Mom moved in to look after our boy, Jake. He's ten now. That works for us and she does a great job. But we really miss Sally. Sometimes I go numb just thinking about her ... she still comes to us in our dreams. And Jake, he gets real still when we talk about her.

That afternoon, it all caught up with me. Soon, my eyes closed and I was fishing a stream with Jake, relishing the flow of cold water around my legs. Sally watched us from the bank while we cast for trout. We weren't having any luck, but I could have stayed right there forever—just the three of us, together. Then, the call of a blue jay cut into my dream and I resisted but the excited voices of two boys about eight or ten brought me all the way back. I lay still and listened.

"Luke, come over here!"

Rolling onto my right elbow, I looked down towards the river. Luke was winging flat rocks out into the still water behind the dam.

"Wait a minute, Tommy. I just about got one to skip five times," he called.

"Yeah, sure. Just come look at this—there's something in here."

Luke failed at one more attempt and then moved downstream to the patch of tall green rushes screening Tommy.

"In here?" he asked.

"Yeah. Take a look, it's a backpack and it's kinda weird." He named articles of women's clothing as he apparently fished them out while Luke supplied suitable sound effects. "There's a bra! And underwear! Here's a shirt and shorts."

"Man, Tommy, some woman left her clothes. I wonder why?"

It sounded to me like someone simply changed to swim or sun bath, but it was strange that she left her things behind. I stretched and went down to the river. I had seen these boys here before, but when they heard me part the rushes, they startled and jumped to their feet.

"Hello," I said. "You boys find something in here?"

"Yes, sir," they said together and eyed my uniform. "Somebody left clothes here in a backpack. It's creepy."

Sizing things up, I decided to check into it. "How long have you boys been at the river today?"

Tommy looked at Luke. "We come down here most days on the way home. I guess we've been here about a half hour."

"Seen anything out of the ordinary—any other people or anything different going on?" I asked.

"No, sir. Just the bunch of guys across the river we usually see. And sometimes, we see a police car."

No surprises there. Some of the regulars always hang out and Clancy patrols this beat on my days off.

"But I know this backpack wasn't here, the last time we came," Luke said.

"When was that?"

Turning to his pal, Luke said, "Let's see. Two days ago, wasn't it, Tommy? The day we saw the turtle—on Wednesday. I hid in here when we played hide and seek, and there was nothing here."

"OK. Thanks for your help, boys. I'll check into it and may get in touch with you."

"Man, that's cool!" said Tommy.

I took their phone numbers and addresses and gave them a number to call if they thought of anything else. Then I photographed their find and the general area and pulled on some evidence gloves to collect the materials. As dry as it was lately, there were no footprints, so there wasn't much to go on. If I reported this back at headquarters at the end of my shift, I risked delaying my vacation...on the other hand, I wanted to look good with that sergeant exam coming up.

Still undecided that evening, I parked alongside Clancy's car and went into the station to the squad room for the daily debriefing. As usual, Clancy ignored me while others returned my greeting. He was seated next to the Commander. I took a seat across from them and sized up my rival. We were roughly the same age, mid-thirties, but at 5 foot 5 inches he was a good half-a-foot shorter than I. His round, choir-boy face and red cheeks might have made him sympathetic, but he was no cherub.

After we ran through the usual lack of permits, littering, and noise nuisance complaints, Clancy cleared his throat and, turning to the Commander, said, "I stopped three cars for traffic violations this afternoon on the roads adjacent to the Forest Preserve District: I had two of them impounded—one with expired plates, another with a tinted windshield, and the third was playing loud music."

That brought a smile to the Commander's face, since it meant upwards of $2,000 in fines and fees.

To have something to say, I decided to report the backpack near Dam One; I mentioned the find and listed the contents. Then, I asked, "Does this match up with anything that's come in lately—a missing person report or suspicious behavior?"

Heads shook. Nobody had anything. Turning to the Commander, Clancy quickly said, "I can check the databases and let you know by morning, sir."

"OK," Commander Thompson said, "Take care of it, Clancy. That's it for today."

I realized I had been outmaneuvered and my jaw tightened.

The sun was sinking into the haze of another stifling day when I arrived home for supper. I wondered if I should mention the possible hitch in our vacation plans as I walked into the trailer and was met by the sound of animated voices.

Mom and Jake were sprawled on the floor in the advanced stages of a Monopoly game. Negotiations for a complicated property swap seemed to be going nowhere, and their money fluttered in the draft when the fan played across the board.

Jake tried again. "But Gramma, you'll never get past my monopoly. Why don't you just swap me?"

I remembered back when Sally was still here: Jake used to make up the rules as he went along. To judge from each of their holdings and cash, this game was pretty even—which didn't stop Jake from looking up and saying, "Hey, Dad, I've got Gramma in big trouble!"

She chuckled and showed her usual good nature by admitting that "things are getting pretty tight for me. He is really sharp tonight."

Though still worried about getting away for a vacation, I managed a smile. Mom had been counting on a visit with her sister in Michigan for some time, and I hoped the backpack wouldn't get in the way. I kicked off my shoes and got down on the floor to take her place while she got supper.

The next day was my day off, but thought I better stay on top of the backpack business and drive to the station where I found a report in my box. A note from the Commander was attached:

> Rick, here is Clancy's report. We don't need more in the papers about crime in the forest preserve! Since it was found in your sector, it has to be cleared before any vacation. See if this backpack is linked to criminal activity that warrants passing it along to a detective."

The report read:

> The inventory of articles found yesterday tally, in part, with the descriptions of persons listed as "missing" in pertinent databases. See attached list. Recommend we investigate. Patrol Officer Clancy Branaghan.

I groaned. Chasing this down could kill my dream of trout fishing with Jake this summer. School started up again for him in a little over three weeks and the sergeant exam came soon after—no wiggle room there. Although I could see the need to pursue this, the urgency escaped me. So far, the only potential crimes the clothing pointed to were public indecency by the owner or theft of the belongings by a voyeur or sneak thief. I also noticed that the database queries were time-stamped four days prior to my find, which was odd.

Ever since I first showed up for work two years ago, Clancy seemed to have it in for me. We both wanted this promotion. Me, I'd settle for more money, but he wanted to be in the catbird seat, to be the boss and stick it to me. Since he had started before me and had completed his probation, the Commander said he should show me the ropes. So, I went on patrol with him my first two weeks.

He insisted that I drive, so he could tell me where to go, how to get there, and what to do next. Now I'm a pretty laid-back guy, but he really got to me. Three days into it, I was ready to shoot him. Any time I made a suggestion about how we might proceed, he would just say, that wasn't in the cards—I should just wait and see. So I sat back, bit my tongue, and followed his directions. Needless to say, we had not become best buddies.

I passed Noreen at the dispatch desk as Clancy came down the hall on his way to clock in.

"Morning, fellas!" she greeted.

"Good morning," he said to her and turned to me with a smug look: "I see you have my report."

I nodded and watched him go down the hall. After the squad room door closed behind him, I asked Noreen, "What gives with Clancy—have I got bad breath or something?"

She laughed and said, "No way, Rick. He just is that way. After a few beers at the Fourth of July picnic this summer, he started telling me things. I asked him how he got the name 'Clancy', and he said, 'My dad's doing—it was good for a lot of ribbing at school.' Seems his dad was Irish and always wanted to be a cop, so he named his boy 'Clancy'," she said.

"I get enough guff about being 'Ranger Rick', but a lifetime of hearing yourself called 'Clancy the Cop' sounds worse," I admitted.

"Then he went on to say, 'Well, I am a cop and it makes my life worth living. Cops get to tell people what to do or what to stop doing. The best time I've had so far was when Rick, the new guy, started and I showed him who was in charge. If I can help it, I'm moving up to sergeant after Harrison retires this fall and staying on top.'"

Seeing my frown, Noreen leaned in closer and said, "One more thing, Rick: That new policy giving us jurisdiction on roads near the forest preserves has got people angry, and the newspapers have gotten onto it. You know how cars get impounded for minor violations? Add that to the tow fees and it means big bucks for us. But the press is turning up the heat."

I knew about this, so I raised my eyebrows with a question mark.

"Yeah, but listen to this: There's talk of a harassment law suit. Half the cars towed are driven by Hispanics, even though they make up only a quarter of the cars stopped."

Quickly looking around, she continued, "And the guy with the most stops by far is Clancy. That could go either way for him."

I gave her a thumbs up as I left and said, "You're always a good person to check with, Noreen. Thanks!"

So it looked like I couldn't count on Clancy for much help with the backpack, but the on-line course in criminal investigation I was taking gave me some ideas. His report listed five adult females from Wisconsin, Illinois, Iowa, Indiana and Michigan who were reported missing within the last eight weeks.

I got on the computer in the squad room and used a new program I'd just learned about to generate images of a person from clothing sizes. Inputting the garments from the backpack gave me an image showing an estimated weight, height, and body-type for the person wearing them. Comparing that to the photos and measurements on-line of the missing women eliminated three of them—one was definitely taller and two were definitely heavier. That left two: a blonde from Illinois and a brunette from Michigan, 5 feet 4 and 5 feet 6 inches, and both about a catalog size 38.

I sat back for a moment. Sending garments to the State lab for DNA testing meant a long turnaround time and would surely nix our fishing trip. I would also have to send DNA from anyone who handled the material—Tommy, Luke, and me—so I approached it from another angle.

I went to the evidence locker and signed out the backpack and its contents. No one else had accessed it since I signed it in. Wearing gloves, I removed the first garment from its paper bag and laid it on a tray for a closer look. Under a strong light and magnification it looked new and was barely rumpled. Several short reddish-blonde hairs showed in the light. I tweezered them into an envelope and marked it. Next, I took the skirt. When I turned it over and shook it, a small earring fell out of the pocket. Another surprise. Following the same procedure, I put it in a separate envelope and realized I had slipped up in not finding and including it in my initial inventory. An examination of the underwear turned up no sign of staining or wear, which was puzzling, as were the rips in these apparently new garments. So I added the earring to the inventory and signed the materials back in to the locker.

I was making progress: Assuming the reddish-blonde hairs were from the owner of the garments rather than a third party would eliminate the brunette from Michigan; the best hypothesis was either the missing blonde from Illinois or some other person who had contact with the clothing. Luke and Tommy and I have black hair, so we were out.

I weighed my next step: I should check with anybody who might have seen something down at the dam and decided to start with the regulars from the river bank.

On the way home, I checked out the Saturday night crowd at their watering hole, the Black Banjo Tavern. The first one came in around 10 p.m. He was still steady on his feet when he leaned against the bar to order a beer and a shot and I greeted him.

"Hello, Artie."

"Hey, how ya been, Rick?" he replied over a low belch.

"You know ... mostly getting callouses on my ass from driving that patrol car all day."

"Hah, hah, hah! Hey, that's pretty good!"

"By the way, Artie, I wondered if you guys saw anything odd going on the last few weeks around Dam One—say, other people hanging out or strange business?"

He pinched his brows down over cloudy blue eyes set in a ruddy face and searched. I knew this was asking a lot, but I needed to start somewhere.

"No, nothin' much. Just the guy walkin' that brown dog most days and the usual tricks Mac plays on me. You know. The guy with tattoos all over one shoulder. Like the last time ..." and he rambled on.

I figured I had drawn a blank and was only half listening. Since I knew it would just get louder and busier the later it got, I kept an eye out for any other guys I recognized. Two more who knew Artie came over to the bar to listen in.

"Yeah, Mac had a pair of binoculars and started watchin' a car across the river," Artie said expansively. "So, he pokes me and hands me the binoculars and says, 'They are really gettin' down over there, Artie, take a look.' Now I had just got back from taking a leak in the woods, so I takes a few minutes tracking around with those damn glasses until I gets the car in view. Then I says to Mac, bullshit, I don't see anything. Just some guy sittin' behind the wheel. What's so hot about that?

"'What do you mean?' he says. 'She was right there beside him. She must be down lower. Use your imagination, Artie!'"

His audience sniggered.

"'Could be, but nothin's in it for me ... 'aw, you're just puttin' me on,' I says."

The other men laughed at this latest round in the pranks the two played on each other. Sometimes Artie succeeded, but usually Mac came out ahead.

Artie's face showed more color as he downed another drink and warmed to his audience: "So, Mac says, 'Honest, I'm not shittin' you, Artie. She was right there! Long blonde hair and either they were wrestlin' or something pretty hefty was startin' up.'"

Wrestling ... that brought me back fully alert to what he was saying. Could this be what I was looking for?

Artie continued, his words slurring: "So he snatches back the glasses, takes another look, and says, 'Sure enough. Just the guy!' So I says, 'Well, I'm not hanging around here any longer' and pick up my bicycle and push it up the slope to the path ... and that was pretty much it," he said with a look of satisfaction.

"So nobody got out of the car, and it was still there when you left?" I asked.

"Yeah and everybody else took off then too."

Further questioning didn't produce much. Artie wasn't sure what day that was or what color vehicle— "either a red one or a green one".

"Red or green?" When he hesitated, I pressed him. "Come on, Artie, just tell me you're color blind and we'll be getting somewhere."

"OK, Rick," he stammered, "You got me there—I guess I am. But I'm sure that man with the dog comes most days."

It was late when I pulled the truck into our trailer park, gravel crunching under the tires. Crickets chirped briskly chirping, seemingly grateful for the evening shadows as I climbed down and the truck door closing set off the schnauzer living two trailers down to end the cricket serenade.

I sighed and remembered that apartment living hadn't been any guarantee against yapping pets either. After Sally's doctor bills took our savings, it only left Jake and me with the trailer court option. This was home for now, and Jake was growing faster all the time.

He settled in to his new school OK. But I couldn't be with him as much as I wanted, and there were no other kids around to play with. So we were counting the days until our fishing trip and Mom was looking forward to visiting her sister. That left me exactly one week to clear this up if we were going to get away.

The next day, I woke to the smell of bacon frying. It was Sunday, my day with Jake. I found him still sprawled on the sofa where he slept, reading. "Good morning, partner!" I yawned.

"Gramma is making pancakes!" he exclaimed.

"That sounds great." I tousled his head. "I'll go get me some coffee and see if I can help her."

I moved on through to the kitchen, kissed Mom on the cheek, and set the table. When I rejoined Jake, I said, "What say we watch that Bears game at noon—it's too hot for us to do much outside anyway."

"Awesome!" came his response. Although the trailer was small, it didn't prevent Jake from playing spirited games of phantom football, silently faking, dodging, pulling in long passes with a nerf ball and collapsing under crushing tackles—no doubt to the wild cheering of imaginary fans. It was the best he could do without other kids around.

When the Bears game ended around 4 p.m., I decided to try my luck at the dam, hoping for a lead on a vehicle or a man walking a brown dog. A blast of hot air met us when we walked outside and drove to the river wearing T-shirts and baseball caps. We tossed a rubber football around until Jake, like Luke, was drawn to the water to try his hand at skipping rocks above the dam.

By 6 p.m. the river had given up no secrets—no man, no dog; but it had stopped getting warmer. So we climbed back in the truck and headed home for supper.

Monday didn't produce anything useful besides temperatures in the mid-80s but, on Tuesday, I got lucky. There he was—a man in a blue T-shirt walking a small, light-brown dog near the parking area. The dog was short-haired and pranced, but the man himself, maybe in his mid-fifties, shuffled and was nearly bald. Certainly worth a try, I thought as his dog got busy snuffling around a tree. I climbed out of the patrol car and introduced myself.

"Good afternoon, I'm Officer Auberson of the Cook County Forest Preserve Police. We are looking into a possible crime in this area in recent weeks and are asking patrons of the Forest Preserve to help us with any leads. Can I have a minute for a few questions?"

He stopped the dog from tugging him off towards a clump of weeds, reeled him in, and said, "Be glad to."

My pant legs got a good sniffing as I learned that his owner's name was Randall Westby. He walked his dog Roscoe there around this time after work four or five times a week. What he said next made my heart surge a beat—"yes," he had seen a red sedan parked overlooking the dam last Thursday, "probably a late model red Buick." What came next was equally interesting.

"Yeah, I recall there was a couple seated in it playing loud music and a woman was singing—almost screaming," he said.

"Which would you say, singing or screaming?"

"Hmmm—I don't know—not my kind of music, in any case. But by the time Roscoe here tugged me back into the woods, I figured out it was probably French," he added, with a self-satisfied look. "The word '*amour*' kept coming up." He pointed upstream and said,

"After that we just kept to our routine and went back up the trail."

"About what time was that?"

"Oh, I'd say five o'clock."

"Did anything look amiss?"

He smiled. "Well, I figured they were folks looking for a place to get romantic—maybe not married to each other and out to sneak some time together. I was married for a time myself," he added with a shrug.

"How would you describe the two of them?"

"Well, she was blonde, with hair down to her shoulders. Didn't see her face, though I did look. Mostly they were kissing and close, so I only saw that he had dark hair."

"How were they dressed?"

"Hmmm. I didn't really see their clothes," he said, "but it's sure they were dressed or I'd have noticed"— this time, with a grin.

I thought it over. They were in the car—probably for the air conditioning—with the windows rolled up; otherwise, she would have her hair up in this heat. And he did say long blonde hair. With the sound turned up high enough to hear, he would have missed any screams or cries for help. "OK. Well, just one more thing. Have you and Roscoe seen any sign of them before or since?"

"Nope. Say, did something happen? Wasn't a woman's body found in the river last spring?" With a worried look he asked, "Should we stay away from here or something?"

"No, sir," I said and, pointing at the clump of rushes thirty yards farther along the bank, I told him: "We found a backpack with some articles of women's clothing right over there last Friday, but there is no evidence of a crime. Do you recall if Roscoe had a look in there recently?"

"He couldn't have. I keep him on a leash, like it says to, and never let him go into bushes or underbrush to keep him out of trouble. You know—skunks and the like."

I thanked Mr. Westby, took his contact information, and gave him my number in case he thought of something else. Halfway back to my car, it occurred to me: Could it be that this red car got stopped by Clancy, maybe even impounded?

I bumped into Clancy just as he was leaving the squad room that evening.

He grinned and asked, "Tell me, are you getting anywhere with match-ups with those missing persons on the clothing and earring, Rick?"

I did a double take. How did he know about the earring? It wasn't in the original inventory. Regaining my composure, I said, "To tell the truth, I keep coming up with puzzling stuff. I thought maybe you could help clear up a thing or two."

"You never know unless you try," he said with a smirk.

"To begin with, I noticed that the data queries you turned in on the missing persons were date-stamped four days before I found the backpack."

"Oh, that!" he said, "Just on-the-ball police work. I try to stay on top of things that way."

Pressing on, I said, "I also wondered if you might have seen anything in the area where the backpack was found when you patrolled my beat last Thursday—the day before it turned up."

"No, there was no one around—I am certain of that," he added quickly, with the shadow of a smile.

"I see. Well, one last thing: I'm trying to track a couple in a red Buick sedan seen there the day of your patrol. Any chance you made a traffic stop on it?"

He looked at me for a moment before saying, "Could be. Could be—there've been so many lately. Why don't you just check the register?" After a moment, he asked, "Say, why are you looking for that one?"

By this time, I suspected that Clancy had something to do with planting the backpack, and felt the heat rise in my neck. I decided to let him squirm about how much I actually knew and said, "They were seen in the area, and I need to know if they saw anything."

"Oh, no! They couldn't have," he said and strode towards the exit.

That confirmed my suspicion, but I had no proof—and it was Tuesday evening already.

It was a simple matter to check the traffic stops for that Thursday, so I stayed on. And, yes, there was a red Buick logged that Clancy had stopped on Milwaukee Avenue just before 7 p.m. for playing loud music. I noted the particulars of the driver and decided to see what I could learn from him. Was that the car with the couple the regulars had seen from their vantage point and Randall Westby had seen while walking his dog? Either way, maybe they saw something that might help nail down the backpack.

Luckily, I found the owner of the Buick at home at an address in Westchester. His wife answered and called him to the phone. I told him we were contacting drivers who were known to have been in the area of Dam One off Milwaukee Avenue on Thursday, August 12th. I had some routine questions aimed at locating a missing person and wanted to come by that evening.

I heard his wife ask who was on the phone and his answer: "Just the police auxiliary looking for contributions," whereupon, he lowered his voice to say he would rather meet me at the Tollway Oasis closest to his house in an hour than talk right now. When I agreed, he thanked me, relieved.

It meant another late evening, but Saturday was coming up fast. The red car and its blonde passenger could be the key.

I entered the Oasis and followed the fast food smells to the coffee bar. A dark-haired man sprang up from his chair and came towards me. I judged him to be about fifty, with dyed hair. "Gordon Brathwaite?" I asked.

At the affirmative nod, I introduced myself and gestured towards a table, willing my stomach to stop complaining. The situation was pretty much as Randall Westby had guessed—a clandestine rendezvous by people not married to each other—both still alive and well seeking an idyllic backdrop. Gordon's description of his blonde lover matched Randall's to a hair. And, like Tommie and Luke, they had seen a police car at the dam on Thursday, the day before the backpack was found and, upon questioning for more details, were willing to testify to what else they had seen.

When I came to breakfast the next morning, I found the Wednesday paper folded open to this article:

Are the Woods Safe?

According to a regular patron of the Cook County Forest Preserve bordering Milwaukee Avenue, Forest Preserve Police found a backpack containing articles of women's clothing and are investigating any connection to missing person reports. Our informant admitted that "the fact that bodies keep turning up in the Des Plaines River and other preserves spooks me. I think I may find somewhere else to walk my dog."

"Isn't that part of your area, Rick?" my mother wanted to know.

"I'm afraid so," I answered. "And I'm afraid this case could mean postponing our plans for next week." I stood up to go and gave her a hug. "I'm doing all I can to clear this up before then, Mom."

"Well, Rick, your job has to come first. We'll just make do some other way if we have to."

As I went down the hall towards the squad room, Noreen signaled me and said, "Rick, the Commander wants to see you in his office." She mouthed, "It's the news story."

"Thanks, Noreen. Wish me well!" She gave me a wave, and I strode down the hall to the Commander's office.

I knocked and entered to find Clancy already seated and was greeted by the Commander.

"Good morning, sir," I responded.

He waved a copy of the newspaper at me and said, "Rick, this just won't do," slapping it down on the desk. "I've asked Clancy to help you get on top of this." I noted Clancy's pleased look as the Commander added, "The last thing we need is for folks to believe that the County Sheriff's police need to run things here because we can't do the job!"

I knew that the coming election involved a turf war over which department could more economically deliver law and order in the forest preserves and realized that my job was on the line in either case—so I decided to go for broke and took a deep breath to calm myself.

I turned to Clancy and said, "It's good you are here, Clancy, because you may be able to clear some things up. First of all, this backpack could simply have been lost or, second, it's tied to a missing person or, third"—I paused for effect—"someone planted it."

In response to the Commander's startled look, I continued. "This is what I've learned so far," and handed him a summary of my investigation. "I reported the backpack on Friday the 13th; the boys who found it played hide and seek in the same spot on Wednesday the 11th and it wasn't there—which means it appeared sometime between 5 p.m. Wednesday and 5 p.m. Friday.

"What about the contents, Rick?" asked the Commander.

"The garments were arguably new, possibly never worn; their sizes eliminated all but one blonde and one brunette female in the missing person reports Clancy ran. I found several short reddish-blonde hairs on the garments, potentially eliminating the brunette. I have tracked down the one blonde seen in the area on the day before the find. She has long hair and is alive and well with no connection to the backpack."

Eyeing Clancy's short blond hair, I continued: "If a suspect is found who might have planted the backpack, forensics could tell us for sure whether the hairs found on the clothing match."

At this, I saw Clancy swallow and heard the Commander ask impatiently, "How do you think Clancy can contribute at this point, Rick?"

Turning to Clancy, I said, "Perhaps you can explain the following. First, why would you run the missing person queries on Monday, four days before the find?"

"I told you, I like to keep on top of things—that was just a coincidence."

"Second, I overlooked an earring in the clothing when I first inventoried them, but you asked me about an earring without having signed out the material— how could you know about the earring, unless you knew what went into the backpack to start with?" Clancy shifted uncomfortably as the Commander stared at him.

"Don't most women take off their earrings, when they get undressed?" he countered.

"Third, your car was seen at the site on the day before the find by two separate witnesses."

Clancy flared up with, "Of course I was there; I patrol your area on your days off! And there was no one else there when I was there."

I pressed on. "You're right, there was no car. But two witnesses saw you there carrying a dark backpack resembling the one found." His ruddy cheeks went ashen. "The occupants of the red car were coming for a lovers' tryst. When they saw your car parked and spotted you walking with the backpack in the direction of the find, they decided to drive on past along Milwaukee Avenue and only came back after you left. Later, you stopped them for loud music on a road adjacent to the district and they recognized you. They are willing to testify to that."

"What do you have to say to that, Clancy?" the Commander asked. "You realize this goes beyond any rivalry between you and Officer Auberson—this puts the Department in a bad light at a time when we are especially vulnerable in the public eye—to say nothing of a breach of regulations."

"I don't have anything more to say right now."

"In view of these circumstances, Officer Branaghan, I am suspending you from the force pending a full hearing. Turn in your badge and firearm and you will be notified when to appear before the hearing board."

"And Rick," the Commander said, "You've earned a vacation."

I walked out of the meeting exhilarated and exhausted. Noreen was busy when I passed, and I didn't have time to spare before going out on patrol. She would hear soon enough what went on in our meeting. I had trouble getting through the day with my mind switching between anticipation of our vacation and a replay of the investigation over the past week.

When I pulled into the trailer court that evening and climbed down, the temperature was beginning to drop, and Jake was caught up in his favorite pastime—an imaginary Bears-Packers game with leaps and turns worthy of a ballet dancer.

"Hi, Dad! The Packers are going down," he called, passing the ball to me with a satisfied grin.

"Why am I not surprised?" I replied and clapped him on the shoulder. "Tell you what, Jake. Let's go in and tell Gramma some good news."

"Oh yeah?" he asked. "What?"

"Well, it's that we need to start packing tonight and tomorrow, so we can get away early Saturday. We want to get our lines wet on the first day, don't we?"

"You said it, Dad!" he shouted and turned to race me into the trailer.

Friday came and went with no further complications. We loaded the truck early Saturday in chill air that signaled the end of the heat wave. The schnauzer two trailers down gave us a send-off as we pulled away, and I wondered how much longer we would be neighbors.

Mom said, "What a relief that everything worked out."

After Jake and I put her on the bus to Benton Harbor, we drove north into Wisconsin to the same cabin Sally, Jake and I had rented four years ago. We unpacked and got our lines wet just at dusk. We caught a couple of small ones for breakfast. More importantly, Jake began to talk about the last time we were here. I secretly hoped this trip might open the door on feelings and memories we both had put away—and help us heal.

Monday after lunch we decided to run into town for supplies and give the fish a rest until their evening feeding. Once back to the cabin, Jake took off to try out his slingshot, and I settled down on the porch to browse the Chicago paper we picked up at the store. The breeze rattling the poplar leaves and the buzz of insects made it hard to keep my eyes open. I turned a page and an article datelined Sunday snapped me back:

Cop Found Drowned in Des Plaines River

Authorities alerted Saturday evening by an anonymous caller found a body floating below Dam One along Milwaukee Avenue. Responders found the corpse of a Cook County Forest Preserve Police officer with over two years of service who was facing a disciplinary hearing. According to our source, the officer's hopes for a promotion had been dashed by charges of misconduct. Preliminary findings point to an apparent drowning with a high blood-alcohol level.

I shook my head. Clancy was right after all—the backpack was connected to a death along the Des Plaines. I couldn't help feeling a stir of sympathy, and I wondered how he had placed his bet this summer.

Just then, Jake called: "Dad, come see how good a shot I am ... I wish Mom could see." And I knew we were going to be all right.

William Geuss

Beyond Buenos Aires

As LAN Airlines flight 216 to Buenos Aires left Miami and banked to climb over the Caribbean and leave the coastline of Florida behind, the blonde woman in seat 21D slid her hand onto her husband's and said, "Vince, what if this trip doesn't change anything?"

He gazed out at the lumpy carpet of clouds passing beneath, his hand inert and his face impassive. He answered: "I don't know, Annie. It really can't make things worse."

By 'worse' she hoped he was referring to the ground shifting under them in mid-January when the school board replaced him as head football coach at Chicago's Roosevelt East High School.

In his ten years at East, Vince had built the program into a regular contender but never managed to deliver a championship. When their archrival Roosevelt West beat them for the title last fall, a faction had formed calling for the team's assistant coach, Todd Brownlee, to replace him.

"I know you're disappointed, Vince," she responded, "but being offered the job of athletic director is no small thing."

"Annie, I'm being kicked upstairs. The fact remains: Todd is going to take my place next fall."

She shuddered inwardly at the mention of Todd's name. "I know you feel betrayed, Vince, but I think you should accept—it's a promotion..." and she hoped her voice sounded more encouraging than strained. "You always worked well with him."

He removed his hand, still looking out into the darkening sky where a first star glimmered on the horizon. "Let's just have something to drink, Annie, and try to forget about it for now."

But she couldn't forget. After the board's action, dressed up to look like a promotion, she had watched the spark dim that coaching and being in the public eye gave Vince and seen worry claim his forehead. Would there be no return to the good years?

The drop in enrollment and budget problems at their school now meant her contract would not be renewed next fall. Coaching and teaching at Roosevelt East, a school with a family feeling, had been everything they hoped for... and the energy and striving of young people around them made the lack of children of their own less important.

While the mirror told her she still looked good at forty-one, Vince's increasing lack of responsiveness over the past month made her wonder if word had gotten out after all about her indiscretion with Todd Brownlee at the Ingersoll's party. He must feel betrayed, and no matter what she tried, his furrowed brow refused to yield and their life began to unravel.

When the flight attendant broke into her thoughts, she was grateful for the distraction. Annie ordered for them both and handed Vince a glass of Merlot and accepted a glass of Chardonnay. She remembered telling her friend Rosemary Ingersoll when Vince first started teaching PE at Roosevelt ten years ago that *he might be the one.*

He was five years older than Annie and looking to settle down. Their brief courtship and short honeymoon in Toronto were followed by dreams of paying down their college loans and saving for a small house ... and for children, a boy for him and a girl for her. But by the time they were ready for them, none came and Vince rejected the idea of adopting. Instead, as only children themselves, they increasingly were called upon to respond to the needs of their aging parents on opposite coasts, hers in New Jersey and his in California.

Annie glanced over at Vince, glass empty, his head against the back of the window seat. She took another large sip of Chardonnay and set it on her tray, alone with her own sense of betrayal. What stabbed at her conscience had happened when the silence between them became unbearable.

She shifted in her seat, unable to banish the memory of her failure that night in early March at the Ingersoll's.

Rosemary Ingersoll and her husband, Harold had served as witnesses to their marriage and become their best friends. However, since the change in Vince's standing, he avoided socializing and only the death of his father from a stroke had saved him from Annie's further coaxing to go to the party: Instead, Vince took bereavement leave and flew to Anaheim to take care of things and Annie was left to attend alone.

When she stepped into the Ingersoll's entryway, she saw Todd Brownlee and hesitated. Should she stay? Before rumors began to circulate that he was a rival for Vince's job, Todd was fun to be around. They had enjoyed his lively wit and sense of humor, but now he was Vince's rival. He was five years younger than Vince, and Annie noticed that Todd still managed to keep off the extra pounds Vince accumulated after football season. She recalled that Todd had been engaged to a woman in another town but had broken it off for some reason at the end of last summer.

When he saw her standing in the entry hall, he came over and said, "Hi Annie, where's Vince?"

"Hello, Todd. His father passed away this week. He's in Anaheim settling up things."

He placed his hand on her arm and said, "I'm sorry to hear that. And, your father passed away last summer, didn't he?"

It moved her that he remembered and she felt torn—she needed distracting from her troubles but the thought that talking with him would be disloyal to Vince unsettled her.

Just then, Rosemary's husband Harold approached and she seized the opportunity to delay her decision about continuing the conversation. She returned the touch on Todd's sleeve and said, "Yes, thanks for remembering." Turning towards Harold, she said, "excuse me, Todd, I'd better say 'hello' to our host. Let's talk later."

"Annie, I'm glad you came," Harold said as he gave her a hug, and immediately she felt better.

"I am sorry to hear about Vince's dad, on top of everything else he's dealing with," Harold said and led her to the punch bowl. "How are you doing, Annie?" he asked as he ladled a cup for her.

"Not so great, Harold."

"Still no prospects for next fall?"

"No. But maybe this party will cheer me up," she said, wanting to believe it herself.

After she'd received her lay-off notice, Annie began doing art again in her studio—just as she had in college when she had added an English major to art to increase her chances of finding a job. To test the waters this winter, she had mounted a show of her latest paintings in a local gallery, but it had closed without anything selling—except the small piece Rosemary and Harold bought: A collage of design elements drawn from the shape of wine bottles and glasses, grape leaves and grapes.

"Annie, you are good," Harold, said pointing to her picture displayed above the punch bowl. "And I know something good will come along for you."

"At a time like this, Harold, friends are what matter most. I think I'll try to forget about everything else tonight."

"Good," he said and squeezed her again around the shoulders. "Now just enjoy yourself."

She went into the kitchen and collected another hug from Rosemary who said, "Annie, I'm glad you came. So sorry Vince couldn't be here. When we hung up this afternoon, I wasn't sure we'd see you. Now, you have a good time and tell me tomorrow how much it helped," Rosemary said and busied herself pulling something from the oven.

As Annie moved off, she told herself it was irrational to blame Todd for what the school board did. She entered the living room and saw him talking with a couple she didn't know. Before she could reach him, he glanced up and excused himself to come and meet her.

"Annie, I really feel bad about everything that's happening."

"Me too, but I think Vince is the worst off. He so loved that job."

"I know and he was good—winning isn't everything. I've wanted to tell him that, but he seems to avoid me." He looked searchingly at her with his startlingly blue eyes. "Do you think he will step up to athletic director?"

Feeling the effect of his gaze, she wondered what had gone wrong with his engagement and answered, "I can't predict, but I wish he would."

"Well, let me introduce you to a few people I've met here," he said. "This seems to be a faculty and neighborhood friends' night. Too bad so few from East High came."

Annie hadn't noticed anyone else from school, but she wasn't sorry. It made it easier to talk about other things. The evening was warm and the punch helped her laugh more easily and forget there was no one waiting for her at home. As midnight neared and the guests thinned, she began to feel unsteady and was afraid it showed.

Todd came up just then and said, "You going to be alright, Annie?"

"I think I'd better call a cab, Todd. I really shouldn't drive."

"I can drop you if you like."

She hesitated, then said, "Thanks, Todd. If it's no trouble?"

"Teachers are family. We need to look out for each other."

Fifteen minutes later, she sat with her head against the seat of his open convertible, her eyes closed. It was warm for early March, but she hugged herself for added warmth as they drove. The radio played oldies from the years she first came to East High kindling a mix of nostalgia and yearning that kept her from talking. Before long, they turned into a quiet street lined with bungalows and pulled up in front of hers. She glanced over at its darkened windows but didn't move to get out.

"Annie, are you OK?"

"That's sweet of you, Todd," she managed. Tears welled up against her will. Panicking, she reached over and put her hand on his forearm as though to steady herself and sobbed, "I just can't seem to get a grip on myself. I'm afraid my life is falling apart."

When she felt his left hand cover hers, it calmed her enough to peer out into the darkness. She began to explain how out of control things seemed, how distant Vince appeared to be, and how alone she felt. She turned and said "I'm sorry, Todd; none of this is your fault." Then, she drew a deep breath and leaned over the console between their seats for the hug and goodnight peck on the cheek that had been their practice before things had changed. With a tear-stained cheek pressed against his, her need for understanding, for affection and comfort broke through all constraints and, instead, she kissed him for a long moment on the mouth. When he did not refuse, she lingered and lost track of time. In the morning, the memory of eventually leading him up the steps into the dusky brick bungalow left a jagged wound.

Two days later when Vince returned, he seemed older, tired and stiff from clearing out his father's things, but his face showed less strain. As they lay in bed that night, instead of turning away from her, he said, "Annie, we're going to inherit some money from Pop's estate. It seems strange that he's gone. But, with no one left for us to worry about, it should make things easier."

The trips to New Jersey and California to visit their parents had been a financial strain and, hence, infrequent. However, their parents' not-so-veiled references during phone calls to the visits their friends had received from grown children and grandchildren invariably brought the intended result. When their parents' health began to fail these visits became a frequent necessity. For Vince, it began one Thanksgiving when they saw his father, who had never cooked, step in and rescue dinner preparations when his mother lost track of things, became agitated, and blamed him for confusing her. Her dementia advanced rapidly and four years later she was dead.

In her parents' case, it came as a phone call in the middle of the night. Her mother had not felt well all day and had gone to bed early. When her father followed to bed two hours later, he found her quite still and only realized she was cool to his touch. When he turned over and his toenail scraped her leg, she no longer complained or moved.

Vince snipped off the light but did not turn away, and Annie moved closer to put her arms around him. He wouldn't have to find out. Now they could begin to worry about one another, just the two of them. What killed his father and hers too—there had been no one left for them to worry about. Those trips to see them, nearly always ill-timed, were over. Their fathers had joined their mothers and lay beside them in the family plots.

After making love for the first time in weeks, they lay still and realized that the inheritance gave them the possibility of getting out of their rut, getting away. While colleagues used summers and Christmas or Easter breaks to travel or study abroad, their own dreams had centered around the wine regions inspired by labels on the bottles that passed through their hands—Chardonnay for her and Merlot for him. But something had always interfered and left them with dreams instead of memories, and now uncertainty about their jobs clouded their imagination.

Ten days later, the production of the musical *Evita* at Roosevelt East High School was to open and when Vince heard that Argentina, Eva Peron's homeland, also was home to wine varieties new to him, he agreed to see the show with Annie. Both of them were hazy about the figure of Eva Peron, but Argentina sounded exotic and they could explore it by proxy in the looming Art Deco auditorium at Roosevelt East.

As they sat watching young people (some of whom they knew from their classes readying themselves to launch their lives) play out Evita's fate on stage, Annie was shaken by the story of cancer cutting short the fulfillment of Eva's dreams and leaving half a nation bereft of their idol.

Before falling asleep that night, she said, "Vince, I haven't wanted to bother you with this on top of everything else ... but while you were in Anaheim, I learned that my cousin Lucy started treatment for cancer, and I went in for a mammogram. There's a funny area in my left breast. I'm scheduled to go back in two days for another x-ray."

He rolled over to face her and said, "Annie, I'm sorry. Of course you should tell me. I've been so selfish—wondering if I died, would anyone miss me ... I'm really sorry." He drew her to him. "How can I make it up to you?"

"This is a good start," she said and snuggled into the crook of his arm. "Vince?"

"Yes?"

"If this test shows there is nothing wrong, why don't the two of us just go away together for a while?"

He kissed her and whispered, "OK … Maybe to Argentina?"

When Annie learned of Lucy's cancer, she began to phone her regularly. Hearing about her treatment somehow helped still her own anxiety. The next day, when Annie was given the news that her own mammogram was negative, it felt like a reprieve from sentencing for her betrayal of Vince.

"Annie, that is fabulous news," he said when she called him. "Now there really is nothing to stop us. Let's use Easter break to go to Buenos Aires. After the streak of luck we've had, we deserve it don't we?"

But, when Vince returned to school on Monday, the unspoken pity he believed he saw in the eyes of others—perhaps even agreement with the decision to remove him as head coach and substitute his younger assistant—began to erode his self-respect. And once again, his ability to sense Annie's needs suffered, stranding her like someone treading water at sea, with no hope of rescue before her strength gave out.

Before leaving Chicago for Buenos Aires, they had searched the Internet for a hotel in Argentina and, with their limited Spanish, found the "Howard Johnson" listing reassuringly familiar. Combined with *Recoleta*, it conjured up colorful images from *Evita*, so Vince and Annie Cooper checked into the Howard Johnson Recoleta Hotel upon their arrival. When they looked out through the glass doors of the lobby at the bright yellow taxis and colored buses passing by, the poignant appeal of retracing Eva's steps in Buenos Aires offset much of their weariness from the overnight flight.

As with many visitors, their destination the first day was Recoleta Cemetery where Eva Duarte Peron lay buried. They set off with the program from *Evita* in Annie's purse and followed a map given them by the concierge, remembering his advice to "look for Eva in the Duarte family mausoleum."

The map led them to an enclosed miniature city of the dead: Four square blocks with narrow, paved walkways that crisscrossed broad avenues lined with imposing monuments and crypts that cast shadows through which a file of visitors slowly processed— people of all ages, drawn like them, from around the world; some out of curiosity, others to scatter carnations and roses at Eva Peron's shrine, acknowledging for a silent moment that "Santa Evita" had tapped something deep within them.

As Annie and Vince filed by in turn and read the name "Duarte," the modest nature of the black marble crypt surprised them, but the bronze plaque inscribed with words from Evita's song—*no me lloras* or "don't cry for me"—caused Annie to bring her hand to her chest and lower her chin as she sought to quiet the convulsive movements of her shoulders. She thought of her cousin Lucy, who was thirty-five and had two young children and that her own doctor had told her the second clear mammogram was no guarantee about the future.

To make matters worse, just beyond Evita's resting place, they came upon another tomb with a life-size statue of a soulful young woman standing at its entrance like a white marble angel. She seemed to be glancing back at them, her right hand resting on the door. They paused to listen to a guide explain that it was a memorial to a sixteen-year-old girl, the age of their students at East High. Although merely in a coma or perhaps narcoleptic, she had been thought dead and was buried alive; despite her efforts to free herself, by the time the source of her cries was traced, only her broken fingernails and scratches on the inside of her sarcophagus lid bore witness to her horrible fate.

As Annie struggled to hold in sobs she found no words for, Vince knew to put his arm around her shoulders and lead her back out of the cemetery into the park.

"I guess you've got a lot of worries these days," he said, unaware of her mixed burden.

"Yes, but perhaps this was a good place to leave them," she replied when she regained control. He took her hand and, as they strolled to a nearby café, she found comfort in the realization that, ultimately, it had been fate that destroyed Evita's life and robbed the girl of her future and, ironically, had made them unforgettable.

They entered the café's shaded, gravel courtyard and chose one of the tables at the same moment as a pigeon that was determined to feed on deserted crumbs. Flushing it away, they sat down and were grateful for a respite after their pilgrimage to the cemetery.

Then, Annie took a step back from her own anxiety and asked Vince, "Does visiting her tomb make you wonder how you will be remembered?"—knowing it might go either way in her case.

"I just know how I will remember you," he said.

"We got so used to just hanging on and getting through life and settling for pipe dreams—I hope it isn't as that boring woman who never wanted to get out of her rut."

"No ... I want to remember you the way you were before I let you down."

"Vince, if anything, we let each other down—but I have the feeling we'll both need to revise our memories after this trip."

"Well let's start with lunch," he said, "and see what happens."

The waiter who came up spoke English and, when asked for something typical, he brought them a number of empanadas stuffed with onion, cheese, or beef and glasses of Torrontés white wine. "It is the typical food that you must eat while you are here," he said. "And you have chosen the very best restaurant in all of Buenos Aires," he added.

They clinked glasses and toasted.

"For better or for worse!" Vince said.

"For better and for worse," she replied. She took a cold sip and her face lit up. She raised her glass again: "Chardonnay move over, here comes Torrontés!" They clicked glasses again and drank.

On the way back to the Howard Johnson, they went through a park with several large trees shading an open area and approached a crowd gathering to watch a couple in costume dance to tango music, the man's sober black pants and jacket over a white shirt contrasting with the daring neckline of the woman's red velvet dress and her fishnet stockings. To get a better view of them, Vince and Annie moved to the front and found places near each other in the crowd.

Dancing was Vince's clearest memory from their courtship. They had first met chaperoning a prom at Roosevelt East High School, and he remembered slow dancing with Annie at the Ingersoll's parties. A picture of them on the dance floor at their wedding still hung in their bedroom, but tango was not in their repertoire. He looked over and realized it had been too long since they had danced and he felt a surge of happiness as he watched Annie move to the music, a dreamy look on her face, until the music stopped.

As the applause faded, the dancers walked around the perimeter collecting tips, the man with his hat and the woman with the pocket formed from gathering in her skirt, exposing even more leg. When they had finished, they bowed and added the money to a pouch under the man's shirt. Another song began and, spying Vince's camera around his neck, the woman stepped over with a convincing smile and beckoned for him to pose with her while her partner photographed them. Vince hesitated at first, though he found her dress and stockings alluring. When she set her partner's black hat on his head at a jaunty angle, Vince caught Annie's eye and saw her broad smile and enthusiastic nod as the woman pulled him by his shirt into the center and handed his camera to her partner. The tango poses seemed more risqué than they were in the photos he saw later. When she had finished posing, she took Vince's hand and indicated to bow with her to the applause from other appreciative tourists. Straightening up, Vince reached into his front pocket and extracted several bills which the dancer took and he watched them disappear down her bodice while some of the onlookers applauded again.

That evening, after a nap at their hotel, he and Annie strolled until they found the small restaurant along the Avenida del Libertador which their concierge said locals favored. The cramped entryway was occupied by an older couple and two younger women waiting for tables. After Vince signaled the hostess with two fingers and pronounced "*dos personas, por favor*" badly, he spotted two free stools at the bar and they stepped over to wait.

"What would you like, Annie, or should I call you 'Anita'?" he asked.

Feeling flattered, she smiled and touched his sleeve. "See if they have Chardonnay, *por favor*, so I can compare."

"And I'll try for Merlot," he said and realized that, since things had deteriorated, they had often neglected their Merlot-Chardonnay habit after exhausting days in the classroom and he wondered if it wasn't time to experiment. He screwed up his courage and signaled the barman that he wished to order.

"*Un Merlot* ... and a ... *un Chardonnay*," he said, holding up one finger on each hand and pronouncing the names louder but the same as he did in Chicago. When the barman nodded with a courteous smile, he felt a surge of relief and, for a moment, it was as though he were home—or at least not a total stranger.

Then, in English, but with a strong Spanish accent, the barman said, "I am afraid we have no Merlot, but I can give you maybe a Malbec from Mendoza Province?"

Instead of saying something stupid, Vince nodded his head not once but twice, and the barman nodded once in return. Turning to Annie, he smiled and said, "This is the farthest away from home we've ever been, but I like it here."

They sat watching others at the bar and listened, trying to catch some of the Spanish. When either of them thought they recognized a word or phrase, they leaned over and shared what they divined about the conversations around them. Before long, they were shown to a table near a pillar at the back of the small dining area.

As they sat afterward to let the meal settle and consider dessert, a man overheard them speaking English and paused at their table. He asked them in English where they were from and why they had come to Argentina. They replied that they were school teachers in Chicago and had decided to come during their Easter break because there was so much uncertainty about their jobs. They also enjoyed wine, and seeing a production of *Evita* had tipped the scales in favor of Argentina.

Their interlocutor, who was American, responded with a tale of reaching the same point in his career when he fell in love with an Argentine woman he met in Miami and followed her to Buenos Aires. Leaning down, he said *sotto voce*, "As luck would have it, I met someone in this restaurant who gave me the chance to become a partner with a group of investors taking over and modernizing a winery—one of the investors had backed out. With just eight days to decide, I stepped in and committed all of my pension money. Now, twenty years later, I can't imagine my life having been otherwise."

Annie looked over and said, "Vince, do you think something like that could work for us?"

"I don't know, Annie. We like wine, but what do we know about growing grapes?"

Somewhat louder, the man said, "That's exactly what I asked myself—but I wasn't the first to invest in this industry. And I won't be the last."

"This is really amazing," Annie said. "To come down here and meet someone who made such a change in his life ... would it be too much to invite you to have a drink with us and tell us more?"

"Not at all," he accepted and introduced himself: "Ralph Bentley." He wore a flannel shirt open at the neck and light trousers with frayed cuffs and, for a man of his achievements, was surprisingly understated. Over the next hour and another glass of *vino tinto*, they listened as Ralph embellished his story, telling of his standing in the winery, his quick mastery of both the business and the production end of grape growing, and the return on his investment. When they could no longer fight off fatigue, the couple thanked him for sharing his story, and the three of them drank a parting toast: "To new beginnings!"

Before they left him, they asked for contact information in case they needed advice.

"I can't see how anything could go wrong," he said. "Argentina is a democracy too, with laws and courts. Look, I don't have any cards on me, but I'm here most evenings after 10 p.m."

With hearts gladdened by the invigorating wine, they returned to their hotel in a rosy mist.

Over breakfast the next morning in the hotel dining room, Vince told her, "I can't get that idea from last night out of my head."

"Is there really anything stopping us from chucking everything, Vince, and using the money from your father to do what he did? I could teach English, and you could learn the wine business. We could make a new start together."

"It seemed within reach last night," he replied.

Annie grasped his hand and said, "We did it once, Vince—now let's see more of Buenos Aires; let's find the presidential palace. Evita addressed the people from the Casa Rosada." She took out her program to look for the picture of Eva on the balcony and caught a glimpse of lyrics from her famous song about never having invited the fame and fortune bestowed on her. And Annie wondered if that might one day apply to the serendipity of meeting Ralph last night.

"OK," Vince agreed, and they saw from their map that the Casa Rosada was on the Plaza de Mayo.

As they walked along streets lined with a mix of new apartment buildings, hotels and ornate French-style mansions, remnants from a century or more ago, that now housed embassies, Annie found herself humming the song.

Listening, all Vince could recall was the refrain, "Don't cry for me Argentina," and thought, with a sinking feeling, no one at East High would cry for him if he left.

On the way, they passed numerous buildings with concierges who were either busy polishing the brass plate lined with buttons for buzzing the apartments and offices within or standing nonchalantly on the sidewalk at their entryways.

Each seemed to strive to make their plate the shiniest and she said, "They must feel like English teachers—with pupils from so many different backgrounds, I have to teach the same grammar lesson day after day."

Then she asked, "Do you suppose we might live in one of these buildings, Vince? After all, Ralph is in the wine business and he lives here in Buenos Aires."

"I wonder," he replied.

Farther on, they came upon a man leaning down to dip into a bucket of sudsy water and wash the windows of a small dress shop. He was in silhouette as they approached against the sun and he looked up then quickly away as they passed. His clothes were fraying and faded. After another ten yards, Vince turned to her and said *sotto voce*, "Annie, wasn't that Ralph, the guy from the restaurant last night?" She looked back just as the man wiped his squeegee with a cloth and glanced towards them before turning away.

They walked on towards the plaza in silence. Then she stopped and, in a stricken voice said, "Yes. It was. Why did he lie to us, Vince?"

The rush of traffic along the broad avenue in the city center masked the silence between them, before he replied. "Maybe he's like some Argentineans we've noticed ... they want to think everything they do is special, is the best."

She looked down and when she raised her face, the glisten in her eyes could have been from the sun.

Before they moved on, he said, "Maybe that was the best he could think of, Annie."

Ten minutes later at the Casa Rosada, Annie again pulled the program from her purse to compare the picture with the pink building across the plaza. It fell open to the same page as before and she read the next words after "fortune" and "fame"—that 'they were illusions, not the solutions we hoped they would be' ... and she thought, as the song said ... the answer was there all the time: to love each other.

She took Vince's arm and sagged against his shoulder and he looked down, unsure of what to make of the smile behind her tears; but it felt good. And he knew that with time, they would find their way— where, did not matter so much.

Dumpster Days

A Novella

William Geuss

Haunted by the specter of alcoholism and dereliction in his family, a young man struggles to find his place in the scheme of things in a big city, first in Berlin then in Chicago, which provides the backdrop. Recollection of your own search for love and stability provides the glue, and this light-handed treatment of a precarious life stage provides the entertainment.

Chapter One

Watching Chicago's Lakeview neighborhood come to life on a chill winter morning after a late night at my keyboard was not my idea of fun. The temperature had dropped enough to show me my breath, and the fat boxer I walked for extra cash moved in slow motion.

"Get a move on, Brody; I've got a deadline to meet. Money won't grow on trees, no matter how many times you water them." I watched my words condense into a cloud and dissipate as Brody grudgingly complied.

I had just bagged and dropped his morning offering in a trash can when I turned the corner and saw a medium-sized, white Maltese squatting on the parkway ahead, linked by a fashionable purple lead to a woman in leather boots, and I quickened my pace to check her mistress out.

She wore jeans topped by a cream cable-knit and peered back along the leash towards her charge. The mane of rusty red hair cascading over her square shoulders caught the first morning sun and lent a touch of enchantment.

I was pacing Brody along the parkway from tree to tree, when I heard her say, "Come on Gloria, I have to get to work," and give the Maltese a brisk yank before reeling her in.

I sped up and overtook them midblock. Then it happened. Gloria saw Brody abandon the trees and bear down on her. She hit the brakes and turned to meet him and they devoted themselves to whiffing what they each had to offer the opposite sex.

"Straighten up, Brody," I said. "That's no way to treat a lady on a first date."

"Gloria, cool it you vixen!" her mistress said as our charges ignored and easily out-maneuvered us as they twisted in all directions and entangled their leads.

Embarrassed by their antics, I bent down recklessly to untangle them at the same instant as the red head, and we gave each other a resounding head butt that left my glasses dangling from one ear.

"Damn," I blurted.

"Crap," she said.

We straightened up together, each holding our head with our remaining free hand.

"They had a nicer way to meet than we," I smiled and repositioned my glasses.

She laughed. "I think they look on it like shaking hands."

"Well," I grinned, "I'm all for that ... shaking hands I mean," and extended mine. "Josh."

"Beth," she said and clasped mine with her leash hand while she continued to rub her head. "Look, I have to get to work, but I hope your head feels better soon."

"Thanks," I said. "The same."

She and Gloria continued on their way, and I muscled Brody down the street and around the corner to the townhouse where he lived.

By the time I stepped into my studio apartment a few blocks away to check the bathroom mirror, a major headache was developing and a red bump showed at my hairline. Fingering it, I remembered the healthy flush on Beth's cheeks ... good thing I had worn my brown leather coat, black turtle neck, and black jeans today. With the haircut last week, this face isn't that far off from the screen mags at the checkout stands. Then I tilted my face and checked the nose hair. Better keep a closer watch on that in case I meet her again. And better find some aspirin if I'm going to finish this translation job.

After some yogurt and cereal, I sat at my computer in a tight corner of the apartment and eyed the list of objectives I had taped on the wall when I arrived in Chicago four months ago. It was short:

1. Find enough work to pay the rent

2. Find friends

3. Get laid

4. Find love

Only the first two had been checked off so far, though *needs improvement* might have been more truthful. I moved to Chicago to try my luck after a stab at grad school and an internship with a translation agency in Germany. So far, the editing and translating jobs had paid the rent thanks to a bit of double-edged luck: my building was going to be torn down as soon as the owner could finalize sale. Since the date remained uncertain, that brought the rent down and delayed the threat of me joining the burgeoning ranks of Berlin's squatters or Chicago's homeless.

As for number 2, Ian, the Irish guy I met jogging along the lakefront was the only person who qualified as a buddy at this point. He appreciated the fact that I'd been to Ireland and would listen to the proverbs he served up with a fluid lilt; like one of them said: "A friend's eye is a good mirror".

As for 3 and 4, I found that getting a love life in a new city isn't as simple as downloading the right smart-phone app. Those only sucked up my time and jeopardized *numero uno*—meeting the rent. It was the classic vicious circle: investing in number four aggravated number one.

I ripped the list off the wall and tossed it in the wastebasket to join other drafts not yet ripe for publication. Thinking about it more just made my headache worse, so I focused instead on the image that floated across my retina when I closed my eyes of early sunlight on Beth's rusty hair. That seemed to help.

The headache had slowed me down but, by two o'clock the next afternoon, I finished editing the website material for a German cell phone network and gave it one last pass before sending it off. With no other work on my desk, I decided to see an Italian film playing at the cinema on North Clark Street.

I walked the few blocks to the Chicago Transit Authority station to catch an elevated train south. Every time I clanked through the turnstile and climbed past the rust-eaten girders supporting the hundred-year-old system, it seemed like time-travel into the past—the one constant being strutting pigeons at both ends of the trip that worked the platforms for handouts.

Depending on the movie, I was usually able to forget I would rather be with someone than alone, but today I was feeling vulnerable. At least in the dark, no one would be able to tell. Soon, the rumble of a train echoed along the rows of brick tenements lining the tracks to interrupt my self-pity as I watched the silver metal cars thunder into the station and set the pigeons in flight.

Near me, a young woman in a short, dark wool coat braced against the damp wind. Straw-colored hair protruded from her Nordic knit cap, and as she moved to board, she clutched a colorful metal lunch box.

When I paused to let her board first, she glanced up and I said, "Nice hat!"

"Thanks," she said with a fleshy smile and happy green eyes.

We slid onto the only remaining seat and the train clattered on. "Nice lunch box," I ventured. "You didn't happen to get that from someone smaller, did you?"

Hugging it to herself, she said, "No, this is my very own!"

Encouraged, I asked, "Does it have a little thermos in there, too?"

"Of course," she said faking incredulity.

I was enjoying this. "Where are you taking your lunch box today?"

"To the Greenhouse Theater. I'm directing crew for a show called the *Klingon Christmas Carol*. That's why I'm wearing black."

That explained her dramatic flair. "Not everybody can pull that off," I said.

Again the smile and happy eyes. "On the day after a show, I put on bright pink just to compensate."

This time, I smiled, and she asked, "And what do you do?"

"I sit at a computer and translate German stuff," I said and pulled out my notebook with drafts to revise. "Oh, and I learn languages."

"I can barely manage English."

"Does it get better or worse as the day wears on?"

"Before it's over, I just make noises," she said.

"Something like Mandarin?"

"Actually, Klingon. It's like nothing you've ever heard." She prepared to get up to exit at the next station and said, "Come to the show and find out."

"Now you've got me intrigued." I stood up to let her out. "By the way I'm Josh."

She moved towards the door and said, "I'm Piper."

"Watch out for hungry Klingons," I called and she hugged her lunch box to her chest in response and smiled as she stepped off the train.

Two stops farther, I thought I'm definitely on some kind of a roll: Two days, two interesting women—but no way to take it any further.

At my stop, I got off and walked over to the theater and bought a ticket, eager for a cinematic visit to Turin. Italians always seemed to know how to get to romance—perhaps I could pick up some pointers.

Once I settled into my reclining seat, the dark theater began to do its work. Before I dozed off, an attractive immigrant woman resembling Piper but much sadder, and a darkly handsome Italian appeared on screen and hooked up at a speed dating event. I was disappointed to see that his style was not that different from mine—if anything more understated. And I thought I even caught a glimpse of nose hair. They had settled in for the night at his place when I dozed off.

I woke in time to try and make sense of several surprising plot twists connected with the enigmatic immigrant woman that nearly cost the hero his life. By the end, however, she had disappeared and he was alone again, but he took up the search for a trustworthy partner—once more with speed dating.

A kindred spirit, I thought: he doesn't give up easily either. Nevertheless, speed dating didn't seem to deliver better results than cruising the CTA El train.

That night, Piper's fresh face and smile brightened my dreams. She was standing on the elevated platform and looking up at me. Her mouth moved, but the rumble of passing trains drowned out her words.

The next morning, a big job with a tight deadline came in, and any thought of taking a theater break to find her went out the window. Besides, Klingon wasn't on my list of languages to learn. Even so, I couldn't resist a surfing break to Google her but only turned up a review of *Klingon Christmas*. Piper wasn't mentioned. Like my Italian *amico*, I drew a blank and was left to add this face to the angels in my heaven and go on with life here below as a gladiator in the language arena. I realized it was time for another talk with Ian.

On Thursday night most of the folks at the Celtic Isle on Lincoln Avenue where Ian keeps bar were Chicago Cubs baseball fans trying to forget another 6-1 loss that afternoon at nearby Wrigley Field. Like me, the northside Cubs were fizzling after a promising start. The southside White Sox were early contenders, but their night game didn't bring in many customers this far north in the city.

That left Ian free to debrief me on the progress with my list, and somehow, it always seemed appropriate to give him my play-by-play in a sports bar.

I sat at the bar and he looked at me with mournful grey eyes and asked, "What will it be today, my friend?" while a smile played around the corners of his mouth.

I ordered a Guinness and watched him as he drew it with a steady hand. At just under six feet, Ian was on the lean side and lacked the beefy face of some Irishmen. He tilted his head as I filled him in on Beth's hair and Piper's smile.

With a thoughtful look, he said, "As brief as those encounters were, you start out well; you get first names."

"It's just that I've been in town four months now and still don't know anybody's last name. Or even how to find them." He set a glass in front of me that was a thing of beauty, a creamy nut-brown cushion of foam shading down into deep, dark chocolate.

"Do you see a pattern there?"

"Yeah, I guess so," I said, unsure of what he was driving at.

"You'll never plow a field by turning it over in your mind."

I raised an eyebrow and hoped what he had in mind still fell within the law.

"You need to take it a step farther so she knows you think she's worth it."

Still, nothing came to mind, so I asked, "Like how?"

"You know a lot about Chicago food specialties, right? So take things in that direction," he said and broke off to tend to refills at the other end of the bar as fans tried to forget today's game.

I weighed the stout on my tongue, black stuff that invited swirling and chewing, just what was called for to match up Celtic agrarian wisdom and Chicago culinary excess.

As I sat and pondered this in my dark clothes among Cub fans in white blue-striped shirts and caps, I felt like a Klingon among earthlings, but a second round of the Black Stuff and an hour of bleary reflection watching the servers and patrons brought the zany insight that pub life resembled theater—with the Ians and Pipers providing direction.

Convinced that Cubs, Sox, Klingons and earthlings all are heavy on improv and light on predictability I left, wondering if the odds of connecting in a tavern shouldn't outweigh those of speed dating or the El train since the hang time was greater. Yet, somehow it wasn't paying off. My only certainty was that I was glad for public transit.

Talking with Ian was like having a shamrock in my pocket. A week later, I saw Beth again in the neighborhood. She waved from across the street and called, "Hey, Josh. How's your head?"

"Mine's fine, and yours?"

"Can't complain. But how about the dog? That isn't Brody."

"Right you are. This is Topper. He lives two streets over. And that isn't Gloria either, is it?"

"Very observant," she said. "I see your head's alright."

Her long, rust-colored tresses were gathered in a paisley ribbon and my mind went blank. Then, thankfully, a few neurons fired. "Small world." I said, plowing on, "Looks like we're in the same profession. Who do you walk for?"

"City Sniffers, and you?"

"Doggie Style. So what do you do when you're not walking the street?" Did I just say that?

"Hah, hah. Tell me this. Are you stalking me?"

She wasn't far wrong. I had kept an eye out for her since last week. I liked the way she dressed, and the smell of her shampoo must have registered either before or after impact.

Taking things a step further, I said, "Tell you what, why don't we meet up for coffee and, uh, compare trade secrets."

To my surprise, it was that easy. Just before she handed over her number, the alarm on my cell phone sounded in my pocket telling me Topper's time was up and time to get back to work.

"Wow, musical underwear," she quipped. "Boxers or briefs?"

"Trade secret," I said and took the slip with her number. "Think you can stand the suspense?"

"Guess I'll have to," she said and waved goodbye and moved down the street.

I was the one having a hard time standing the suspense but, ten days later, we got our schedules to mesh. I suggested we meet at my favorite place, the Dollop Coffee Company over on Clarendon in the Buena Park area.

Beth had arrived first and was taking advantage of the uptick in temperature and sitting on one of the benches along the sidewalk in front of the two-story brick building. I faked going inside but stopped short and turned to her. "You know, I barely recognize you without a dog."

"Very funny. What did you expect, protective head gear?"

We went inside, filling our lungs with the aroma of fresh-roast Metropolitan Coffee beans while we scanned the menu. A barista in black with a nose-ring took her time chatting with another customer before taking our orders. *Easy does it* was tattooed down her left arm. She's right, I thought. It really is about connecting and that takes time. Maybe I've been trying too hard.

"So here we are," I said inanely and we found space on a couch along the wall to wait for our drinks and pastry.

"This place looks like a fixer-upper still on its way down," Beth said. "I think it would be hard for me to sit here and not think of what could be done with it."

"Don't spoil it. The chill factor is awesome," I countered. It was an abandoned pharmacy that had been rehabbed and I camped here whenever I could. "The Wi-Fi is free and the Chicago roast is great. My second office, I guess—maybe third, after the Chicago Public Library."

The drinks came. She took a sip of her coffee and said, "Hmm. This does make up for the decor."

That was close enough to a stamp of approval for me, and I sank back into the cushions.

Our trade secrets turned out to be pretty much the same: we were part-time walkers and both of us had invested in cradle harnesses to increase control over our canine charges. Gloria's owner had insisted that she be walked with the fashionable purple leash that complemented her white coat so nicely but provided little control—or we might never have butted heads.

I shared that my days were mostly spent in my apartment translating. But, rain or shine, I hit the pavement with my little buddies to break up desk time. In return, I learned that Beth commuted to her job at the Chicago Convention and Tourism Bureau in the Loop and walked evenings and weekends. We both did it for the extra bucks to keep a roof overhead, but her situation sounded steadier than mine.

"Well, at least your work takes you somewhere else," I said. "But that is a lot of time on the El."

"I can't believe how jammed it gets," she said. "You'd think the Cubs played five days a week. I'd give anything to live downtown, but I can't afford it alone. And my roomie doesn't want to get that far away from her boyfriend."

"Well, I've been happy enough here in Lakeview. But I've learned that my building is scheduled for demolition in June, and I haven't found another place I can afford."

She had her mouth full of the lemon custard Hoosier Mamma pie the barista had recommended, and I was licking some icing off my fingers when the light bulb went on for both of us. We kept looking at each other and then our heads began to nod.

I think I said it first: "I don't suppose you would consider teaming up?"

"Just what I was thinking," she said and smiled, "though here we are, imperfect strangers with an affinity for canines."

"It would just be sharing a place," I hastened to add to avoid spooking her.

Then her smile vanished. "I couldn't stick Rhonda with the rent. I'm not on the lease, but it wouldn't be right."

Her loyalty impressed me and the spontaneous synchronicity of our brains intrigued me. "Too bad—but still intriguing," I said out loud.

We finished up and paid. As we left, I said, "Let's talk some more anyway."

"Yeah. Nobody got hurt this time," she agreed. "Let's."

Ian would be proud, I thought.

I had read somewhere that it's best to wait three days before phoning a woman after you collect the precious number, but it was hard to still sound cool when I reached Beth after leaving three different messages.

There was no need to worry. She answered on my fourth try: "Hi Josh. I'm glad you kept trying. My schedule at the Convention Bureau has been hectic lately. It occurred to me, we ought to talk about backing each other up on walking jobs when one of us gets tied up."

"That sounds good to me," I said and was unsure where to go from there.

She spared me by saying, "So tell me more about yourself. Where are you from?"

"I grew up in Ohio. My dad was a mechanical engineer and traveled a lot. The company he worked for designed large presses for automobile companies. That took him to Italy and England a lot. I guess it got me interested in other countries."

"How about your mom?" she continued.

"She's a kindergarten teacher and before that mostly was home with my brother and me and my older sister, Amy. Our parents split up when we were in grade school, but they never divorced."

"Where does everybody live now?"

"My dad is Canadian and all his relatives live in Canada, but he works for a company in Brazil and my mom is still in Ohio."

"Where does your sister live?"

"She's back in Ohio, too. In Columbus. I'm glad I had Amy to grow up with. She married a guy during her senior year at Ohio State and they have two kids. She's a stay-at-home mom. How about you? You mentioned a younger sister last time?" I asked, relieved she hadn't asked about our brother.

"Yeah, Suzy. She's lesbian. She lives in Milwaukee and is a graphic designer. I really like her partner, Franny. In fact, they're hosting Thanksgiving dinner this year."

"Everybody in the family 'OK' with that?"

"My dad had the most trouble with it. But, I think he's about up to speed now. It's been three years," Beth said.

This was as deep as I had gone with any woman or anyone for that matter. Somehow, it was easy to talk with Beth and I asked, "Do you feel any pressure to be the one to spawn the grandkids?" and I realized this definitely was deeper water, but I had just read something about the baby question and was naïve and curious enough about women to raise it myself.

"Yeah, some. My parents had us late, and now they feel out of it since their friends' children are busy making babies. How about you? Your sis took the pressure off, but have you got ideas of your own?" she asked.

"I keep my eyes open, and I don't rule anything out," I said, hoping to sound more self-assured than I felt.

She waded in deeper still. "I mean about kids. Does that appeal to you—when you didn't see how it's done. With your dad gone?"

"I think nowadays a man can parent kids as well as a mom. You know—read to them, play games and sports, help with the home work, cook together"—all things I had only read about.

"That makes sense. I guess there's no formula for how to do family today, is there? I plan to see mine again at Thanksgiving."

"I haven't given it much thought yet. But maybe it's time I checked back in too. I didn't see them the year I was in Berlin." That had been a trying time for me. Money was tight and it was a place that drew lots of people looking to drop out and drift—like Travis—but I got through it.

My brother was probably the most obvious casualty of alcohol in our family and I wasn't anxious to share much about him. Not that I escaped unscathed. As the puppy of the family, my craving had always been for love and I approached people without knowing whether they wanted to scratch my ears as badly as I wanted them scratched. As for Travis, as hard as he tried to please dad, it was never enough. He gave up trying. And drugs pretty well finished off his attempt at college.

By the time I hung up, I gathered that I had passed muster with Beth, but I wasn't sure as what. She suggested we meet for coffee again on Sunday. This time at Julius Meinl's Cafe on Southport in Lakeview. "The *CRÊPES* and Viennese coffee and treats are authentic," she explained. "And they serve this amazing breakfast all day if you happen to sleep in."

I gladly agreed and got the message: something more upscale next time, but I couldn't resist saying, "Well, I bet they don't have Hoosier Mama pie."

The slowdown in new translation jobs had sharpened my antennae for ways to expand my client base and keep the coins dropping into my cup, so I decided to attend a program at the Goethe Institute on Michigan Avenue. It's one of the few opportunities in Chicago to directly network with people who might provide a link to someone needing German translation.

I had texted Beth to ask if she wanted to join me after work, but she had a meeting with convention planners. Although I was late leaving for the 6 p.m. lecture, the Purple Line Express train downtown to the Chicago loop was running and saved me a few stops on the way south. Once past the Merchandise Mart and across the Chicago River, we followed tracks that snake 90 degrees eastward and send standing passengers lurching as the train threads through a mix of Chicago architecture. The richly stylized older stone and concrete buildings we passed contrasted with soaring sheets of glass that splintered light and dazzled this small town boy, sowing doubt about whether I would be able to afford life in the big city.

Desperation, however, inspires ingenuity. Like Berlin, Chicago disgorged enough discarded and castaway furnishings, so keeping an eye on bulletin boards, throw-away newspapers, and alleys on trash pick-up day turned up enough discards to outfit my apartments in both cities for next to nothing.

At Lake and Wabash Streets I exited the train, walked across the suspended wooden platform, and felt the departing train set the floor swaying enough to give any visitors from earthquake-prone San Francisco, New Zealand or Japan the jitters.

Ahead of me, a tall brunette in a dark trench coat left through one of the turnstiles that ratcheted around its axis like a human shredder. Despite the menacing clatter, she emerged unharmed and hesitated as though deciding which direction to go. I left by another turnstile and was caught up in the throng moving towards the stairs down to the street.

Once below, I headed east against foot traffic streaming homebound towards the station I had just left. The alleyways were flooded from afternoon rain and concentration was needed to avoid wading through puddles. By midblock, I began to notice the staccato beat of boot heels behind me.

If I turned to check out the source, I would risk a head-on with some determined commuter—not an ideal way to meet—so I left it until I reached the corner of Michigan Avenue and sheared north across the pedestrian flow to enter the bank building housing the Goethe Institute. I paused and heard the boots follow. It occurred to me we could be going to the same place and I might get a look anyway.

The Goethe Institute was on an upper floor, but just which one escaped me. Cutting through the bank lobby, I passed the battery of ATMs and stepped up to the security desk in the elevator lobby. I heard the boots enter through the street door and looked over to see it was the tall brunette who had survived the shredder on the El platform. A bright-green silk scarf showed against her dark raincoat and I guessed she was in her mid-thirties. Stepping up to the desk after me, she repeated my question: "What floor is the Goethe Institute on?"

"That's where I'm headed," I volunteered. She faced me and the words "sophistication" and "class" came to mind at her clear gray eyes.

"How convenient," she said with an accent familiar to me from my year in Germany.

Once in the elevator, I switched to German and asked, "Are you already a fan of Herr W. tonight's speaker?"

"No, I must confess, I haven't read anything of his yet," she replied.

"Well, I haven't either. But I did pick up a used copy of one of his novels and from time to time I hear some mention of him."

When we exited the elevator on the second floor, she turned right and looked down towards the wall where the hall dead-ended.

"*Hier entlang,*" I said, turning left to the reception area of the Goethe Institute, her footfalls softening as she followed along the carpeted surface.

A woman wearing a nametag identifying her as Ursula Binder greeted us and directed us to the cloakroom on the left, adding, "Registration is at that table over there."

I hung up my windbreaker to bring my appearance more in line with the formal dress of the German academics and consular people in evidence in order to pass at least as a graduate student. I stepped over to Frau Binder and heard the lady in boots ahead of me being given the news that "all the seats are presently reserved. But if you choose to wait, perhaps a cancellation will allow accommodating you."

I had registered by phone and, when my turn came, gave my name and said, "My friend had to cancel, so one of my places is free." Gesturing toward the lady in boots, I said, "Perhaps she would like to have it?"

"I'm afraid we have a number of requests," Frau Binder said, "So she'll have to wait."

The lady in boots overheard and rewarded my gallantry with a smile followed by a shrug. I put on a sympathetic face and stepped over to where she sat. "Maybe you'll get the place my friend reserved."

"How nice of you. Well, hold a seat and we'll see."

"Glad to," I said and entered the conference room, already two-thirds filled, and found two seats on the edge fairly far forward.

The crowd was a mix of elderly Germans, young graduate students, and Goethe Institute staff. I didn't have long to wait before my damsel in distress came in and searched the room for a seat. I half stood and signaled her with a nod. She smiled and sat next to me as the program began.

With characteristic German punctuality and formality, the director introduced representatives from the Swiss, German and Austrian missions in Chicago, thanked those responsible for sponsoring the event, and introduced the moderator, who would introduce the novelist, who would read from his work.

After several introductory homages to the aging author, the great man himself returned the compliments and led off with remarks he had recently prepared for a German newspaper in which he took issue with an interpretation of his last novel that had appeared several years ago. This was followed by an extensive reading from said novel and proved to be altogether as mind-numbing as anything I could recall from my one brief semester in graduate school before I left for Berlin.

After the program, I persuaded my attractive acquaintance to join me at the Pastoral Artisan Bistro around the corner on Lake Street for a glass of wine. She accepted, which may have been her way of returning the favor with the seat. Her name was

Stefanie. She was from Hamburg where she had taken acting classes before coming to Chicago and was working in Chicago's Lufthansa offices.

The second—or third element of my strategy, if you include the knight-errant gesture earlier—was to invite her to a foreign film at the Siskel Film Center.

That was when I learned that she lived with a filmmaker from Barcelona and they were due to leave for Las Vegas in two days. "He is shooting a movie in which I play Verena, a high-class hooker who meets a Catholic priest on the airplane. The priest is on his way to Vegas to visit his mother who is dying of cancer."

I could see her in that role but didn't risk saying so.

"They meet again when Verena is brought in to the hospital where Father Joseph's mother is being treated after suffering an auto accident. He comforts us both during a week of visits, falls in love with me, and has to decide what to do about it."

I began to strongly identify with the priest and had just offered Stefanie a third glass of wine, when she glanced at her watch and jumped up.

"I completely forgot. I'm meeting Lluis at the Swissotel for dinner with an agent. He's arranging for product placements in our film, and I need to get freshened up to make a good impression."

As I stood up, she thanked me with a peck on the cheek, and I barely had time to wish her good luck with her career before she rushed out the door.

Ordering another glass of the fabulous red blend we had been drinking seemed the obvious way to compensate—but I remembered reading about the alarming incidence of alcohol problems among Father Joseph's fellow Catholic clergy and reluctantly called it a day.

That night, I dreamed that Ian's pub had added pari-mutuel betting on greyhound and horse racing, but when I next stopped in there, the most hotly debated wager was the odds of my accomplishing numbers 3 and 4 before my building was torn down. The odds were dropping each week, and Ian sent me off with something that gave me small consolation: "Even a blind squirrel finds an acorn now and again," which I took to mean "you never know what will turn up in the next dumpster."

I woke the next morning feeling sorry for myself. It was St Patrick's Day, so I decided to stop in and see the real Ian and give him a status report on my list.

"Ian!" I called out over the hubbub, "I'm having a worse season than even the Cubs." Since I was planning on staying awhile, I said, "Give me a Bud Light."

He gave me a skeptical look and shook his head. "If it's drownin' you're after, don't torment yourself with shallow water. Try Irish Car Bombs and get right on with it."

That surprised me. "The only time I ever ordered one of those," I told him, "was at a pub in Dublin and it went silent. Everybody turned to look."

"When enough damage's been done, some things can never be taken lightly," he said, "but here in Chicago, it's safe enough now."

So my next plunge into deeper waters came in Chicago. I watched the whiskey drop into the Guinness and Bailey's and heard Ian say, "Now, don't tarry lad. Drink before it curdles."

I never imagined a Guinness milk shake could taste so delightful. I had another and soon was promoting its virtues to those jammed up to the bar to my right and left.

Between breaks in the singing, I stood a round or two to someone at my side who seemed to appreciate them as much as I. The rest of the night was a blur of foggy images.

The faint ringing of a phone grew louder and I fumbled to answer, "Hullo."

A female voice said, "Josh, is that you?"

"Hold on a minute," I said. "I'll check the mirror. Yeah, I can't find my ID, but the chances are pretty good it's me."

"Well, don't bother checking. That's one reason I'm calling. You left your pants here last night—with your wallet. Maybe I better come over and identify the body. It looked pretty good last night."

"Last night? Say, who is this?"

"What! Are you saying you can't remember? St Paddies Day? The show at the Green Shamrock after we left the Celtic Isle? The pool filled with green beer? The body painting? For God sakes, we were runners-up!"

"Uh, you must be Colleen ... er Doreen, or Bernadine, right?"

Frosty silence.

I glanced at my watch. "Yeah, well it was a while ago." I still felt addled.

"Look—I called to see if you want your pants—and your ID."

"My ID? Say, are you so sure I'd fall for that? I mean, I just told you, I can't find my ID and you pretend to have it—what's going on here?"

"But, I just ..."

I pressed on. "I've read about stuff like this on *craigslist*. They've got your number sweetheart. No way, I'm not falling for that."

"The only reason I was willing to come over there is I was hoping there would be more to fill your pants this afternoon than there was last night. Suit yourself," and the line went dead.

Then I woke up—for real this time—and shook away some of the cobwebs. My head was pounding.

Damn. I thought, *That* was pretty crazy. Deeper waters can be pretty shallow. No need to strike item 3 yet.

On Sunday mornings, the pace slows in the city, but business picks up in the coffee houses. When I got to Julius Meinl's Cafe, Beth was sitting at an inside table near the window, and I was fifteen minutes late. She looked out, smiled, and checked her watch.

I thought about how much the tabs at the Celtic Isle and coffee houses were costing me and lost my appetite. I locked my bike and went in to join her. "Sorry I'm late. I had a deadline to meet and didn't count on having to air up a bike tire."

She was wearing a belted, soft beige sweater with a dark-blue scarf knotted around her neck. Seeing the large, half-finished latte, I asked, "Have you been here long?"

"Long enough to decide what I'm having for breakfast."

"What do you recommend?"

"Easy. The brie and ham crêpes rule."

"That does sound good. Great way to end—or start the week."

"But it's too much for one person. Want to split an order?" she asked.

Grateful for the suggestion, I said, "OK, that is what we're talking about, after all."

"Well, listen to this. My roommate dropped a bomb last night," Beth said.

"She's pregnant?"

"I don't know, but she has asked Henry to move in and I don't relish being around for the fun."

"I guess that opens up new horizons then."

"That's the truth. Do you still like the idea of teaming up?"

The end of my lease was approaching faster by the week, so drastic action was called for if we really wanted to go through with this. On the other hand, I had read that romancing a roommate was high-stakes gambling, and I still found Beth quite attractive.

Hedging a bit, I said, "OK. This is a pretty big step," I said. "Why don't we take a look at how we each live now and see if this is such a great idea. You know, visit each other's apartments."

Just then our brie and ham crêpe arrived along with a second plate and a major refresh on the Viennese coffee. Beth sectioned the crêpe into equal portions, maneuvered one onto the plate, and passed it over to me. "I guess you're right," she said. "For all I know, you live like a cave man, and I'd jump out the window after a week."

"Maybe it's been long enough that some men have mutated beyond Tarzan," I said, not completely convinced, since I remembered beating on my chest when I saw Stefanie at the Goethe Institute just the day before yesterday. "Besides, guys like him who work with animals should be able to work with people. Right? Think Tarzan and Cheetah," I offered. "You know, the chump with the chimp."

She inhaled crêpe aroma and quickly plied a forkful into her mouth, stifling any urge to respond to my meandering.

I wondered what she wanted to do with her life and decided to take a different tack. "How about you? I didn't learn much on the phone about your plans for yourself. Are you one of the young and restless?"

When she had swallowed, she said, "Actually I am. Restless at least. When I first gazed into my crystal ball after college, I saw a fabulous future—a woman commuting into the city with a brief case and having lunch with handsome men in suits who posed in underwear ads in their spare time.

"So I started commuting and, after three years, I still haven't run into those men, and the commute has started to suck, so I shook the ball again. I saw myself decorating a large home in the suburbs while the children played with a big dog in the yard. Then I realized, someone has to walk the dog and scoop the poop and mow the grass, so I shook it again, and up came an apartment, high in the city, with all kinds of excitement down below." She poised her last forkful close to her mouth and said, "If that doesn't work out, I'll just keep shaking it."

By the time we left Meinl's, we were full and also had filled in our thumbnail biographies: She was from a small mid-Wisconsin town, had gone to Ripon College where her parents went, and came to the big city to escape the smell of cow pastures. She also knew that my monthly free-lance income could fluctuate widely and give me sleepless nights, but so far, it had paid the bills on time. Since this didn't bother her, we agreed on the next step: sniffing each other out with home visits.

My turn to visit came first. She had me to dinner that Wednesday with Rhonda, her roommate, and Henry, who practically lived there already. The apartment was in a typical three-story brick walkup. Theirs was on the second floor.

This time, I arrived early since I wanted to make a good impression. Beth answered when I rang. She was wearing a light purple running suit, and I got treated to another whiff of herbal shampoo as I stepped past close to her long red hair gathered in a pony tail that left strands trailing down each side of her face.

I had spent some time thinking about what she would be wearing—bun-boosting jeans? a mini skirt over tights? work stuff? But then I didn't know much about corporate dress codes these days or just how far "business casual" went.

"It's Josh," she hollered into the apartment, and I trailed behind her as she moved towards the kitchen and saw that her running suit betrayed a slight spread in her bottom which led me to guess that, like me, Beth must be approaching thirty.

"How was the commute today?" I asked to mask my uneasiness at being on display myself.

She gave me a wry smile over her shoulder. "It's sardine season. It rains, everybody packs in, and we all marinate together."

She led us on along the hallway with doors trimmed in dark varnish that led into bedrooms, bathrooms, and, finally, to the kitchen.

"Rhonda, this is Josh," she said. And to me, "this is Henry. He's a teacher at Roosevelt East High School."

He sat on a stool with a Bud Light in his hand and two empties already lined up on the counter.

"Hi," he said. "Nice to meet you."

"Hello," I replied. "Looks like the bar is open."

"Can I get you one of these?" he asked.

"No thanks," I said. "I want to be on good behavior tonight."

"Making an exception are we?" Henry said.

"Sometimes, we have to make sacrifices," I rejoined. "Besides, I came to scope out how Beth lives and whether we could share a cage. I don't want my judgment impaired."

Turning to Rhonda, who was stirring a pot of spaghetti, I asked, "So, what kind of dirt have you got on Beth? Who does more of the housework?"

"Oh, we have that pretty well split down the middle. We each do our own bathroom. It's clean up after yourself in the kitchen, and weekends, we each put in an hour or so to tackle the common areas plus any special stuff that needs doing."

"Who cooks, who shops?"

"Well, you certainly are covering all the bases," Beth said. "Who am I going to ask about your habits? Some talking dog?"

"Aw, come on, Beth," Rhonda said. "Girls can tell whether a guy is a slob. Just go and look in his drawers."

"Ha, ha. High time, if she hasn't already," Henry chimed in.

"Shut it, Henry," Beth said. "Clean your ears. We're talking roommates, not romance."

"OK, OK. Then go for the sock drawer, while you're at it." Turning to me, he said, "Dude, I don't envy you. I'd never pass."

"Can't say I wasn't forewarned," I said. Inspired by Henry, I asked Beth, "Does that mean I get a peek into your drawers tonight?"

"I guess. Turnabout is fair play."

"Yikes," Rhonda said. "The garlic bread is starting to burn. Could you grab it, Beth?"

We sat in the dining area and labored over plates of spaghetti with pesto sauce and a salad flanked by spears of garlic bread.

Afterward, I said, "OK if I pitch in?" and jumped up to begin clearing empty plates.

"Hey, Henry, are you watching this?" Rhonda said.

As he handed me his plate, he clipped his partially emptied glass. Red wine sprayed over Rhonda's placemat and left her blouse sprinkled with an irregular swath of polka dots.

"Jesus, Henry!"

"Sorry, my love," he managed and began blotting up the spillage, stopping short of her blouse.

"Bad luck, old man," I said. "But thanks for taking the pressure off. That raises the bar to a point I doubt I'll clear tonight."

Turning to Beth, I said, "So, what about those drawers of yours?"

She gave me a frown. "You are serious, aren't you? OK, mister," she replied to my smile, "come into my parlor," and led the way down the hall.

"Tah dah," she said and stepped into her room. I closed the door behind us.

"What are you doing?" she asked.

"I know enough to look behind doors. That's where I hang stuff I don't get around to putting away and where amazing dust bunnies breed." None were in evidence.

"Are you satisfied?" Beth asked, as the sound of a row back in the kitchen penetrated the closed door.

"I wonder if Rhonda is having second thoughts," I said.

Beth shook her head. "It's what they do. Seems to be what they need and not everybody can supply that. Now what?" she asked.

"Well, this is your private space, but if you opened up your drawers …"

"Are you some kind of pervert?" she interrupted.

"The drawers over there, I mean. Better to know these things ahead of time. Now I'm wondering if you're afraid I'll discover you are a scrambling crammer—someone who might turn kitchen cupboards into hell on earth."

"Look. I can tell the difference between undies and utensils. You do realize we are only talking about splitting the rent and common areas. You know, separate bedrooms? It's not like an eHarmony screening."

"Say, we're starting to sound like Rhonda and Henry out there," I said and realized the warm and fuzzy images in my mind were not an easy fit over the flesh and blood reality before me. "Let's face it, unless you're the total neat freak and I the Ditzy Dora, why shouldn't that work? Every lease has an end—no divorce necessary."

"You've got a point there. Your drawers are safe, but I'd still like you to come play at my place."

"Maybe we should skip the preliminaries and just move right in together," she said.

"Aw, humor me," I said. "Day after tomorrow, OK?"

"Well, OK."

That gave me time to prepare before Beth stopped by after work. I had straightened out my sock drawer and the other two just in case and cleaned the bathroom and kitchen. That, along with vacuuming, took a chunk out of my morning.

When she knocked, I let her in and asked, "Wanna start with the sock drawer? I didn't bother ironing them like my grandmother used to, but you'd be passing something up."

"Keep talking, Josh, and I'll let you keep my drawers in order, too. Let's just get down to business."

I was disappointed but not surprised. I had looked forward to having a woman in my place and felt playful. But realizing we both had a real problem to solve, I said, "OK. I'll order a pizza Margarita and make a salad. I've got beer, some red wine or tea. What do you drink?"

"Beer is fine."

While we ate, it was clear that Beth's mind was set on planning, not play. By the time the pizza box was empty and the beer gone, we had decided to think big. If we were going to live downtown, we'd go for a landmark building—Marina City on the Chicago River, maybe Precinct Towers near the Metra Station, Lakeshore Tower along the Outer Drive—nothing was ruled out.

We agreed to think about it for a week and meet again.

To be honest, the idea of uprooting from familiar haunts for a postcard view wasn't exciting me. A high-rise cell wasn't that different from one in the outer neighborhoods, and I didn't spend that much time staring out the window. Regular breaks from my computer screen and chair were essential for my sanity, and I needed to get outside. That's what my pals from Doggy Style did for me. Cold, rain or snow got my blood moving and cleared my head for another few hundred words until I got bogged down again or reached a gap only a nap would bridge. Losing my link to the outdoors made me consider backing out, but I realized that Beth was counting on liberation from her commute. Since she didn't appear to have other promising housing options—nor did I—we went into overdrive in our search.

The main hurdle to clear was whether the convenience of living in the Loop within walking or cycling distance or a short bus commute from Beth's job was worth the price differential to living in one of the closer-in neighborhoods.

We both worked, so there was no time to visit and check out so many buildings. The next best thing was to tread the path trod by millions before us: We used the Net and our networks, and the apartment-search sites made our job much easier. Each time we got a lead, we simply bracketed it on several sites and ended up with a virtual tour, reviews, rental conditions and prices. The photos were obviously showcase units, so we didn't have any illusions about what awaited us.

A woman Beth worked with lived in one of the Marina City corncob towers on the Chicago River. The idea of living high in a silo was quirky enough to appeal to me, but Beth had visited her once on the way to the Fourth of July celebration in Grant Park. The balcony was huge and the view dynamite, but after living in an old place, low ceilings and rooms with tapering walls gave her claustrophobia. So we looked further.

Although the West Loop contended with the Streeterville district north of the river and east of Michigan Avenue's Magnificent Mile for the most expensive digs in the city, what decided us was the availability of a six-month sublet to fill an apartment in Precinct Towers on West Madison Street not far from the Loop. That would give us a chance to get our feet wet and see what the future brought.

I was torn between curiosity about life downtown and nostalgia for the neighborhood haunts I would be leaving, but it was too late for that. Next up was to arrange for the move.

Before the big day, I decided to have a nagging problem on the bottom of my right foot taken care of. It was now late April when I pedaled my bicycle a mile and a half to the podiatrist's office up from the Polish-American Museum. Bracing against the saddle to gain leverage set my leg muscles burning as I sped past the sun-fueled spring foliage lining Ashland Avenue. Splashes of bright green honey locust alternated with lower voltage elm and walnut.

Dry pavement and luck with the traffic lights brought me to my appointment with Dr. Ortega twenty minutes early. The first ten were spent filling out paperwork essentially granting every fellow human on the planet permission to access my data without explicitly naming them all.

Although Chicago's version of Cinco de Mayo was still a week away, Dr. Ortega's practice was ready. A fringed fiesta banner hung over the reception desk which sprouted a dark green, plastic cactus. Colorful wooden maracas lay at the ready on the magazine tables in the seating area, and sombreros hung around the necks of the secretary and nurse.

I sized up the magazine selection and, even though this gentleman usually prefers brunettes, I passed over the *GQ* cover showing a dark-haired senorita, sans sombrero, in just a short tee upstairs and a tiny black bikini bottom which was imprinted with a raunchy saying and triangulated her bare essentials downstairs.

Instead, I filled the next ten minutes surveying the cheesy decor meant to whet my appetite for mariachi music and enchiladas. First prize I gave to swathes of green, white, and red webbing that was scotch-taped to the walls and had swarms of tiny plastic spiders in sombreros traveling across them, like minnows caught in a net; a large marble foot, truncated at mid-calf, from which a green cactus sprouted, was a close second; and the chili pepper shaped piñata hanging from the ceiling got third.

I had just exhausted the possibilities when a young woman limped into the office and went up to the reception desk saying: "I'm terribly sorry, I'm late. I've never seen traffic like that."

"No problem. Just tell me your name and birth date."

"Jennifer Stanfield, 08/18/88."

"What a lucky number you picked," the receptionist said.

"I know. Just rolls off your tongue. And I've never met anyone else with my birth date."

Then Jennifer took her sheaf of paper and sat opposite me, crossing nice legs in patterned black tights that descended into shiny, mid-calf leather boots. She set to work and, after a first go, looked up and smiled.

"I couldn't help overhearing that about your birthday," I said. "That's my story too."

"You mean we share a birth date?"

"No. I've never met anyone with the same birthday in October as mine either."

"Well, that makes two of us, then," she said, sounding a little startled, perhaps a little pleased.

"Sorry, didn't mean to interrupt. They really need a lot of information before they see us, don't they?"

"Oh, don't worry. That's true." She returned to finish filling out the forms she held with a hand unmarked by telltale rings.

I returned to proofing printouts of a job for an automotive parts manufacturer due tomorrow at 8 a.m. to check for completeness but only saw my companion's face with dark eye brows and red lips set in alabaster skin float across the pages.

Finished with her paperwork, she sighed, brushed back her shiny, medium-length black hair, and looked over. She smiled and asked, "Well, that's that. Are you doing extra credit paperwork for here or is that something you brought from home?"

"Oh, it's work stuff. I'm a freelance translator and it takes several passes to get things up to snuff. This one is a final read through for completeness."

"Really? What language do you work with?"

"I do German to English."

"Oops. I tried to learn German in high school. The only thing that saved me was that the teacher died. I got to switch to Spanish."

"That was a close call," I said. "It wasn't easy for me either. But learning any language, even your own, is a life-long project. What do you do, when you aren't visiting podiatrists?"

"I do market and survey research for a company headquartered downtown."

"My clients are mostly in Europe," I said.

"Wow!"

"Last month I translated a newsletter for a Swiss-based vacation village consortium. It touts the benefits of membership which give Europeans access to these resorts all around the Mediterranean."

"Did you sign up?" she asked.

"Nope. Basically, I don't like to be fenced in. Besides, it's a whole lot easier to go to exotic places in your head than to put up with the grind of travel."

"I envy you that you can say that," she said. "I guess I haven't had time enough to travel yet."

"So what does your work involve?"

"I ask people how they rank a group of destinations according to certain criteria. Then we might invite certain subsets of the respondents to different focus groups, depending on the products or services being explored, and dope out the best approach to use for each subset."

"Do you get many surprises along the way?"

"Not really."

"Jennifer?" the nurse called.

"Yes, right here."

"You can come in now. And sir, Dr. Ortega will be ready for you shortly."

"OK."

"Uh, Jennifer, I tell you what. I'd like to swap stories with you some more. Here is my card. Call me and we can give it a go."

She took it and went through the door with a gracious smile on her red lips and wished me "Good luck."

I hoped there was no irony intended and settled back to see how far I could get with the self-edit before my number was up to have a wart taken off the bottom of my foot.

By the time I peddled homeward, the sun had shifted lower in the darkening sky, muting the spring palette along my route but for the occasional flair when a burst of sunlight between buildings illuminated a blooming honey locust.

After three days and no call, I popped my browser open to area phone directories and searched for *Jennifer Stanfield*. Sure enough, there were three—one in Evanston, one in Rogers Park and one in Lincolnwood. What the hell, I thought and, picturing her smiling face framed in that stylish haircut, dialed the first one.

It rang five times before voice mail picked up. "Uh, hello, Jennifer, this is Josh. I hope you are the one I met at the podiatrist's last Wednesday in Lakeview. If not, sorry for the mix-up. If so, I really would like to swap stories with you some time soon. Give me a ring. My cell is 773-604-6721. Bye."

Same story with the other two. So now came the hardest part—simply waiting … and watching the image of her face fade.

It was the Friday before our move when my phone rang and Beth caught me before she left for work. I had stayed up later than usual packing and was still groggy.

"Hey, roomie, it occurred to me that some watershed moments are upon us."

We were set to move the next day, and it was the last night we would be walking pooches.

"Let's go out without a head bang," she said, "and walk together. I'll meet you at ground zero at 10 pm."

The idea appealed to me. "Deal. I'm all packed. How about you?"

"Well, as for clothes, let's just say I won't be carrying in the stuff you haven't seen over my arms."

I instantly regretted not having pushed on into that territory during my home visit and wondered if she was teasing. "When we finish," I offered, "I'll buy you a drink at the Four Moons," a watering hole a couple of blocks from where I was spending my last night in this neighborhood.

"Who's up tonight for you?" she asked.

"I've got Frieda—the usual." I had been in a rut with male boxers and labs. Tonight it was a bitch though. "Who have you got?" I asked.

"Plimpton, that miniature Schnoodle you saw me with last week," she said. "He's loyal, affectionate, easily trained, fun loving and good with children," she elaborated.

"Why do women bother with men?" I asked.

"You got that right. See you at ten."

By evening, I was ready for a walk to clear the cobwebs out of my head and stretch muscles stiff from packing.

The moon shone brightly and the air was cool when I met Beth where we first bumped heads.

"Hi, Beth. Meet Frieda. And, hello Plimpton."

"Plimpton, this is Josh. Now mind your manners and give Frieda a sniff—but watch your head."

"I wonder how they would do sharing a kennel," I said.

She smiled and suggested we walk along the railroad embankment and then turn into the neighborhood.

"Good idea," I said. After ten in the evening, not many people were about—except a few with dogs in tow.

Beth and I had known each other three months now and done well together finding an apartment. Planning the move and working out the scenario for sharing space and expenses had gone smoothly, too. Her red hair and her spirit had hooked me, but I still wondered if deciding to share space had been a mistake: She had said, 'We're talking roommates, not romance,' and that disappointment might be hard to live with.

We walked until we reached the corner bordering the park where bushes reach to the sidewalk. Beth had Plimpton on the inside and Frieda and I were on the street side. Something darted in the shadows and both dogs barked and veered after it, too quick for us to jerk them off balance. A rustling in the leaves and barking turned into yelping as the god-awful smell of skunk engulfed us.

"Oh, crap," Beth said.

"Worse," I said. "Skunk." And we saw a white-striped tail disappear into the bushes and the dogs begin pawing frantically at their noses.

"Omigod, now what?"

"Follow me," I said, and led the way to my apartment a block-and-a-half away.

Frieda and Plimpton followed us up the back stairs and into the kitchen. "Should I close the door?" Beth asked.

"This place is slated for demolition," I said. "Who cares how it smells."

"Yeah, but you have to sleep here tonight."

"God, that's right. Leave it open."

I grabbed some baking soda and dish soap and continued on into the bathroom past the cardboard boxes holding my limited kitchenware.

To give us more room, I closed the door on the four of us and, this time bumped bottoms with Beth as I leaned down and dug under the sink for a bottle of hydrogen peroxide. I poured the ingredients into a pail to the sound of the dogs whining as they kept pawing their noses.

"My neighbor told me about this formula when her dog got skunked just last month. Get them into the tub, and we'll sponge them with this stuff."

"Should I use this wash cloth?" Beth asked.

"Yeah. But just on the fur and feet. Watch out for their eyes and noses."

I knelt alongside her and we went to work. Fortunately, Plimpton and Frieda must have been trained to tolerate baths and they began to enjoy the romp.

As we reached around to swab our charges, we bumped into each other repeatedly and Beth didn't object. I realized it was the closest we had gotten since our head butt. But this time, her aromatic shampoo didn't come through.

"Hold them both by their leads," I said, "and I'll turn the shower on to rinse."

She turned them away from the spray, and I hit the control and helped her hold tight to keep the frisking to a minimum. We rinsed Plimpton and Frieda clean, sending the worst of the skunk down the drain.

I had just cut the shower and announced "That should do it," when they began to shimmy, sending a wall of water at us. We ducked and grabbed towels to hold against the spray until it subsided, then dove on our charges to blot and wrap them.

Hugging them to us, we sagged to the floor and leaned back against the tub. Beth turned to me. Her eye makeup was running and, for the first time, I noticed that her hazel eyes and saw a light sprinkling of freckles stretching across her cheeks that must have normally been hidden by makeup. Warmth heightened my sense of satisfaction as we rested in the narrow, humid room.

"I feel like I've been through a car wash with the windows down," she said.

Wanting to give the good feelings time to take hold, I suggested, "Let's throw our clothes in the dryer, take the doggies home, and go get that drink."

"Uh, hello," she said, pulling at her streaming hair and releasing Plimpton. "I can't be seen in public like this."

I let Frieda follow him out of the bathroom. "Yeah. I guess we don't smell so great either. Let's just come back here for a night cap. The movers don't come until ten tomorrow."

Midnight found us warmly clothed and sprawled on my sofa bed converted back into a couch, draining tumblers of Syrah and munching our way through a bowl of nuts. "You know, this isn't such a bad way to close things out," I said. "Let's drink a toast to Brody and Gloria. We owe them a lot."

We clinked glasses, and she said, "Thank heavens, we won't get skunked in the Loop."

"Maybe we should consider ourselves lucky tonight. Remember the mountain lion they killed near here in the Roscoe Village district last year?" We both reached for nuts at the same instant and our fingers touched.

"Sorry," she said.

"Don't be," I said, "We've got to learn to share space," and, without thinking, I leaned in and surprised her with a mellow smooch on her cheek.

Beth pulled away. "I think that could confuse things, Josh—kind of like cougars in Chicago. Our cage will be small enough without roaming wild animals, don't you think?"

"Well, you never know what's gonna git ya, woman," I said, joking to cover my hurt. "Coyotes are back too," I told her. "There was one running right down State Street in the middle of the night not too long ago."

"What's a girl gonna do," she smiled and relaxed. Then she got up and collected herself and thanked me before heading home.

Crestfallen, I consoled myself with the prospect that our joint tenancy would be on firm footing: Adversity and animals usually prove to be bonding.

Chapter Two

On June 1st we moved into a two-bedroom apartment on the twenty-sixth floor of Precinct Towers on West Madison with a six-month sublet. Beth got the large bedroom with full bath and I the small bedroom and half bath—as much as I could afford and all I needed.

We were standing in the living room when the movers brought her mattress in. Beth told me when we decided to move in together, she would never tolerate anything less than a queen-size. I couldn't see the sense of all that real estate for just one person—besides, it filled a room. To test her sense of humor, I said, "I think it belongs in the living room. It's the only room with any space to spare with that thing in it."

She took it more seriously than I thought she would. "That's stupid, Josh, how could you have anybody in without a real living room? Did your friends simply come in and all jump in bed together?"

I hadn't mentioned how few friends I had and said, "Of course not. I've never had a mattress large enough to give me ideas like that ... but it might be a set up worth trying."

"Josh, how could you have anyone over to sit in the *bedroom* and pretend it wasn't the *living room*," and she waved the movers on down the hall.

"OK, just a passing fancy." This was not the first sign of grave differences in how our minds worked.

At least she eased up on my room. It had the sofa bed along one wall, a table in one corner with a computer and file cabinet tucked underneath, a keyboard and large-screen monitor on top and some reference works on a shelf above. And so it went, as we installed the limited amount of stuff from our apartments in Lakeview into our new roost twenty-six floors above the West Loop.

My share of the rent matched my share of the acreage: 60/40. That came to fifty bucks a month more than my cut-rate studio, but this was deluxe living in comparison and enough work had been coming in the last few weeks to make it worth a try—no matter what happened by January. As for Beth, she would be closer to her job but it was her first try at living with a man—and mine at living with a woman.

I had recovered from the move and ordered my meager universe when, a few days later, something unexpected happened. I had joined the knots of tourists with their cameras on the State Street Bridge across the Chicago River in clear air under a vivid blue sky. Perfect conditions for photographing my impressive new neighborhood.

Peering through the telephoto, I panned around for subjects until a splash of iridescence and color at the north end of the bridge filled my viewfinder. Backing off the lens a little, I saw Piper's happy eyes and sparkling smile pop into focus, her face radiant beneath a feathered hat—but no little lunch box this time. She stood on the far end of the bridge, turned like a sunflower following the sun, and faced my camera.

The green eyes I remembered looked out from her peaches and cream complexion, and her flaxen hair waved in the soft river breeze. Once more, I couldn't make out the words as her pink lips moved, but I kept my finger on the shutter release and heard the device chug away, storing images of this peacock-feathered goddess as they burned into my brain. Somewhere I read that the bright feathers of male peacocks distract predators away from the hens, but that's exactly the opposite of what hers did.

I saw an arm close around her waist from behind and a man's face came into view when he leaned against the bridge railing and pointed over to the famous corncobs with his other arm. Overhead, a gull from Lake Michigan let out an insolent screech, as though he too had spotted the couple, before circling and plying his way westward.

My rival's face remained shaded by one of the taller buildings, and when Piper turned toward him, her face too was lost in shadow. My fantasy bubble drifting aloft with my goddess over the Loop suddenly began to wobble and barely cleared the Wrigley Building before crashing. She and her companion continued across the bridge and I lost sight of them among noon-time pedestrians.

Although I was managing on my own so far in Chicago, an underlying feeling of dissatisfaction never left and moments like this shook my confidence. I was alone and still adrift and wondered if the pattern of fantasy and failure in my chimerical love life might be a legacy of the role alcohol played in my parents' marriage.

The next hour I spent strolling the riverbank, hoping for distractions before returning to my cell, and told myself that, no, I'm not a stalker on parole, just a translator away from his desk: After all, exposure to wireless radiation and heat from a laptop computer might zonk the motility of sperm, it didn't seem to impair their determination. I'm simply prone to the same yearnings as my cloistered brethren in ages past—and realized it was time get back to work.

The latest jobs were about as close as I would get to matching the glorious, illustrated manuscripts produced by the monks, namely marketing material for cell phone operators, brochures for vacation colonies, press releases for industrial parks newly minted out of abandoned land in blighted areas—at best, I was gilding ephemeral lilies into bouquets for publication in airline magazines, Sunday supplements and web sites.

After two weeks more of that work, Jennifer's face, but not her catchy birth date with all those eights, had extinguished along with Piper's face when I found a voice mail from Jennifer on Saturday afternoon.

"Hi Josh, really nice to hear from you after we met at Dr. Ortega's. I'm sorry I didn't call. I won't go into details. Let's do meet up somewhere and talk. I work at home in Rogers Park. If you're downtown by now, I like coming down there. Suggest a time and place."

Finally, I'd connected with someone after a first meeting! She had looked pretty classy in the foot doctor's office, so I racked my brain to think of someplace that might impress her. That eliminated bars, ethnic eateries, and sporting events. Too early for high-end restaurants or a show. Maybe a movie? Or why not the top of the Hancock Building? I had met friends from out of town up there once during the day. It must be spectacular at night and, always conscious of the expense, for some reason I thought she wouldn't drink that much.

I messaged back and suggested any night next week around eight-thirty at the lounge on the top floor of the Hancock. Then I got going on a job that had come in that morning and worked straight through until I ran out of gas around eleven that night. One last check for messages left me wondering when I would hear back.

The next morning I woke as usual, around eight, after Beth left and went into the kitchen to put the coffee machine to work. Then I sent several questions off to my client asking for clarification of the context and a fact or two. It would take me the rest of the day to review the material I had drafted the night before, break for lunch and a breather, and come back to it for a final read-through. Some days I simply got up from my chair, locked the door and climbed up six or eight flights, and then back down; after drinking some water, I went back to my keyboard and felt my pulse return to normal while I checked email.

I found what I was waiting for. Jennifer's message suggested Thursday night, and she sounded excited about getting up on the Hancock at night. I immediately fired off a "Yes."

That night was my night to cook with Beth. We had agreed on quiche and salad. Fairly routine, but one of my favorites. I was the crust guy, she was the filling woman, and we both had a hand in the salad. While we worked, a glass of white wine usually smoothed the path.

She told me about the latest installment of the saga featuring her over-controlling supervisor at work and the overload expected of her while her coworker Corinne was out for surgery.

When she reached the end of that episode, she took a long sip of Riesling and sat down heavily. "My God, Josh. I haven't even asked you how your day went—or is going, in case you have to pull an all-nighter."

"I think your story takes the prize actually. Today, good things happened."

"So tell me," she said.

"First, I nearly finished a job that will pay well, and second, I finally heard from a woman I thought was out there blowing in the wind."

She gave me a quizzical look and raised her 'I'm waiting for more' eyebrow. "So which one?"

"Uh, did I tell you about Jennifer? Works in survey research in the city, met at the podiatrist's office maybe two weeks ago?"

"You mean you got off on the right *foot* with someone?"

I groaned appropriately. "Nope. I confess. I had to make the first call."

"Oooh, not the best foot."

"It paid off this time, though. We have a date Thursday night on top of the Hancock."

"Very nice. I've been up there. Just with the girls, but still—good call, Josh."

"Glad you approve." I peeked in the oven. "The quiche looks done. Let's eat."

She hauled it out and said, "Smells divine. Have some salad."

We topped off our Riesling, clinked glasses, and made short work of the quiche.

"So much for leftovers," Beth said, pushing back her chair. "My mom never saved stuff. We all tended to overeat so as not to throw anything away. That's why I have to go to the health club four times a week or I'm doomed."

She looked pretty trim and I told her so.

That seemed to please her, but she said, "Oh, my God, Josh, if I ever get sick or can't exercise for a week, I'm afraid I'll explode. Thank heavens, walking to work makes up for City Sniffers."

"It really doesn't show," I said. "Is weight an issue in your family?"

"Both my parents are pretty ample but not mega-large. My sis and I both have always struggled with our weight."

I felt lucky to have my father's slender build and was grateful that getting personal with Beth was this easy.

Thursday was a humid day in early July. Ideal baseball weather. But it took its toll on me as I rushed to arrive ten minutes early and wait for Jennifer in the lobby of the Hancock Building. I wanted to score any points I could by being on time and escorting her up to the top. Her first visit up in the Signature Lounge was bound to impress.

When she arrived, ten minutes late, she said, "Hello, Josh. Sorry, if I kept you waiting. Seems to be my thing."

It was worth the wait. She wore a wine-colored silk blouse and a curve-hugging skirt with smoky tights on her legs. She also carried a light-gray sweater against air conditioning. I stepped to meet her and said, "You look great tonight," and led her to the elevator.

We stepped off on the 96th floor and, leading her by the hand, I threaded a path through to the lounge. It was nearly full, but the lights were dim and the atmosphere muted since the main event was the cityscape of lights spreading away below us. Just then, three people left a window table to go to dinner and we quickly sat down.

"Wow, what a view, Josh. This is really cool."

"Yeah, I'm so glad you could make it. Have you eaten?"

"Of course. I never go out on an empty stomach. That's asking for trouble."

"What will it be for you folks?" the waiter asked and set down a small tray of olives and crackers.

I looked at Jennifer. "Let's do things up in style and order the signature cocktail of the day."

"OK, what is it?" she asked.

"It's a Sidecar—basically brandy, prosecco and lime juice," the waiter said. "Or, instead of brandy, you can have it with vodka or gin if you prefer."

"Umm, I think, I'd like mine with vodka," she said.

"Make mine with brandy, please."

"How is your foot coming along, Jennifer? Mine has pretty well stopped complaining if I wear the right shoes."

"That's great. My toe healed really quickly. That doctor knows his stuff."

"Doesn't he?"

"What a coincidence to meet someone else with a rare birthday at the foot doctor," she enthused.

Our drinks came and we toasted our birthdays.

"Mmm. I like this," she said and took another sip.

"So how do you like to celebrate your birthday, since it's coming up?" I asked.

"Well, last year my parents drove in from Des Moines and took me out to dinner because I turned twenty-five. This year, I'll just have to wait and see."

"What haven't you done yet, that you look forward to?" I asked.

"Travel, I think. My mom just got back from two weeks in Italy. She and her friend, Sheila, were college roommates and since Sheila knows her way around in Italy and wanted company, they went together."

"Where would you like to go?"

"I think France. It just must be so romantic." She took another sip of her drink and asked, "Do you think they have Sidecars there?"

"It would be worth the trip to find out," I said. She laughed more than I thought my remark merited, and I figured the drink tab wouldn't soar out of sight if she was already that far along.

"How do you celebrate your birthday?" she asked.

"If I had friends around, I'd cook for them or, if not, like the year I worked in Berlin, I'd let the sow loose—it's a German expression for going hog wild. My version would be to eat in a fancy restaurant and then go dancing. But that year I didn't have the money for either one."

"Oh, I like to dance too, but I'm really bad at it—even worse than my cooking." More laughter and heads began to turn.

I couldn't quite place the laugh—I didn't remember hearing it in the doctor's office, but then her foot hurt.

Lightning flashed to the west, followed closely by a clap of thunder. She laughed again. "Ooh, how exciting. We can sit this out right here and stay high and dry. I think I'd like another Sidecar."

And high and dry pretty well summed up that evening.

The storm closed in and swallowed the city lights. I couldn't think of a good reason to go out in it and saw no way around another hit to the bar tab—but when the waiter showed up, I asked, if we couldn't split the third round. He acquiesced and brought us two diminutive versions.

Try as I might to hold the wit, Jennifer commentated everything I said with squealing laughter punctuated by snorts. Then, I remembered where I had heard it before—in a pet shop from alarmed guinea pigs.

After our third drink, we went down and I walked her to the subway to put her on a northbound train. Before she climbed on, she thanked me for a "really spectacular evening." "Imagine," she said, "sidecars on top of the Hancock in a thunder storm," and laughed one last time.

We agreed to talk, but I couldn't imagine hearing that laugh even once a day, so I decided to let items 3 and 4 rest and appreciate the fact that someone thought I was a witty guy.

Friday night I stopped at the Mystic Celt to tell Ian about getting high with Jennifer and to check the mirror of my friend's eye.

After the conclusion of a major soccer match, the place cleared out a bit, and I told him my tale about meeting her.

He asked me which kind of 'tale' I was talking about here.

"Normally, I'll take either spelling," I said, "since my social calendar isn't exactly full. But this woman was too much for me."

He smiled upon hearing how her laugh kept pace with the bar tab. "Just remember," he replied, "If you have a roving eye, it's no use having the other one fixed on Heaven."

I pondered that one for a minute. "Are you thinking, I'm being too picky? Or are you saying, I won't recognize heaven, even if it's staring me in the face—as long as I'm on the prowl?"

"That's the best part of proverbs, my friend. Some part of us is always ready to take something from them—and that changes as we change."

That night, I turned things over in my mind and wondered: Do I have to make up my mind between items 3 and 4, getting laid or finding love?—that's a lot to ask.

Beth and I had been living at the Towers six weeks and the kitchen schedule was working well. Sunday night was our night to cook together. Otherwise, we each cooked separately because Beth sometimes ate out with clients at noon or in the evening, and I ate whenever I got hungry—so Sundays made the most sense.

We played it safe in the kitchen the first six weeks—spaghetti, pizza, sloppy joes, sweet potato fries, green beans—with no complaints. But my palate was starting to get restless. I felt like Curious George the Monkey looking through the window at the fruit market—I had to get in there or else.

"What about walking on the wild side now and then?" I asked. "Try out something different?"

"I'm game," she said, "but don't expect me to plan out something with new recipes and all. My job takes too much out of me, and grocery shopping is not my idea of fun."

"Fair enough. How about this: Since you work for the Chicago Convention and Tourism Bureau, you really oughta be up to speed on Chicago culinary specialties—you know, Chicago-style hot dogs, pizza, Italian beef, Polish, pulled pork, sliders, chicken wings, Mexican."

"I suppose you're right, but I miss Sheboygan brats."

Our opportunity to break out came sooner than I expected. Sometimes I do field work to find clients so that I feel comfortable with jobs I bid. It gives me a leg up to see what style and level of material a client is using. So when I spotted an ad in the *Chicago Tribune* for a cooking class at a German kitchen store on Michigan Avenue, I said, "Hey, Beth, listen to this:

Here is a pizza workshop advertised in the *Trib* at that Kochstudio stove place on the Magnificent Mile.

"They promise to teach you 'the ingredients and techniques that make your deep dish pizza rival Chicago's best'."

"Homemade *is* good," she interrupted.

I continued: "'Learn the importance of a cool rise followed by intense heat to produce the perfect pie'."

"That should be a snap for you," she said. "You'd just have to reverse your technique with women."

"Some things shouldn't be joked about," I said. Did she have feelings about me and other women? Could she be jealous? Instead of asking, I said, "I'm not so sure sixty bucks is worth it," and did a quick calculation out loud—"Sixty dollars for 180 minutes comes to thirty cents a minute. For that money we could get maybe six pizzas if we picked them up."

"Halve that with delivery," she said. "And don't expect it to still be warm by the time you get down to reception to pick it up and back up twenty-six floors."

"That starts to change the equation," I said. "I'll have to think about it some more."

I waffled up until the day before class to give it a chance to fill up. However, the more I thought about it and browsed their stove and cookware website, the more I realized this class was likely as close as I would ever get to a kitchen of that quality.

What settled it was checking the company's brochures on line and seeing that their translations were due for an overhaul. Key phrases were awkward and the syntax sometimes clumsy. So I decided to roll the dice, submit a proposal to review their material, and enrolled in the course.

By five that evening it was decided. I had snagged the last spot in the class, and my proposal was being considered.

After a late breakfast the next morning, I decided to dress for the part, dug out my "Chicago-style Hot Dog" T-shirt, showing a fine specimen on a bun with all of the ingredients properly labeled, and headed down to the street to start Pizza School.

Sunshine washed over me as I walked east and spotted a banana-yellow water taxi waiting down on the river. I decided to take it over to Michigan Avenue. When our craft churned past the two Marina City corncobs jutting sixty stories upward, I craned my neck and regretted that Beth and I hadn't taken a closer look when we were apartment shopping; wedge-shaped living isn't something you would soon forget.

I jumped off the taxi at the Michigan Avenue bridge and threaded my way a quarter of a Magnificent Mile north through tourists and shoppers to the Kochstudio kitchen store.

Up until our move, I had always made do with kitchen appliances in rental units that had taken a beating. Now, the ones in our new dwelling in Precinct

Towers were state-of-the-art and offered more functionality than I knew how to coax out of them—which slowed me down. Maybe this class would change that.

Whenever I ventured into most cookware stores, I was a kid in a toy store: bold-colored pans and utensils, gadgets that challenged the imagination, fascinating designs—all to accomplish what my grandmother used to do with her bare hands.

The image of her smiling, wrinkled face brought a moment of relief from the vague, rootless feeling that gnawed at me, although I knew her only from infrequent visits. My father seldom sought contact with her once he left home. Maybe the soothing memory would help me resist the urge to carry home more kitchen toys to jam our cabinets.

As I waited for the class to begin, I browsed the aisles of the Kochstudio. Alas, I saw a sterile array of stainless and synthetic materials on metal shelving where wood, pottery or natural fibers would have been glaringly out of place. Perhaps Koch*labor* or kitchen *lab* would say it better.

At precisely noon, we were summoned to gather near the stoves bearing the Kochstudio brand. They formed a ring, like an altar in a temple where offerings were to be brought for scrutiny and approval by the high priest. He wore a white smock and apron—why not a toque I wondered—and would direct us in placing our creations on the stove tops for flaming or in the ovens for roasting or baking.

Our class of nine had come from far and near; for some, the class had been a gift from family members; others, like me, were responding to a notice in the paper showing a steaming, deep-dish pie, a wedge of pizza trailing fiercely resisting strands of cheese as it was hoisted from the pan. The flaky crust had been the clincher.

Once our high priest had initiated us into the origins and mysteries of deep-dish pizza with a spiel worthy of Wikipedia, he directed us to form teams of three. This plan, however, was foiled by a short, stocky woman with a severe face named Marusya who insisted on working alone—which left me paired with Cassie, a skinny young blonde with stringy hair and slightly bug eyes.

As the afternoon unfolded, I learned that her all-time favorite movie was *Ratatouille* and Cassie's resemblance to Linguini, the awkward, not terribly bright, yet appealing garbage boy *comme sous-chef* was too obvious to miss. She had little success kneading and shaping or pouring and spreading, and this brought out my paternal instincts; I did my best to shield her from Marusya's bossing, who bulled her way through the exercises with critical comments to spare.

Our late luncheon for sampling our *Kochkunst* was meant to convince us that we were now privy to the secrets of Chicago-style crust and fillings—but there were a few holdouts and doubters: Marusya knew she could do better and Cassie wasn't sure she could do as well. By the time we gathered up our recipes and aprons and headed out into splendid weather, there was still no consensus on where to find the best deep-dish in town. The sunshine and the thought that Beth will be surprised—I didn't hit on anyone—plus the possibility of gaining the Kochstudio as a new client quieted the lurking specter of spending the future feeding from dumpsters and made me smile.

After a day indoors, the weather was too good to waste, so I headed back down Michigan Avenue, crossed the river, and went on past Millennium Park. South of the Art Institute, I decided to stroll over towards the lakefront to Buckingham Fountain before heading west to our tower.

It was around five when I reached the bench I sometimes chose to watch the colored light and water show at dusk and to take in the amazing skyline—something I had never done before I left my Lakeview neighborhood.

When I arrived, my bench was already occupied by a woman in her thirties in airy clothes that complemented this early burst of midsummer weather. She seemed to be caught up with simply watching the traffic flow past on the road beyond the meadow. I hesitated, aware of the contrast of her summery pallet with the garishly autopsied Chicago hotdog splayed across my T-shirt, but I risked it and, when I sat down, it startled her.

"Oh, hello," she said.

"Sorry to intrude. I sometimes hang out here awhile before going to work. I guess I was surprised to find someone else here."

"That sounds like a nice routine," she said. "I love it here. It's like being on your own island and still being part of the world streaming around you."

"That's true."

"Why do you come?"

"Why?" I reflected a moment. "I think it´s a way to connect some of the strands of my life that don't necessarily fit together. I'm from a small town and the one park had benches like this where I would sit. Sometimes alone, sometimes with someone else. Sitting here and watching all the streams of water collecting in the basins makes me think that my strands will come together."

She swept a hand through her honey-blonde hair and stretched her legs. "This is a good spot for that. I get down to Chicago from Madison, Wisconsin, once a month to check on an older relative. Before going back, I always come here to clear my mind."

"That's nice. I guess your strands are connecting."

"You could say that. So what other strands are there for you to connect, here in Chicago?" she asked.

I thought of Beth. "It's mostly trying to see into the crystal ball. What lies ahead, with whom—that sort of thing."

"Maybe we're all looking for that," she said.

"I guess so," I said. "At least it's true of everyone I know."

She laughed. "This is like talking to the stranger next to you on an airplane you'll never see again." She continued, "I know a lot more about the *what* and *where* in my life, but not so much about the *who*."

"I'm unattached and managing alright, but part of me is looking for something more," I said. "Finding someone to share a life with in the big city is taking time. Is it any easier in Madison?"

"No. After I graduated from college it got harder, if anything. Work and career and just coping seem to soak up most of my energy. So far lightning hasn't struck."

"Well, it's not quite lightning, but meeting on this bench is pretty serendipitous. I'm Josh."

"Meredith," she said and gave me a pleasingly warm hand.

I checked my watch. Five-thirty. "Tell me, Meredith. Did you say you get down to Chicago every month?"

"Every month. My aunt is ninety and lives in a retirement setting here. I'm her only living relative anywhere near and she's my favorite aunt. And she's the only one I have left."

"You both are lucky then. What time do you leave for Madison?"

"I take a bus from the Amtrak Station. It's simpler than driving and I can read. I spend the afternoon with her, get a bite to eat, and get the seven or eight-thirty bus back."

"I've got it easy; I live just west of the Loop in one of the apartment towers—I'm a freelance editor and translator and work out of my apartment. Any chance you'd like to get something to eat before you go?"

"You know, that sounds like a welcome change. Eating alone is not the greatest experience, unless you have a good book."

"Great. Today I learned how to make deep-dish pizza. You can probably tell from this shirt, that I'm a fan of Chicago food. Are you up for a Chicago-style hotdog?"

"Being from Wisconsin, I'm afraid I've always been a cheese girl. Oh, and brats, of course."

"Well, it would be unpatriotic, if not downright treasonable, not to introduce you to a genuine dog."

"OK, I'll bite—forgive the pun. What makes them Chicago-style?"

"First of all, the hot dogs themselves. They aren't boiled or grilled—they are *bathed* in water at 190 degrees for about twenty minutes. That gives them that nice snap when you bite into them.

"Then you pile on peppers, maybe celery salt or tomato slices, and dill pickles or hot onions. Or you could add sweet relish. Mustard is OK, but catsup is a no-no. And *voila*! One of the tastiest and craziest hot dogs in the world!"

"I don't know, Josh. It's a long bus ride."

"I'll tell you what, why don't you try a bite of mine first to ease into it?"

"OK"

"Let's stroll around the fountain and take a turn through the park. There's bound to be a hot dog cart patrolling here somewhere."

We hit pay dirt about fifteen minutes later on the far side of the fountain, its mighty jets sending streams high into the air to splash back down with a spluttering clatter. This dog man knew his stuff and served it up without once cribbing from the diagram on my T-shirt.

We moved to a bench with our feast, and I was flattered to be the one to introduce Meredith to this particular taste of Chicago. Holding it away from her to avoid fall out, she closed her eyes and took a big bite. She held still and chewed once, twice; her eyes flew open and tears came and a choking sound had me worried until she grabbed a napkin, put it to her mouth, and turning away from me, disposed of her very first bite.

"Oh, dear," she said, "I'm so sorry. I guess I just don't have what it takes."

"Don't say that. I'm the one who should apologize," and wondered which condiment had gotten her. Inspired by Ian, I ventured: "Even in Wisconsin, not every farmer was meant to raise cows."

She wiped the perspiration from her forehead and looked at her watch. "You will really think me ungrateful, but I do have to get going. Just to show you I am not, I will bring you my favorite cheese the next time I come down."

"I will count on it," I said, between bites and she apologized again while I made short work of my truncated dog. We stood and walked over to her bus at Union Station where I gave her a wave as she boarded. Sadly, a culinary chasm separated us, and we left it, that we would meet at the same time on the same bench, when she came down next month.

My deep-dish pizza the next day was fabulous and the recap of the class, especially me running interference for Cassie against Marusya, scored major points with Beth. The evening ended with Beth promising to come up with something to match my pie the following Sunday.

When I told her about the class, I left out meeting Meredith afterwards at the fountain and the aftermath. Even though the setting and the company made it the best Chicago dog I'd tasted, I guess I oversold it, and I wondered if I would **ever** see her again.

Sharing the master bath with Beth was not working out quite as well as the kitchen. It was off Beth's bedroom, and my stuff was in the half bath. When she was at work, I could bathe to my heart's content. So far no complaints about that.

But the tooth brush spray on her mirror and the smudges on the sink and sink top—things she never seemed to notice, cried out for attention. Each time I wiped them away, I told myself, another four months is not forever.

Another thing that began to get to me was the underwear hanging around her bathroom—mostly bras—as if she was decorating for me.

I had to unhook them from the shower rod, faucets and shower head, drape them on the vanity top, and return them to their places.

Maybe she thought I have a serious thing about underwear. If I'm any judge, her stuff was getting racier as time went on. To begin with, we were talking about two potholders linked together in plain standard-issue garments. Before long, those began to disappear in favor of lace and net contraptions that scooped and swooped. Colors became a standard feature, too.

These developments weren't something I could simply bring up, since we hadn't been through her undies drawer during my home visit. What if she was signaling something to me? Was she teasing me or was she oblivious? Or was it all for someone else? I didn't see any way of finding out.

Fortunately a translation job with a five-day deadline came in to distract me. A tourism consortium in Germany was promoting a reclaimed rustbelt region famously known as the "Ruhrgebiet." Since the late 1800's, it had been synonymous with the steel, coal and manufacturing backbone of industrial Germany but now was being reinvented as a recreational paradise. I was making little headway up in my tower cell and my conscience was nagging ever louder, so for a change of scene I headed after lunch over to Gotham Library— my nickname for the Harold Washington Chicago Public Library in the Loop.

After running a few errands north of the river, I arrived by El train at Library Place and saw the phantasmagorical gargoyles of weathered-copper looming from the rooftop. They keep watch over a structure suggestive of a Renaissance fortress-cum-Bat-garage that could have been spawned by Batman's imagination during a film shoot in Italy.

As I left the El platform and took the stairs to the street below, I kept one ear open for the swish of a cape, in case he swung down from a rampart. Rounding the corner, I found the entrance and, once inside Gotham, the doors reduced the random honking of cabbies and corner traffic cop's shrill whistle to a distant soundtrack.

I decided not to cross the soaring lobby to the elevator banks beyond the information desk but headed instead up the long escalators to the third level where books were kept. If ever it flooded downtown, they were safe up there.

The time spent getting up to them each visit would be annoying but for the veined Carrara marble cladding the walls that never failed to work its magic as it slid past my gaze. Beauty does soothe ruffled spirits and perhaps this accounted for the ever-present contingent of homeless patrons.

Like other users, some strayed in to watch porn on the Wi-Fi, or nap in the stacks, or use the toilet. In any case, all of us used books in some way as props to explain our presence.

Eventually arriving on level two, I defocused from the marble panels and moved around the landing for escalator transit up to level three.

As I rode up, I recalled a recurring nightmare in which the guards declared an emergency; the escalators quit, the elevators failed, and the stairwells were dangerously jammed with a stampede of guards and homeless persons stumbling over the jumble of books abandoned by fleeing patrons. But I had been prescient enough to wear a parachute and could descend directly to the lobby from the upper floors. I yelled "Geronimo!" and jumped, but my chute got snagged on the wing of a gargoyle surveying the lobby below, and I was left swinging helplessly under the creature's mocking gaze until I would wake up perspiring.

Since I was in no such hurry this morning, I looked back down at the mortals dwarfed by the lobby's monumental scale and listened to the background murmur of exchanges between patrons and personnel checking out books punctuated by the jolt of carts wheeling materials around the floors.

Like the Great Hall in Union Station a few blocks over, any semblance of discrete speech was set awash, blurred and smoothed high above the speakers' heads, ending as dampened reverberations, blunted consonants, and flattened vowels.

On the third floor, I found a desk where I could tackle the next portion of the translation job. Warmer weather today had brought more nap- and knowledge-seekers indoors than usual. I turned down an aisle until I managed to find a free table and set myself up far enough away from the check-out area which generated intrusive noise that was persistent enough not to break my concentration. There was no one to my left and to my right, just a man in a nondescript clump of dark clothing.

The next half hour, I read through the section describing the near miraculous transformation of Westphalian coal works and slag heaps into performing arts venues, museums and nature preserves. The area had once provided the livelihood of miners and workers who watered at the network of taverns sprinkled throughout their habitat and brought to mind the underbelly of bars and flophouses along West Madison in Chicago which zeal for urban renewal had swept away and given me my present domicile: the Precinct Towers had driven a stake through the hearts of the wraiths who once haunted that district.

Just then, the lump of clothing sprawled on the table near me stirred, and a human form began to take shape. A man lifted his head, and long, white-blond hair and a scraggly beard framed his ruddy face. He turned and regarded me through blood-shot eyes, and the rancid scent of an unbathed body triggered a memory.

"Queenie?" I said.

He blinked and squinted me into focus, trying to make sense of what he saw. "I know you?" he asked.

"I remember you from last fall. Near the corner of Broadway and Belmont. In front of the Walgreens. I used to pass by there. We would chat sometimes."

At one point, Queenie was thinking of heading back to West Virginia where he had a daughter and once had a wife. I had asked him if he might have run into my brother, Travis—he was out there somewhere too—but Queenie couldn't recall.

"Where have you been?" I tried.

"Ah. I used to crash along west Madison—til they built them towers that pushed us further west. This winter I'm headin' back down to New Orleans. There's plenty goin' on down there in the winter to live off of."

"Can I buy you a cup of coffee?" I asked.

"Naw, I been sick some. Can't stomach coffee much anymore."

He truly didn't look well.

"But I wouldn't mind somethin' towards a meal or a bottle."

I fished for some crumpled bills that had been easier to stuff in my pocket than insert into my wallet when I was hurrying to catch the El.

"Here," I said, "Take this fiver—for old time's sake."

He rose and shouldered his day pack, then approached to accept the bill and mumbled. "Thanks." Turning, he shambled away from the guard station towards the restrooms, trailing the unmistakable odor of the unwashed.

I took the opportunity to stand for a moment and stretch. He's probably grabbing a bath in the restroom, since this was his place. The thought of anyone's life coming to this made me shudder and wonder how immune I was.

I was certain Queenie had no idea who I was, no memory of our chats on the sidewalk where he perched on stacked milk crates and held a cup, placid as a Buddha, and spared unresponsive passersby the menacing rattle of the cup and the sarcasm-twinged wishes for 'a nice day' meant to fester until the next opportunity came along to salve an uneasy conscience.

How fruitful was such labor? I never knew for sure but guessed it was enough for vodka or schnapps—judging from the empties that collected at the edge of Queenie's alleyway—and kept him and others coming back, regular as clockwork until they disappeared. Like Travis.

It was some time before I could shut the door on memories of my brother who, as far as I knew was dumpster diving back East, like Queenie, canning for aluminum at a nickel a pop. Maybe I had something to do with it? Or sister Amy? He couldn't keep up with her—she was three years older—and he wasn't easy; so she chose me to play with instead of him. The image flared up of Travis sweeping the Sorry board off the table and pushing my chair backward, and I automatically checked where the stitches had closed the gash opened in my head by a metal radiator.

Refocusing, I picked up the thread of the well-paying fairytale lying on my table about large-scale urban renewal.

Eventually, my eyes began to grind in their sockets, and I rose to leave and dutifully present my bag for inspection at the guard station. Queuing up, I found myself behind a slender young woman with short, bronze-colored hair. She carried a slim messenger bag over one shoulder and her turn came quickly. She opened it and the guard, a Black woman of imposing mass and a voice to match, said, "You're not holding it so I can see inside. You'll have to take everything out."

I watched the young woman unhook herself from the bag and unpack it on the desk. Everything you would expect—except purloined library materials.

"OK, that's it," the guard said. Then, the reverse process began. "Can you speed it up? You're holding people up," she said.

"I'm in no hurry," I offered.

"Yeah, honey, but take a look behind you."

I saw two others waiting. One was reading and one looked like he was headed back to his shelter for a meal.

The young woman's keys slipped to the floor, and the reverse process slipped a cog.

"Crap," she said and bent down and crammed them back into her bag before she stormed off.

The guard muttered something about "dumbass" as I quickly passed muster and, forgetting my earlier fatigue, hurried after the fleet messenger.

Below, I could see her already emerge from the second floor down-escalator and slow her pace somewhat. By clipping along down the escalator and passing other patrons, I caught her just as she prepared to push out into the street. I moved to open the door for her and said, "I was right behind you up there and saw the grilling you got. What was there not to like about you, do you suppose?"

Surprise, then delight lit her face. "That bitch and I have a history."

Not wanting to go into it further, I smiled. "I like to work here sometimes. You studying here?"

"Yep. I'm a third-year vocal major at Roosevelt University, a few blocks over," she said, as we stepped outside.

"No kidding. So when do I get to hear you?"

"Oh, well 'never turn down an audience' they say. My semester recital is next Friday at 3 p.m. in Ganz Hall. On the seventh floor."

"I've been in there," I said. "What are you going to sing?"

"Two songs by Mahler. Are you seriously coming?"

"Mahler nails it. I didn't mention that I work with German. I'm a translator."

"Awesome. I'm taking German this semester and I so suck." The sun glancing off the building opposite turned her hair coppery.

"Thanks for telling me about the concert. We could talk afterwards, if you like. About some tutoring. I used to teach it."

"I'm Thea, and that would be really super."

"I'm Josh. Well, good luck and I'll see you then."

With that settled, she turned east and I headed west back to the Towers.

I got up the elevator in record time and found Beth in the kitchen. "Hey," I said, "let me help stow those groceries. Tonight's the night we cook together, isn't it?"

"Bravo," she said. "When I found the place dark, I figured you might be out somewhere."

"Nope, just on my way back from worshiping at Harold Washington Temple."

"I'm not sure some people would appreciate that. He was much loved and dying of a heart attack like that hit everybody in the city hard."

"Well, the ultimate sacrifice got him a whopper mausoleum. I saw somewhere, that it's the biggest one in the Loop—and full of the unwashed undead." I couldn't completely shake off a sense of foreboding after running into Queenie, so I tried changing the subject. "What's for dinner?"

"This pasta dish I saw in Corinne's *Cooking Light*—those photos always hook me. Plus some of the last green beans of the season. Anything going on at Harold's place?"

"Well, one of the hobos turned out to be a regular from my old neighborhood. He catches up on his sleep down there—and his reading, I guess."

"How could you stand the smell?" she asked, as she marshaled the ingredients along the counter.

"I have a bit of sinus congestion, so I wasn't up to sniff, so to speak. My lucky day, I guess, because I also met an interesting woman."

"Why am I not surprised? How many is that since we collided?"

"Who's counting? Ian kids me about that too. But, this gal really has spunk. She's a voice student at Roosevelt. And I'm a sucker for divas and actresses."

"I've noticed. So are you going to enroll there or what?"

"Nope. Going to her recital next week, and then I'll tutor her in German. She said she sucks," I said and waited to see if the intentional ambiguity provoked a reaction.

She winged a carrot at me and said, "You nasty man. I almost pity you."

I caught it midair and took a bite. "Just wanted to stir the pot a bit," I said.

"So what are you looking for in a woman? Is predictable and reliable more than you can deal with, my friend? Why this pursuit of the empty grail?"

"Who can explain these things? Maybe I'm compensating for the dull core beneath my fascinating exterior."

She gave me a look that was hard to read and shoved a bottle over. "Just open this wine."

"*Si, bella,*" I said and set about leveraging a stubborn synthetic stopper out of a bottle of red and poured us each a generous glass of a blend that got through my touch of sinus trouble. "Would a glass of this right now oil your waters?" I asked.

"Damned right. Now let's get to work," she said and we clinked glasses.

"It's been six months since we first butted heads," I said.

"Ouch. I try not to remember that."

"To head butts," I said, raising my glass towards her.

"To butt-heads," she said, raising hers towards me.

"Say, now that you bring it up, how are Henry and Rhonda getting along in your old place?"

"Well, they're still there. I haven't seen her for a month, but we talk now and then."

"How is Henry wearing?"

"About as well as you could expect any guy to wear over time, I suppose."

That didn't tell me much, so I asked by way of clarification, "Is that better or worse than our track record?"

She dropped her guard for a moment and gave me a look I didn't know how to interpret, then glanced quickly away and said, "I don't know if it could be better or not, Josh. But I'm content to stay with it for now. How about you?"

"Count me in," I said.

It had been a slow week for me and the rent still had to be paid—but at least I would have time for Thea's recital at Roosevelt University. I changed shirts, gave the mirror a quick check, and took one last look at my inbox. Damn, a job request from an agency in India was waiting for me to translate order invoices for a German supermarket chain in Portugal. Fine and good, but by tomorrow noon. How I hated that—I already had texted Thea that I would come.

Screw it. I shot back a 'sorry, can't this time' before hurrying to the elevator and punching "Down." The next few minutes I spent trying to picture the face that went with the sassy voice and short coppery hair, but like the elevator, nothing came. That was serious. Rent anxiety, I supposed.

Roosevelt University was across the Loop and arriving late would be uncool. After eight minutes and counting, I thought, 'Here we go again,' and bolted for the stairwell leaving a young Asian woman waiting at the elevator with her stroller. I started the plunge down twenty-six flights of stairs. Checking my watch a second time after five flights, I estimated I'd need another eight minutes to hit terra firma—not too far off what the elevator delivered when traffic in the tower was heavy. I stepped into the lobby on rubbery knees and hurried outside with twenty minutes 'til show time. Crap. Another cab ride. Cross-town buses get bogged down too easily. By the time I climbed out of my cab at Roosevelt University and kissed seven bucks goodbye, my knees were steady again, and I ran into the building with a wave at the concierge. "Ganz Hall?"

"Seventh floor," he said.

The stair well gaped to the left, but I went for the elevators. With three minutes to go, I punched and prayed. Thirty seconds later, a *ding* invited me in and the doors slid shut behind me. What was at stake? Maybe a candidate for tutoring. Maybe some spirited times with a woman ten years my junior who knew her way around the club scene. And a stream of income from a summer of tutoring.

I arrived just as the lights in the art deco hall dropped and the students and parents making up the audience settled down. I found a seat near the back and waited through a recital program that included two other students before Thea. A stunning green dress complemented her hair and wrapped to advantage around her slender figure. Her voice, a promising soprano with appealing richness, was equally pleasing. And the two songs by Mahler came off well enough musically but challenged her mastery of German phonetics. I could see possibilities here.

After the enthusiastic applause by her cohort of student friends died down and the lights went back up, I walked to the edge of the stage and called, "Hi Thea, remember me? That was first class."

"Josh, it's cool that you could make it. I'd like you to meet my teacher," she said, indicating a raven-haired woman in her forties in a red dress who had just finished congratulating her.

"Hello. I'm Carmella Frampton. Thea mentioned that you tutor German."

"Yes, I do. I'm also a translator, but tutoring is a nice break."

"My husband is the chairman of the music department at Newminster University and I can pass the word, if you like."

"I'd like that very much. I can get your email address from Thea, right?"

"You bet, Josh," Thea answered. "And by the way, can you join me and ten of my best friends to celebrate tonight?"

That put my integrity to the test and it took me a minute before I stammered that I was afraid I had another commitment, but I gave her my card and asked her to call or mail me so we could talk about tutoring, if she liked.

Friends gathered around to congratulate her and began talking about their plans for celebrating and the excitement in her face covered any disappointment over my response.

Before turning to leave, I said, "Congratulations again and hope to hear from you soon." She gave me a quick wave and a smile.

Next time I stopped in to see Ian at the Celtic Isle, he brought up the crucial subject: "You've been rooming together now what? Three months or so? How is it going?"

"Things are pretty smooth. Lots to get used to though, and I do miss the old neighborhood."

"I can understand that. It's farther away from the pub here and your coffee shop."

"And even my grocery store," I said. "I miss not seeing the clerks at the Jewel check-out."

"Cute ones?" he asked.

"Not even. Just plain people to talk to. It made me feel at home."

"Right, I think that's why half the people come into the bar here, too," he said.

"I used to hear the craziest stuff when I was waiting in the check-out line. Last time, my favorite clerk, Laila, said to the guy in front of me: 'Hey, how's my favorite fireman?'

"He said, 'Laila, I just got off my shift driving the tail end of a damn ladder truck around corners all day, barely missing cars too stubborn to yield or even move an inch. That's what most of the horn blowing and sirens is about ... it means: won't you just move over, you damned idiot.'

"'Sounds rough,' she said.

"'Yeah,'" he said. "'Coming to the Jewel is one place I can literally chill out. I stroll up and down the frozen food aisles a time or two and my blood pressure drops. I couldn't go straight home to the family, or I might kill somebody.'"

"That rivals anything I've heard here lately," Ian said.

"She told him, 'Well, you just keep coming in here as much as you like, sweetie.' Then she asked me where I'd been and, when she heard I had moved, she scolded me for abandoning her."

"Where do you shop now?" Ian asked.

"At the minimart on the third floor of Tower Two. Different people are working there every time I go in. It's not the same."

"OK, so now tell me the good news ... like, Beth is after your tail or something."

"Hate to disappoint, but we both are still behaving like good roommates. The trouble is that's how things end up with other women I meet too." I told him about playing the Chicago food card with Meredith and getting skunked.

"Well, at least you know more than when you started."

Ian's effort to help fell flat. Knowing more than I started with was small solace and sent me down an alleyway with an uncertain end. In my darker moments, I saw myself in Queenie and the others, alone and reduced to seeking warmth and a clean bathroom in the nearest library.

A few days later, I ran downstairs to the lobby to mail some things and then stepped back onto the elevator. We started up to the 26th floor. At the fifth floor, a young Asian couple with a small boy and some groceries got off. At twelve, a man in a dress shirt, slacks and loafers exited with a *Wall Street Journal* under his arm leaving just me and an attractive young Indian woman who looked to be a student. At fourteen, her floor, we heard a clunk followed by a clank and overshot the floor.

"Wait a minute!" she said.

Then, we ratcheted upwards by starts and stops what may have been several more floors before we jerked to a halt.

"Crap," I said. Then silence, broken only by the rustle and whirr of cables from the movement of other elevators in the column. There was just time to exchange glances before the lights cut out but for a small bulb above the translucent ceiling.

She clutched my arm instinctively, and I put my hand on hers and sensed her relax a little.

"Let's try the 'Alarm' button," I said and reached over and pushed on it.

"I don't hear anything," she said.

"Me neither, but I have my cell phone. And we can try the phone here in the control panel."

"Good," she said, sounding relieved.

Feeling manly, I released her hand and searched along the panel to open the glass case and take out the phone. I dialed zero and listened to it ring. This should be easy enough. Service and maintenance have always been prompt before. What was it, the last time I called? Burned out bulbs in the hallway or the air conditioning? The phone continued to ring. Anyway, they should have picked up by now.

I hung up and tried again. Looking over at my fellow traveler, I said, "Say, I'm Josh. What's your name."

"I'm Chandra."

"Are you a student?" I asked, with the phone ringing in my ear.

"Yes, I'm doing a master's at UIC in anthropology and sociology."

"That's great. I moved in a couple of months ago and work as a free-lance translator from my apartment—just a minute."

I hung up again and said, "Let me try calling the desk with my cell phone. Maybe that will work."

I took it out, retrieved the number, and hit *Call.*

At ten rings I said, "What the fuck is wrong with these people," adding, "Sorry about that," and felt my throat and chest tighten.

"Do you have a phone with you?" I asked Chandra.

"I do," she said and pulled out an iPhone. "Shall I try?"

"Here's the number." I reached over and held the screen of my phone near her appealing face. She quickly registered and transmitted the number through her fingers to her phone.

She looked thoughtful, but as time passed with no answer, her face showed signs of tension. "Can't we do something?"

Ten minutes had passed. The tightness in my chest yielded to a couple of deep breaths. "Let's sit down and take a few minutes to keep calm and see what comes to mind. If we can think of a plan, we'll be alright."

I slid down against one wall, drawing up my knees and encircling them with my arms. She mirrored my position against the other wall in formfitting dark jeans.

"How are you doing?" I asked.

She looked over with luminous eyes. Shoulder length ebony hair cast shadows across her face from faint light falling from above. "I think we'll be alright," she said. "I'm glad I'm not in here alone."

"Me too."

That brought a smile, which felt like a small reward and encouragement. I liked looking at her and thought I was in no hurry to get away from here. And I can think of worse ways to meet.

"Look," she said, "it has been about fifteen minutes since we stalled. I think we should keep calling the service desk every five minutes and hope they get back on duty. It is only four o'clock. They have to show up."

"Good," I said, "Plus, we can try signaling other people around us. In fact, let's try standing up and give it a try." I offered my hand and helped her to her feet. She was about six inches shorter than I and dressed in a light, long-sleeved sweater.

"Let's try banging on the door. Use your palm," I told her, "so you don't hurt your hand," and we began smacking the metal door. Then we moved to the wooden wall of the elevator cab and stayed with it a minute more because that made more noise and felt better. I stopped and said, "Let's listen."

The quiet was broken only by the whirr and rustle of one of the neighboring elevator cars passing.

"Let's yell *help* when the next one passes," she said.

I nodded. Our eyes met as we leaned against the wall and listened. When the next one seemed to be approaching, she nodded and we yelled and banged on the walls at the same time. The faint *ding* of the bell signaling doors opening on an elevator on a floor close to us triggered another flurry of our banging and yelling.

After a few minutes of listening for some response, she said, "I think we better phone again. You try the elevator phone and I will ring from my cell."

We went to work and set distant phones ringing somewhere and hoped for the best.

Fifteen minutes later, when I rang through on the emergency phone, someone picked up and said, "Security."

"Where have you guys been?" I barked. "Two of us are stuck on the elevator in Tower Four somewhere above the fourteenth floor. Come and get us out of here."

"Alright, sir, I will notify the elevator service people right away," he said and hung up.

"Now, there is nothing to do but wait," I told Chandra.

During the next hour, we learned a great deal more about each other. Her parents had emigrated from Mumbai. Her father was a software engineer and had found a good fit at Motorola where he still worked. She was one of three children, all in college in professional programs, and her mother was a mathematician and taught high school math and physics.

What drew Chandra to her fields of study was her curiosity about her family's origins and the complexity and diversity of social customs and patterns in India. She explained how nearly every imaginable constellation of kinship and leadership roles could be found in families somewhere on the Indian subcontinent. Talking about the subject made her eyes shine even brighter.

When she told me about the insurmountable strain that arises in her country when a person marries into a nearby village, I thought about the troubles that arose in the relationship between persons even as outwardly similar as my parents, a woman from Ohio and a man from Ontario. My own story, which I didn't like to think about, paled in comparison to hers. She knew enough, however, to draw me out with questions that opened doors I had thought better left locked, and I began to see my parents in another light.

By the time our rescuers had located us and extracted us from our cage, I was left with a sense of the profound difference between her realm and mine but drawn to this woman's dark beauty and intellectual passion, like a ship in distress to a lighthouse marking a foreign harbor.

When we finally stood free before the elevators on the sixteenth floor, I said, "Look, I've never met anyone under circumstances quite like this. We didn't do too badly in there either."

She quietly smiled.

"I wonder if you'd like to get together to talk some more. It might be easier out here."

"Well, OK. But my schedule is pretty full. And this set me way back. I'm a teaching assistant and midterms in the sections I meet are next week. That puts me on overload."

I noticed that the brighter light in the lobby revealed sharper edges and harder features on the face that had floated in the half-light of the elevator.

I tried another tack. "I tell you what. I have to eat and I guess you do too. What if we met for lunch or dinner some time?"

"Could you come to campus and meet for lunch?" she asked.

"Great. Why don't you call me? I'm chained to my desk through tomorrow by a job that came in day-before-yesterday. I know of an Italian beef place over there I'd like to show you. It will give me something to look forward to." At my mention of Italian beef, her face betrayed something I couldn't decipher, but she nodded.

I gave her my number and we both entered the stairwell to move in opposite directions—me to 26 and she to 14. I was in no mood to trust my luck on an elevator twice and liked what stair climbing did for me.

By the time I got upstairs and let myself in, Beth was home and talking on the phone. Her door was cracked, and I heard her say, "I don't know, Rhonda, I like this arrangement. And sometimes I even think it might grow into more ... no nothing yet, really. But there is a lot to be said for someone like him."

Then she must have heard me in the kitchen and said, "Oops, gotta go."

She came out into the living room, and I said, "I'm starving. I'm going to open a can of soup. Do you want anything?"

She looked at me differently somehow—like she was turning over some idea in the back of her mind—and sat on the couch.

"No, but thanks for asking. I stopped with Corinne after work to get something. How was your day?"

Beth and I didn't always cross paths, even though we slept twenty feet from each other, and I welcomed this chance to talk. "Well, aside from getting stuck in the elevator for over two hours on the way up this afternoon, it was pretty routine."

"No shit," she said.

"The damned thing stalled around 16 and nobody answered the hotline for twenty minutes. It took forever to haul us out of there." I tactfully omitted the fact that the other part of 'us' was a very interesting female who lived eight floors below.

"You poor thing," she offered. "I bet you avoid that one next time."

"On the bright side, the stairwell always works. Besides, it's good for us." Beth was not enthusiastic about climbing stairs and was used to my teasing about the irony of taking the elevator down to the fitness studio in our tower.

"To each his own," she shot back.

"How about you?" I asked.

"Rhonda called. She says Henry sure makes a mess, and she's getting tired of it. In some ways, it worked better when he wasn't so permanent."

"You were lucky to get a guy who picks up—my boot camp was canine school. Maybe Rhonda should insist he start walking dogs."

"Yeah. I don't have any complaints in that department—but I would draw the line at you straightening my underwear drawer," she quipped.

To be honest, I hadn't given Beth's underwear much thought lately, but after overhearing her on the phone with Rhonda, I wondered if she was just teasing or this was some kind of veiled invitation.

The rain and wind during that night had coated the sidewalk with wet maple leaves, and I slipped a few times in the three blocks from the subway to the Celtic Isle. I supposed that Chicago's corner taverns with their bartenders had long served as churches to the faithful flocks that gathered and, sooner or later, made their confessions.

I, for one, was glad to have a male friend who cared to listen, even if I didn't have Ian all to myself. I only went so far with Beth in sharing my love life. And she shared even less with me. Maybe because she had Corinne. Though they were both from Wisconsin and could drink their beer, the shorter commute meant that Beth worked out now in the club in our building and her bottom certainly had not spread any further.

I was thinking about Beth, but I had come to tell Ian about Chandra. As usual, her face with dark, liquid eyes had filled my dreams for several nights after meeting.

"It's been a week and no phone call and I haven't seen her since," I told him.

"Are you content to leave it at that?" he asked.

"I'm reluctant to play the sleuth and hang out on her floor, if that's what you mean."

"What will you do if you run into her again?"

"Oh, probably be friendly and, if it feels right, tell her I've been really swamped. Then ask her if she wants to meet for lunch."

"That should tell you something," he said, which puzzled me.

"Well, tell me this," I said, as he wiped off the bar and set another pint down in front of me: "I notice that the more disappointments I chalk up, the more I find myself thinking about Beth—as a woman and as a person."

"Didn't you tell me your sublet will be up the end of December?"

"Right. We need to decide whether to renew or not, but that gives us plenty of time."

"I can see why you'd think about her. It's easier to halve the potato where there is love."

"Does that one apply to you and Margaret, too? Do you have some kind of lease?"

"No. It's her place. When I moved in, we agreed that it was open-ended."

"How long has it been now?"

"It was just after St Patrick's Day."

"Any predictions?"

"No. I don't like to live like that. It puts the cart before the horse. I'm content to pull my cart along until the road forks."

Just then, Jerry, the owner called to Ian to mind the register while he went downstairs to see about the kegs.

"Well, gotta go now, Josh. Good to see you."

"Til next time then," I said.

I had knocked off after a day at the keyboard and was looking out the window watching the dark profile of a jetliner drift along a landing pattern towards O'Hare. Like my sublet deadline, the plane loomed ever closer. Closer to me, a darting swallow veered off from a collision course with his larger-winged counterpart at the last instant and interrupted any further thoughts about the matter.

Mindful of the need to troll for clients, I had spotted a panel discussion in German listed in the Goethe Institute bulletin. In my old neighborhood, Queenie, even if he didn't shake his cup, had taught me how important it is to get out there, so I decided to attend the program and shake mine.

When I arrived at the Goethe Institute, I discovered I had misremembered the week.

The receptionist said, "This one must really interest you—you're a week early. We're glad you came though. Why not take a look in the library. We've got current periodicals and you are welcome to browse."

After an hour of flipping through *Der Spiegel* and *Stern*, and the most recent German daily papers, I lost interest and decided to head back home and try again next week.

It was mid-September and any Chicago bar worth its salt was promoting Oktoberfest. As I passed the Elephant and Castle at the corner of Lake and Wabash, I realized that on the money I was making this was as close as I was likely to get to Munich for a while and even this ersatz would be stretching things. So I said to myself, *nichts wie hin!* or *why not?* and dodged through the door to escape the numbing clatter of a passing El train overhead. I was met instead by a wall of sound from the crowd of well-oiled, after-work patrons; laughter and stray words cut through the din—beer-tent ambiance without the oompah band.

The hostess' mouth was moving but the only words that came through were 'dining area', 'bar', or 'sports bar'.

Appreciative of a second warm welcome in one day, I squelched my impulse to flee and pointed to an empty stool at the end of the bar and mouthed, "Thanks. This looks good over here."

She handed me a menu and I shouted, "Wow!" gesturing at the throng. Groups of three and four, dressed in office attire, filled the place. Many held nearly drained steins, and some sounded like they had been there awhile.

I ordered a plate of fried calamari rings and a Wahrsteiner Festbier by pointing to the menu. Neither was likely to disappoint.

As I waited, a man in a gray company uniform came through the door, claimed the stool next to mine, and leaned in to ask, "How's the food here?"

The festive atmosphere combined with the Wahrsteiner prompted me to reply, "You can't go wrong with either one of these."

He looked over at my calamari rings and beer and nodded.

"What brings you to town?" I shouted.

"I'm here with a crew to install lighting for an event at one of the hotels."

"Are those guys out there with you?" I asked and pointed to the sidewalk where three other similarly dressed men were conferring and pointing in different directions.

"Yeah," he said. "They are. I wonder if they're looking for me. Better check."

He reluctantly put down his menu and disappeared through the door to join them as the after-work crowd continued to pour in and stoke the decibel level accordingly. Outside, his buddies seemed to have a different idea and convinced him to head across the street with them.

Left to the solitary enjoyment of my rings dipped in pungent garlic sauce and laved with quaffs of golden German beer, I thought Munich couldn't be better, until a woman entered and hesitated before replacing my fugitive neighbor.

"Piper?" I said. "What are you doing without your lunch box?"

"Oh, my God," she said. "You're the guy on the El train!"

"You got it. And I think I saw you once on a bridge over the Chicago River—from a distance."

This time the roles were reversed. She strained to read my lips as I faced her and asked above the noise, "Do you come here often?"

"I've seen this place but never came in," she managed. "I just wanted to get something light, before I read for a casting."

I was getting good at reading lips. "Well you could do worse than these calamari rings. Want to try one?"

She looked them over and smiled. "I think I'll see about a sandwich."

After a mostly fruitless attempt at conversation, we finished up and paid, and I walked with her the few blocks to the Goodman Theater for her reading.

I learned that she spent her time waiting for that big break while she taught elementary school on a temporary credential, but I figured that running into her for the third time must mean something—maybe my big break.

She seemed pleased that I remembered her and over the next five weeks, I managed to attend some of the open rehearsals and performances she was part of; but I couldn't tell if she had acting talent. She was usually behind the scenes and hadn't landed more than a walk on or bit part so far. But she had been told that perseverance and good looks eventually paid off. I couldn't say exactly how it applied here, but hoped my perseverance and her good looks might be good for something.

On the phone, I learned that she too had a fondness for old Hollywood movies, and we swapped titles of films we liked. I had gorged on them in Berlin where they were popular on late night television and which was all I could afford. But getting together to see them was another thing. My rent had to be paid, the words had to be translated, and she had to fit readings, rehearsals and work into her weeks, narrowing the windows of mutual opportunity down to a few slots every week or so—barely wide enough for phone calls or a late night drink with each of us exhausted and, most often, home alone in our own apartment, me sipping domestic brandy and she Baileys while we talked on the phone.

Hence our relationship developed slowly. I was one of the smaller planets revolving around this sun, a marginal body in her heavens. The few times we met together with gregarious theater people for a drink, she blossomed while I was more inclined to play the audience and only step in with a few zingers when inspiration struck since one-liners were my strongest spoken suit. My strength lay with written material, paragraphs mulled over and reworked, kneaded into smoothness like dough, until an even loaf resulted.

On a warm afternoon with a breeze off the lake and nothing doing with Chandra and things on a slow simmer with Piper, I decided to take a walk. Beth was hanging out with a book in the living room, and I asked her if she wanted to join me. She said, "OK. You know, Josh, our sublet is up the end of December. I'm thinking we ought to talk it over."

We decided to head across the Loop on Madison Street towards the lakefront and the cooler air eddying around the corners of cross streets. At the corner of Madison and LaSalle Streets, I said, "It's cool that we bumped into each other back on Feb 29th—as a kind of anniversary." That made it easier to remember.

The idea of closing my roving eye and concentrating on the woman strolling beside me had occurred to me more than once, even without Ian's proverbs. But as I looked south to the end of LaSalle Street, its walls plunging down to earth, a surrealistic canyon blocked by the looming Chicago Board of Trade building, I wondered if choosing would leave me feeling trapped like this box canyon did.

We continued east across Michigan Avenue and entered the south end of Millennium Park near the pools that reflect the giant, animated human face displayed on two towers. Though only midmorning, a fair-sized crowd had already gathered. Tourists watched the few hardy children splashing around in the shallow water, arms planing the air, as if about to lift off, oblivious to the early October chill and the calls of their parents.

We watched for a while in silence before walking up to the Cloud Gate terrace holding the giant silver, bean-shaped sculpture that had become a world attraction. Two bridal parties gathering to pose for photos near it that would include a reflection of the dramatic cityscape added to the carnival atmosphere. As we approached, our images joined those of the throng mirrored on its curving surface and a magnetic force took hold and drew us in closer. Parents held children up to watch themselves morph into fun-house images, preteens mugged and made faces at each other. An adolescent couple, embracing and kissing, took turns watching themselves over their partner's shoulder in the curvy, mirrored surface.

We stood underneath and watched them all and pointed out zany behavior to each other. The first bridal party took its turn when their photographer motioned them into place and directed them to look up at the bean and smile.

"That is really a cool idea," Beth said. "Got to file that one away."

"Wedding plans?" I asked.

"Things happen," she said.

"Well, what if someone sabotages your plans?" I asked and stepped forward, so my image appeared at the edge of the wedding tableau. Facing the camera, I looked up and put on the most hideous face I could retrieve from memory of childhood contests with my sister.

"Shame on you," she said, pulling me back by my sleeve; but she couldn't help laughing.

We stood and watched, and the next wedding party stepped over for their moment at the bean.

Somehow the idea of photo-bombing a wedding party seemed to please her after all, because the next instant, she stepped forward, dragging me with her this time, and led off with the silliest face I had ever seen her make. When she saw my surprised look, she punched my arm and gestured for me to join in.

I laughed and cranked out a face I remembered Amy giving me when our contests heated up.

Soon, the bridal party moved on and, feeling enclosed and exposed all at the same time, we walked slowly underneath.

"Well, we haven't gotten very far with that talk, have we?" Beth said.

"No," I agreed, as we walked back over to Michigan Avenue. "This turned out to be more fun."

"Yeah, I know what you mean. This was good."

Beth had to stop by her office, and I needed to pick up a book at Gotham Library. So, we parted, seemingly in tacit agreement to postpone the talk.

I didn't see her during the next week because she was working late and I kept busy with small jobs, but it was becoming clear to me that I wasn't earning enough to sustain this life style. The Towers were too pricey and renewing here or elsewhere in the Loop looked out of reach.

On Friday night, the next time I saw Beth, I said as much to her. She had been out late staffing a networking reception for the Convention Bureau at the House of Blues. I wasn't asleep when she came in and joined her in the kitchen.

Hearing this news, she said, "I guess that takes care of the lease question."

"I suppose we could think about finding something else together. That is if you are still interested."

"Wouldn't you miss being down here?" she said. "Like the view from the Hancock? You know, I never even asked you how that turned out."

I hadn't volunteered it either. So, I told her about the fiasco that culminated in the storm-foiled view and Jennifer's guinea-pig laugh.

She cracked up and then apologized when she saw I wasn't laughing. She stepped over and gave me a hug. "Sorry, Josh. You deserve more."

My first impulse was to pull back, but the smell of her shampoo stopped me. I relaxed and lay my cheek against hers. She tensed up for a moment then relaxed too.

"Nice," I said.

"This helps me too. After one of my days turns to shit."

"I think you're onto something," I said and supposed I should release her. "I'll tell you when to stop," I said.

"Just a minute," she said, "where are we going with this?"

"How do you tell unless you keep going?" I asked.

She didn't step back, but she did pull her head back to look at my face. I met her gaze and hadn't remembered how good it was to be comforted and held and said so.

She smiled and hooked her chin over my shoulder. Just then, her cell phone rang, and it was over as suddenly as it had begun.

"I better get that," she said and stepped back to reach for her purse.

I saw her face change. Delight and embarrassment alternated as she said, "Hi, Burt. Great that you called. Just a minute."

To me she said, "I've got to take this one—it's work," and she turned to head for her room.

Confused, I didn't want to hear whose call she had to take and went into my room and closed the door.

William Geuss

Chapter Three

The next several days I kept my head down. I realized that my feelings for Beth could complicate things in a way that might not fit neatly into the decision-timeline whether to find a more affordable lease. She seemed to have pulled back too, and I wondered if I was headed for my Henry moment.

I had just sent off a job Tuesday morning, when I got this message from a Julia Bärlund in the production department of the Lyric Opera:

> For the upcoming production of Alban Berg's *Lulu* this season, the staff person who normally does English supertitles for German opera is not available. We are seeking a translator to rework the texts for our production. Please submit a translation

of the following material by October 25th
for consideration.

An aria and some dialogue were attached as files.
The material intrigued me, the pay was good, and the
timing right.

From hearing a radio broadcast in Berlin, I recalled
that, despite three hours of opera and nearly a dozen
suitors, love remained elusive for Lulu. She did not
pursue it but remained a blank canvas upon which the
men projected their image of a *femme fatale*—always
with disastrous consequences for them.

In an odd anti-Lulu way, I had a certain affinity with
this figure, so I mailed back to thank Julia Bärlund and
promised to submit the material as requested.

Lulu proved to be a peculiar type of *femme fatale*, not
flighty or flirty, but inscrutable, defined only by her
relationship to others. I was hard at work, when Beth
came in after her workout with her bag over her
shoulder.

"Hello," she called and came into my room, stepping
out of her open shoes. "Am I interrupting anything
big?"

"Not for long," I said.

She unzipped her hoodie and flopped across my bed.
"I always feel great after a workout," she said and
rolled over to face me. The red tights and black stretch
top clung to a convincingly female body—full upstairs,
with a waist giving prominent hip bones their due and

leading my eye to the region clamped between thighs encased in bright red spandex.

Focusing instead on her reflection in the mirror, I filled her in about what amounted to my audition at the Lyric Opera. "Something came in I would love to do. It's supertitles for a production about a woman who goes through men like a hot knife through butter. You lying here like this is actually good practice for me—a real-life Lulu distracting me from my keyboard."

"Oh, I didn't think you noticed any women within reach."

I suspected from her grin that she enjoyed my fruitless efforts to hook up, always losing out before things developed or getting distracted by someone else before fully exploring the previous candidate.

"Are you feeling unsafe?" I asked.

"Not really, with you chained to that keyboard."

"Look," I said, "What would I have to do to get you to take over my turn cooking tonight so I can meet this deadline?"

"Hmm, I wouldn't want to stand between you and great things. What if we trade? You take my night Friday. I want to stay late after work and hit the bars with Corinne."

Her request to see her BGF fell on a sympathetic ear, and I saw an opening here. After being cloistered in my doomed domicile, first in Lakeview and since then in Precinct Towers, Ian was still my only go-to guy. Maybe Beth's social life in a city of over two million was as pathetic as mine. I had heard that Friday nights at bars were good for quick hook-ups but mostly didn't deliver anything solid enough to invest in. For me they hadn't delivered anything at all even when my budget didn't keep me home—beyond the hangover dream on St. Paddies Day.

"By the way, Beth, some complementary tickets to an opera's dress rehearsal are normally part of the deal. What do you think? Maybe you could pick up some tips from Lulu," I said— "Sharpen your knives, you know."

"Are you asking me out?"

"Just say … returning the favor."

"Well, try me when you know more. Too much butter isn't good for anyone."

Meeting this deadline meant another trip to Harold's place the next morning to listen to Berg's opera, since I wanted to capture the emotion of the scenes in my supertitles.

Three days later, I sent my file to Julia Bärlund and heard back from her that same afternoon suggesting we meet at 12:30 the next day for lunch at Lloyd's, kitty-corner from the opera house, to go over the particulars of the job. I took it that I was in and fired off to say it was a date.

The Civic Opera House was only five blocks east along Madison and an easy walk. I entered the restaurant a few minutes early and inquired about a table for two under the name Bärlund.

"Of course," came the answer. "Right this way. She said you'd be along shortly."

As we approached a table near the far window, I was greeted with a friendly smile from a thirty-some woman in dark-framed glasses and a vaguely European look. I was not mistaken. Her voice had an appealing Swedish lilt.

"Hello, I'm Julia," she said, rising and extending her hand.

"Josh," I said. Short blond hair curled around a face with signs of smile wrinkles beginning to show at the edges of her eyes and mouth.

"I like to know the people I work with," she continued. "What a coincidence that you live just down the street from the opera house."

"Right, that doesn't happen often in my work either," I said and sat down. "My clients are pretty much spread around the world."

"I like the feel you have for Lulu. You seem to know her," she smiled, her wrinkles blossoming.

"Let's just say, I'm always open to gathering new experiences, and I've met women who have that effect on men. And, not to forget, I'm a man myself."

Her look conveyed energy and interest and she asked, "Would you like to order something to drink? I started with wine while I was waiting."

"Uh, I think, I'll stick to Perrier with a twist since wine slows me down too much at the keyboard."

"Sensible," she said. "Well, let's talk about *Lulu*. I'm free until 3 p.m. when I have a production planning meeting."

"OK. Something that ruffled sensibilities for so many years interests me," I said. "Do you think that was because of male assumptions that women should be shielded from the portrayals of elemental sexual forces in this opera?"

"I think that it's due more to a bad conscience on the part of men who deny their vulnerability to raw feminine wiles," she said, swirling her finger around the rim of her glass. "In modern Scandinavia anyway, women are more willing to own themselves as sexual beings and would find such protectiveness distasteful." Her finger swirled around the rim of her glass again.

When she looked up, her direct gaze prompted me to ask, "So do we want a voice that speaks to that kind of woman?"

"Yes," she said, "that's what will free up women— and men—to feel the full charge of sexual energy that Berg packed into his music."

Her words led me to mirror her movements and gaze right back. I had already noticed the absence of a wedding band on either hand, telling me that she probably was not bound to any particular context.

"This is helpful," I said. "I'll work towards that. Meanwhile, if you don't mind my asking: the life of an artist like yourself who performs throughout the world has always fascinated me. Most of my creative moments take place in a small room at the same keyboard and get sent around the world—in proxy, so to speak. Your life is nomadic, but you deliver in person. Where have you come from and where do you go next?"

"I just came from Edinburgh, and I move on to Toronto next." She thought for a moment and said, "I'm forced to improvise as I go. That requires a fair amount of creativity in itself. That's one reason I suggested lunch. Meeting people face to face from outside the production team frees me from some of the constraints of my work context."

I pondered just where her thoughts might be tending and what kind of freedoms she had in mind. "Do you sometimes find that Lulu speaks to your situation as a woman—meeting new men in different cities and continents?"

"I'd say what she experiences drastically condenses what it's like for an unattached woman in the arts. Like Lulu, I see many of the same people again elsewhere, and don't forget— your reputation follows you."

"Have you been to Chicago before?"

"No. This is my debut production at the Lyric. I will only be here long enough to get the supertitles in place. Rehearsals start next week and once the show opens, I leave for Toronto to prepare another production there."

"Well, I've only been here about a year, but I love this town. Will you have any time to get around a bit? I could show you some things not everybody knows."

"That's generous of you."

"Where are you staying?"

"I'm in an apartment on Taylor Street. Near the University of Illinois. It's convenient. And it's an interesting neighborhood."

"I don't know that corner of the city. How about *you* showing *me* around?" (Thank you, Ian, I thought).

"OK. When are you free?" she asked.

"I pretty well lose my edge by dinner time. Not much good comes out of my fingers after dark."

"That's too bad," she grinned mischievously. "Why don't you call me Monday morning—but not too early. My weekend will be crazy with production planning. We can start with my neighborhood since it's all I know—then take it from there."

On Monday, I took a bus south to Taylor Street and walked west to her apartment above a restaurant. I rang and she buzzed me up. I followed the second floor hallway to her door and knocked. She opened and said, "Come in, Josh."

An earring consisting of a feather, some wire, and a few colored beads of different sizes hung from one ear and the scent of jasmine registered when I stepped past her. It was a tidy one-bedroom with windows opening over the street.

"This is home for now. Would you care for a cup of coffee?" she asked. "We Swedes never get enough."

She wore a pleated folkloric skirt in a dark floral pattern, but it was the open, black bodice layered over a cream poly top pressing against braless nipples that were most distracting and caused me to hesitate an instant before replying, "Yes. I'm curious about what qualifies as coffee for a Swede."

She stepped into the kitchen and soon came back with two mugs.

"How's the production planning coming?" I asked and took a swallow of coffee. I decided it must be a blend of French and medium roasts and would stand up well to what Meinl's and Dollop Coffee Company served.

"I like this team. Partly because everyone is so different. Very creative and willing to take risks."

We talked about the costuming, and I noticed her own choice of wardrobe seemed to reflect some of Lulu's appeal.

Setting her coffee down, she said, "Well, Mr. Downtown, let's take a stroll in my neighborhood," and wrapped a shawl around her shoulders. She followed me out the door, locking it behind her.

On the street, she said, "I suggest we just walk since you say you've never been over here. It is really charming." With that, she linked her arm into mine and we started east.

I liked the feeling of her nestled into me as we walked along and gazed into shop windows. Boutiques traded off with used record and antique stores. Bars, restaurants, and eateries predominated. Toward the middle of the third block, we came across a gallery that stopped us. A sign announced "*SPRING WILD FLOWERS* photographed by Jan Gallagher."

"Let's look, Josh," Julia said. "These photographs are beautiful. I love wildflowers."

We entered and were greeted by the attendant who said, "If you have any questions, please feel free to ask."

Stretching along both walls, close-ups of delicate blossoms in shades of yellow, ivory and blue revealed veins and stamen as design elements of fascinating compositions. The back wall displayed panoramas of hillsides carpeted in flowers.

Julia stood transfixed and I thought of Lulu. "At home in Sweden, I walk every spring and follow them up the hillsides as they bloom. They are different from these," she said and took my hand. "But the effect is the same. I can't resist them."

Turning to the attendant, she said, "These are marvelous. The photographer is really talented."

"Yes, she is. She had a near death experience in Australia and her work evolved after that."

"What happened?" Julia asked.

"She was on a photo safari with a man who didn't survive. In fact, a movie was made about it back then."

"Fascinating," we both said.

We left the gallery and after another hour of strolling, Julia steered us into the Italian restaurant she had fixed upon as her local favorite. A neon sign in red featuring a rose blossom hung above the doorway. Inside, we found bistro-style décor with tables for two along one wall. A bar stretched along the other. She chose to sit near the back and our knees bumped as we snugged up to the small table.

"Well, Josh, how are you liking the tour of my neighborhood? Do you think you can match this?"

I took the challenge and said, "Wait until you see Chicago at night. From my window, twenty-six stories up."

"Oooh, I don't get invited into a high rise every place I visit."

William Geuss

"That surprises me," I said, "Because I can't imagine that men in the artistic community wouldn't at least try when you come to town."

"It's like I told you, Josh, a woman can't be too careful about her reputation."

"What makes you so sure, it's safe with me?"

"Well, you are outside of my bubble. That makes you safe for me. I spend 99 percent of my time inside the bubble. What I do outside might as well not exist."

We ate a fabulous dinner and then grabbed a cab to my tower for a nightcap up in the sky.

Beth had gone to a movie with Corinne and left a note. That made it possible to keep this excursion outside of my bubble too.

Julia opted for a brandy and, while I poured, admired some of the best views nighttime Chicago has to offer. I handed her her glass and suggested we enjoy the skyline from the couch.

She kicked off her shoes and drew her feet up under her, showing her legs to advantage—like wildflowers the world over, though each is different, I thought; and there is no escaping their appeal. "Where is home in Sweden?" I asked.

"I grew up in a town in the provinces. Now I rent a small apartment in Stockholm as home base. This definitely wins in comparison," she said, sweeping her hand across the twinkling panorama.

328

Though I was tempted to take my cue from the lights and the seductive setting, I realized we hadn't talked about my supertitles. As a compromise, I eased over closer and left my arm resting partly on the couch and partly on her shoulders and asked, "Are those supertitles going to be OK?"

She leaned back and said, "Your language is gritty but still singable. Almost a shame it will be sung in German."

I liked where this was going.

Then she asked, "Do you think men are as predictably dysfunctional as the librettist paints them?"

I wondered if I was being tested, so I hesitated, trying to look thoughtful.

She complicated things further by asking, "Do you see yourself, for instance, in any of them—in how they react to Lulu?"

"I suppose it all depends on what experiences and disappointments a man has had and at what life stage he finds himself," I improvised.

"Is that all you've got, Josh?" she said coyly and snuggled closer. "There are no wrong answers here."

"Me," I said, "I'm drawn to women with flair and spirit," *and nice legs*, I thought. "It can show in the way they dress or how they carry themselves. Maybe it's the energy they give off. And if they take life with a grain of salt and a dash of humor."

"Well that adds up to a fair number of possibilities. How do you make up your mind?"

"To tell the truth, I'm mostly here in my bubble at my keyboard. Deprivation seems to sharpen my antennae when I go out though, so I could meet an interesting woman just about anyplace."

"And how well do I fit your template?" she asked, giving me a look that said more than it asked. Her green eyes narrowed and her lips parted slightly.

I set my drink down and met her gaze. "I'd rather show you," I said, even as I felt her hand on the back of my head, pulling me towards her.

She laced her fingers in my hair and our lips met. It was a while before one of us could speak.

"I see," she said. "That is very demonstrative."

The demonstration continued, the energetic expression of our appetites alternating with periods of respite and repose. When we both had come to the end of our discourse, we went into the master bath and showered and dressed.

Around eleven, I went down to the lobby with Julia and put her in a cab. By the time I got back upstairs, Beth had come in.

"I saw you putting someone new in a cab downstairs," she said.

"Yeah, it's the client I am doing the *Lulu* supertitles for." I was feeling drained, and relaxed, and satisfied that item number three was now behind me.

"Gee," she said, "from all the water in the master bath, someone must have gotten skunked. And here I said that couldn't happen in the Loop."

I had no comeback for that, but I caught an edge to her jesting, so I asked, "How was your movie? Pick up any guys at the popcorn counter?"

"One turned out better than the other," she replied and turned away.

I knew enough to leave it alone. "Sorry about the water," was the best I could come up with. Then, as she headed back to her room, I added, "I really would like to hear about the movie sometime."

The next thing I heard was the sound of her door closing.

Two days later, to make up for popping her bubble by bringing Julia home, I invited Beth to the dress rehearsal of *Lulu* the next week at the Lyric. She surprised me by accepting.

I was anxious to see what my supertitles did for the production. And I was anxious to see Julia again. She had been hard to get hold of since my audition, and time was getting short if I was to show her any more of Chicago before she left.

At the entr'acte, Beth and I headed for the lobby and queued up beneath the tear-shaped chandeliers for something to drink. I had only been there once before and when Beth said this was her debut, I said, "This calls for bubbly. And it's on me."

"Thanks," she said and, while Beth kept busy looking at the fluted columns capped by art-deco Egyptian ornamentation adorned with sprays of leaves, I eyeballed the randomly milling crowd in the Grand Foyer, hoping to catch sight of Julia—she had left me a note that she might see me here.

After a few sips, I suggested we go up to the mezzanine for a better view. The red-carpeted staircase took us to the upper level where we leaned on the balustrade and enjoyed a view extending from the lobby below on up to the vaulted ceiling.

"I love this place," Beth said and tried to gaze her fill of the brocaded patterns in mauve and gold tones above.

"Uh, huh," I said and continued searching for Julia below.

Soon, chimes began calling us to our seats, prompting a flurry among those holding last-minute glasses of champagne. Before I stepped back from the balustrade, I caught sight of Julia. Her royal blue blazer stood out from the more prevalent somber tones of others.

She turned her head as though searching for someone. There was no way to signal, and I hoped she would look up. Just then, I saw a tall man in a white shirt on the bottom landing of the staircase watching patrons begin to troop back into the theater.

Julia turned in his direction, smiled broadly, and waved. He returned her wave and nodded before he knifed through the crowd towards her. They met half way and stood facing each other for a moment before he took her hand. She moved closer and they kissed cheeks.

"Shouldn't we head back?" Beth said.

"Yeah. Definitely," I said and saw the couple slowly move against traffic towards the street doors, still holding hands.

"Too bad you didn't see your client," Beth said as we took our seats. "I don't think I've met anyone from Sweden before. She sounded interesting."

"Yeah, well something must have come up," I said. Mixed feelings short-circuited my ability to carry on a coherent conversation as I tried to convince myself: *It's just as well; don't get wound up with a moving target—be glad we met and let her go.*

I was applying these Band-Aids to my ego, when Beth said something.

"What?"

"I'm really glad you brought me, Josh. Opera is such a romantic night out. And I see what effect a diva can have on men."

By the end of the first act, two men had already foundered on Lulu's shoals and more were setting the same course to liven up the next acts. I thought of how many times I had done the same as they and wondered how many more times it would be.

Beth leaned over and whispered, "Aren't you having fun, being a part of this?"

"I'm glad you're here, Beth. That makes it a lot better."

She gave me a curious look and settled in for Act II.

The ache between my shoulders from a morning at the keyboard brought things to a halt. It had been two weeks since I had seen Julia head out the door. She gave me a call from the airport two days later to thank me for my contribution before she headed off to Toronto. We wished each other luck, and she said she would keep me in mind for future opportunities.

After I hung up, I sent off a completed marketing piece for E-Plus, a German cell phone company, and walked out to the living room to check the weather. Lumpy clouds scudding in from the northwest announced rain.

I flopped on the floor to stretch and flatten my shoulders. Curling up into a ball, I held it for a minute and, after weaving my hips from side to side, lay back to reflect: Is this a good situation for me, a pinball bouncing off targets, flipped around until, at some point, I drop off the board like my dad? Was that the kind of life I wanted?

Moving in with Beth had been rolling the dice. So far, so good. Now I knew that it is possible to share quarters with a female without getting tangled up in fantasies and yearning—we had actually worked out a pretty good routine.

Was something going to come along and upset things, like Rhonda's Henry? I had since learned that Burt, my imaginary rival, was married and, as far as I could tell, Beth wasn't connecting with any Henrys out there either.

Then my stomach began to growl, and the smoky aroma of a pastrami sandwich at the deli counter in the French Market popped into mind. That would be reward enough for today. So I got myself together and went down the tower, like Jack from his bean stalk but with far less treasure in my pockets.

Outside, wind met me, but the rain was still on hold. When I reached Canal Street, I turned north and continued a couple of blocks to the French Market beyond the Metra Station. Inside the entry hall beneath the tracks, office workers and matinee opera-goers shopped or funneled towards the food stalls. I elbowed my way past displays of everything from textiles to pottery to find food—patisserie, fruit, cheese, and ethnic fare—with French cabaret music crooning in the background. Once in the dining area, I made a beeline for Howard, my deli man, and put in an order for his pastrami on rye with Dijon.

While he turned to whack at a slab of pastrami, fragrances drew me over to the soap counter across from him. Sniffing around at the pastel-colored bars, I tried to identify the herbal mix in Beth's shampoo, but my bulging sandwich was ready before I'd cracked the code. I collected my feast and set about threading through the crowd to find a beer and a place to sit.

At the one table with an empty seat, a blonde, maybe just over forty, in a quilted black coat and leather boots sat before a soft drink and belabored a pink smartphone with one lacquered fingernail. She peered through brown-framed glasses that had slipped down her nose while she pecked away at the tiny keyboard. Her face looked seriously sad and contrasted with legs that splayed to disclose eye-catching, black net stockings that did not look out of place in a French Market.

"Mind if I join you?" I asked. "It's pretty busy here today."

She peered at me over the glasses. "Please do. I'm just killing time before going over to the matinee at the opera."

"What are you seeing?"

"Something new for me," she said. "*Lulu.*"

"What do you know? I had a hand in that show."

"You're kidding."

"No. I'm a translator and did the supertitles in English. They sing in German."

"I'm impressed." Her gray-blue eyes lit up.

Maybe I was on some kind of roll—from her features and coloring, she was of Scandinavian stock—though who could tell about hair color anyway.

"Are you going to see it too?" she asked.

"Already have. I live in Precinct Towers and just popped over for the deli-man's smoked pastrami." I took another appreciative bite.

She finished her tapping and clapped the phone shut. Her gaze returned to me and signaled interest.

I noticed that she wore no rings. "Do you come far?" I asked, trying not to be too direct.

"About a half hour on the Metra," she said. "Oak Park."

"Have you been an opera fan long?"

"If you can believe this, I used to sing in an opera chorus. In Lyons, in France. I was a voice major and got lucky."

I could believe it.

"I landed a job over there," she said.

"Wow. How long was that for?"

"The first two years were the most incredible experience of my life. Imagine someone that age on the loose in Europe for the first time." She paused.

"Then I had a motorcycle accident and injured my vocal chords. And that was that."

Now it was my turn to look seriously sad. "Rotten luck. What did you do after that?"

"Well, I had to come back to the Midwest and start over. I married for a time and moved around with my husband. He was old-fashioned. When I got serious about a career and managed to get a degree in arts management, he couldn't accept it. That finally led to a split." After another pause, she continued. "Since we didn't have children, it wasn't quite so awful."

She saw that I had taken a pastrami pause to give her my full attention. "How nice of you to listen."

"I'm Josh," I said, and wiped my hand.

"Paula," she replied and shook it.

"Truth time for you now. How did you get into translating?"

"I studied in Germany three semesters before I finished college here—just long enough to warp me out of shape for living comfortably in the States. I just moved back from working in Berlin. I plan to go back over there when I can afford it. To refuel."

"I miss France, too." She glanced at her watch and said, "Say, would you like to meet after the performance for a drink, and we can talk about it and about Europe?"

"You know, I was thinking along those lines myself. I'll meet you at the bar across from the Lyric at five. In case anything changes, here's my cell number." She's old enough to still honor the social niceties, I thought, and calculated the odds of her showing up or calling. Fifty/fifty for the former and sixty/forty for the later.

She uncrossed those interesting legs and said, "OK, Josh, see you then. I better head over to catch the lecture so I know what's going on."

"The great supertitles should help," I said.

"Definitely." She stood up and her boots resounded nicely on the tile floor as she walked away.

That settled it. I decided to place my bet and show up myself and, as another loop of French music-hall tunes kicked in, headed back up to my bean stalk for a few hours to count my remaining treasure.

Back in the tower, I logged on to check for new work and, finding none, puttered around my bedroom to recover from accumulated neglect during the rush to finish the E-Plus material.

Then, I grabbed my umbrella and went back down to earth to tack against the wind—off the lake this time—as I walked east along Madison, risking my umbrella each time I left the shelter of a building.

When I reached the river, I gave up and took the sting of light rain in my face as I moved against the added hazard of departing opera goers. At the Civic

Opera House, I turned south on Wacker Drive the few doors down to my rendezvous with Paula.

It was shortly after five o'clock when I gave the umbrella a shake and pressed through the jam of customers in the foyer. Just as I reached the hostess, I saw Paula seated at the bar chatting with a man next to her. She turned and saw me and waved.

Great. Just take a number. "I'm joining a friend," I told the hostess and stepped over to the bar.

"Hey, there you are," I said. "How did you like it?"

"Hi, Josh. This is Larry, we were in seats next to each other and wanted to talk some more about the opera. I told him I had an inside source and he should come along and meet you."

Wonderful, I thought. He's even dressed like Leisure Suit Larry in the Land of the Lounge Lizards, the video game so popular in Germany.

The next half hour I listened to Larry regale us with stories about Lulu, his Labrador retriever, who had been quite the diva herself. Every time she got into heat she managed to attract a different male counterpart, and her love life resulted in as many surprises for her as for her operatic namesake.

From the glee with which Paula followed this saga, I gathered that seeing her with a soda earlier had possibly been uncustomary. She finished her first round and ordered a second before Larry's Lulu whelped her fourth batch of amazing puppies.

Somewhere between Lulu's fifth and sixth conquest, Paula suggested having dinner. I was hungry enough, but realized I was rolling along like a third wheel that had developed a serious wobble. So I said something about a deadline, put money in for my drink, and excused myself.

Judging from the lack of protest from Larry or Paula, my exit was well timed. Armed with my umbrella, I withdrew back across the river to my tower—and my comforting standard, grilled-cheese with a tomato slice.

The next night, I caught Ian at the Celtic Isle and he greeted me as usual: "Josh. How's the love life?"

I was reluctant to feed him my Lulu episodes so, in between his spurts of serving new customers and giving refills, I fed him some blarney instead.

"I fell in love last night."

He smiled and took me up on it. "What did it feel like?"

"It only lasted, maybe, five minutes."

"Better than nothing."

"An airy, light feeling. It was spring. I was driving a motor scooter through a vineyard near a lake. The girl was in a light blouse and shorts and the more we took corners, the more she leaned into me. She had her head on my shoulder, and I thought she must feel as giddy as I."

341

"Is that how love feels?"

"I just know I didn't feel that way with my college sweetheart," I said. "I think we began dating because it was on her check-list of things to do before graduation—the romance was pretty thin."

"Bad luck."

"Anyway, I thought maybe it's because I'm driving this thing for the first time and she's scared. So I got to a safe stopping place, and we took a walk in the vineyards, and I put my arm around her waist."

"What did she look like?"

"Short, red hair and a nice smile, full lips. I started talking in German, and she did her best to answer back. She looked like a girl named Thea I met at the library."

"So, what happened?"

"We hugged and her body was soft and her cheek was warm against mine. And most of all—I was happy that someone wanted me."

"Please don't stop there."

"Then she kissed me, and I said, 'I hope my breath isn't too garlicky', and she said convincingly, 'Not at all!' So I said something like, 'I wonder if we can find some Italian beef and garlic fries around here?'"

"Josh, you've got to get help with this food thing."

"You may be right. Her last words were, 'Gross, I'm a vegan.'"

"So how do you know you were in love?"

"I woke up and there was the proof."

Ian shook his head and set another Guinness down in front of me.

"Has anything like that happened to you before?" he asked.

"Mostly when I sleep on my stomach."

"I figured as much," he said.

"It's a good thing dreams turn out better than reality some of the time. The one last night, for instance, had a happier ending than my date with the woman I just met." I told him after all about how things ended with Paula. We had a good laugh when I told him what a diva Lulu the lab was.

"And, here I was hoping it might be my Margaret moment."

Then, he asked, "Are you sure you missed kissing the Blarney Stone during your time in Ireland?"

"I don't think I'll tell you," I said.

The words I took away this time had more of a Disney than an Irish ring to them: "Stay out there and give your dreams a chance to come true."

Piper was due to open in a show the following week, and I had invited Beth to go, but she was tied up. After the opening performance, the four cast members sat around in the lobby of the storefront theater drinking Miller Lite and talking about this show and others they had been in and swapping gossip and rumors about fellow actors they had known: Who had given up, who had climbed up the ladder, who was playing somewhere else in another show, and who had slept with whom for how long before moving on.

An audience of one, I sat and looked on as Piper gave the director her ardent attention and laughed the most at what he said. I felt like an American at a cricket match trying to divine the rules according to which their game was played and came away thinking of Sudoku: it would remain an occult puzzle I would never crack. I envied them their camaraderie and wondered if I was always going to be Piper's audience and never given a role with her myself.

Afterwards, we walked towards the subway station at Diversey and Clark and she said, "Josh, I really appreciate your coming tonight. It's hard enough to get an audience for an off-beat show like this."

"You were really good," I said and her face lit up for a moment before doubt clouded her sunny features.

"I don't know whether I have what it takes or not, Josh. I've been at it two years now—in theater, I mean, and what you saw is as good as it has gotten so far." After a pause, she continued. "I came all the way from Sioux City, Iowa, to sew costumes, manage a box office, handle lighting, run on and off stage with chairs and props, and speak four lines in a play no one will ever hear of again."

After a wry smile, she fell silent and I realized I had no wisdom to offer. It seemed pointless to share scenes from the humdrum of my own drama—so I linked my arm through hers and we continued walking to the stairs down to the subway station. A southbound Redline train rumbled in and we boarded, making any further absence of conversation less noticeable. She left me at Lake Street to transfer to the CTA Blue Line and gave me a smile and a squeeze on my arm.

I thundered on south to exit at the Jackson station and climb to the street. A front had passed through that afternoon and left the air clear enough to see stars despite all the light from the Loop. I decided a brisk walk twelve blocks west to my perch in the sky would do me no harm and give me think time about this strand of my life.

My role in Piper's story added up to an interior monologue so far. If it weren't for Ian's ear and Beth's provocations, it wouldn't get beyond a soliloquy.

I rode up in my tower without seeing anyone and felt isolation something like what the patron saint of translators, Jerome, must have felt as he wrestled with his demons in a Bethlehem monastery while he translated the New Testament into Latin.

A light under Beth's door when I got back told me that she was still up reading, so I went down the hall and knocked. "It's me," I said.

"Come on in," she announced, "I'm decent." She had a Chicago Bears T-shirt and snug blue workout pants on and lay propped on pillows on her queen-sized mattress.

"How was the late show?" she asked. "Did you get any autographs?"

"Not really. But I did get a look behind the scenes at way-off-Broadway theater life."

"So tell me about your orgy."

"Surely you mock. It was pretty depressing; listening to five people take turns telling about who they knew and what they thought it might be good for; oh, and some of the meanest talk about their rivals and competitors and saboteurs of their careers."

"Well, how about your sweetie, the pie-eyed Piper?"

"She had a few lines as an old lady, but I knew what she really looks like, so it was hard for me to believe. There were maybe twelve people in the audience besides me. And most of them were friends from other productions. I think she's pretty discouraged by the whole scene."

"I guess there are no free lunches anywhere," Beth said. "That could describe my career in the city so far too. I think the mistake we make is expecting it to be glamorous with a big break around the corner and a handsome leading man thrown in to boot."

"So life basically sucks, huh?"

"In most of the magazines I read at the hair salon, the stars talk about just hanging in there until something happens—or doesn't. Kind of like waiting until the planets line up. Sometimes what happens is that they marry a normal person and settle down raising kids and play a starring role in a real life drama."

I didn't want to hear it but had to admit I hoped it was true.

"The number of people whose names ever get into lights is pretty small, and the ones anyone remembers for long pay a big price. They get murdered, kill themselves or someone else, or let themselves get screwed by lots of self-destructive prominent people— like that Lulu figure you worked on."

That was starting to hit home and didn't make me feel any better.

"We play a role there, too," she said. "Without us to buy magazines and gossip about the stars, they'd be out of business. I guess it only gets out of hand if we take their world to be the real one, and we forget to get on in our own."

"I knew I could rely on you to cheer me up," I said. "I think I'll retire with a bottle and try not to think about either one. Good night."

"Good night, Josh."

Soon after that, Beth sort of asked me out. I had been going on about an Italian beef joint so good you wanted to swim in the juice. She cringed and said my fixation on Chicago junk food was killing her and it was going to kill me too—I needed to try some *good* Italian.

"I know just the place. Corinne told me about it," she said. "Let it be my surprise—I'll get directions from her and make reservations."

Since 'Italian' still qualified in my mind as 'Chicago food', I didn't argue.

Sunday came and, instead of cooking together, we went out for brunch. It was mid-October and fall was in the air. We took a cab west to Little Italy and along the way, passed the first Halloween shop of the season with large posters of costumes for adult females in the window.

The red-lipped specimens, shown with saucy smiles and encouraging cleavage, were meant mostly for men wanting their women to liven things up in a nurse's uniform, stewardess outfit or as a pirate lass.

I couldn't tell if Beth took such things in, while she was telling me at some length about a problem that came up at work, but I couldn't imagine her in any of these disguises.

"Here we are," she said, as we pulled up under the familiar neon sign for The Rosebud, Julia Bärlund's favorite. "I bet you are going to like this."

I decided not to spoil it by mentioning what had unfolded here just a month ago and said, "Cool. Looks like honest-to-goodness Italian."

Once inside and seated, we placed orders and I waited for her to finish up about her problem of the day, so I could tell her about my latest project.

Eventually, she began to notice my eyes wander past her towards the bar. The woman who had been preparing to remove her coat as we entered now sat alone near the front window and faced away from us. What caught my eye was the deep, open, back to her dress which revealed the presence of a black lace bra with straps looping up over bare shoulders.

Beth's words, "The last thing I needed was for that bitch to come over and tell me she couldn't use what I had written, right where everybody else could hear," as she rapped her finger on the table for emphasis, brought me back.

"That does sound extreme," I said and listened to her wrangle on about what kind of revenge she would like to take.

My mind wandered back to the open dress and my eyes soon followed. By this time, a businessman sat next to her and the next time I ventured a glance, she was flanked at the bar on either side by men stopping in for lunch, liquid or otherwise.

Did this woman know her dress was coming apart? Was it not a dress at all, but a costume from across the street and she was working for lunch at The Rosebud baiting in more trade? Either could be true and hearing more about the lack of support Beth got from her friend Cindy at work concerning her run in with the supervisor was distracting me from these questions.

Finally, as I straightened up in my chair to see across the barrier into the bar room and get to the bottom of things, or at least of the plunging backline, Beth caught me staring outright at the source of distraction.

She interrupted herself and turned to follow my gaze.

"Why that is really insulting. I tell you what's eating me and all you can think of is devouring that tramp with your eyes."

I couldn't deny it and had to think of something fast.

Just then the waiter came with our orders and slid a plate of Zinfandel-braised beef ravioli in front of her which distracted her long enough for me to come up with something.

"It's just that she looks like somebody I know, but I can't figure out from where."

"Is it the underwear or the dress you can't forget?"

"No, it's the hairdo. I think my high school crush had hair like that. 'Harriet' something. She lived on my bus route and sat in front of me. I'll never forget that hair."

Her features softened as the hot, savory pasta began to do its work like it had at the beginning of our relationship at Meinl's, proving that there was at least one other appetite that guided us along our pathway, like invisible hands.

I looked at my order of Mama's Lasagna and challenged her, "I'll let you taste mine, if you let me taste yours."

She looked over and, somewhat mollified, said, "Well, OK."

As we left the restaurant, I made a show of taking a closer look at the face in the mirror as we got abreast of the lady on the stool and turned to Beth with an expression of complete dismissal. When we got through the door, I shook my head and finished off with, "Nope. Not her. That would have been too freaky," and thought, *Damn, talk about blowing it. What's wrong with you?*

A week later we were cleaning up after our Sunday cooking and Beth said, "Josh, don't you think it would be cool to have people in for a house warming? You know, while we still have a chance to show it off?"

"Haven't we been here too long for that?"

"We can call it a Halloween party."

"That should work. My deadline for this job falls Friday morning. Friday or Saturday evening would work for me. Should we make it after work or later on?"

"Well, let's see who we want to invite and how that fits," she said.

I already had an idea of how extensive her social network was—Facebook tells no lies. A look at her page told me she was mostly linked up to girl and guy friends from her Ripon College days and a few from high school still. Like me, not much seemed to be happening for her in the city.

I supposed she would have found out that the only friend requests I had gotten since I signed up four months ago were from Scientology recruiters seeking out the friendless. Dodging the question of what that said about me, I rationalized that I was lucky Facebook wasn't an enormous time suck for me yet.

"I'll invite Corinne from work," she said. "Who would you like to have?"

"Well, there's Ian and he might bring a lady friend. And Piper. Her show closed last weekend, so maybe she'll be free. And Chandra.

"Who?"

"Someone I met on the elevator who lives downstairs. She's a really bright grad student at UIC."

"You are just full of surprises."

"Never say die. Who else do you want?"

"To tell the truth, besides Corinne, I really haven't gotten much beyond Rhonda and Henry and a few of their friends since I've been here."

"No luck in the bars, huh?"

"I've met some real dogs in bars. I'd rather invite the ones I walked."

"Well, think about their owners—anybody there that appealed to you? You never know when a cross-connection might develop into something."

"They were mostly couples who both worked and had me fill in on the walking. The ones I knew the best were Helen and Willard, an older couple that lived nearby. I'd walk when they were out of town. It didn't really go beyond that."

"Well, this place isn't that big. It's OK if it's a small party. We could have some games or something. I think people used to do that more."

"Why don't we put you in charge of the games?" she said.

"Oh no. I'm a total bust at that. Like what? You mean Charades?"

"Yeah. And Guess the Animal," she said. "You write a kind of animal on pieces of masking tape and put one on each person's forehead without them reading it. Then they walk around and ask each other 'yes' or 'no' questions, like 'do I have four legs?' to figure out which animal they are."

"OK. That reminds me of one: the Alphabet Category where, if you pick 'food,' the first person says, 'Avocado', the second says 'Banana', the next 'Coconut', 'til only one person is left."

"You'd always win that one, you have so many words."

Was that admiration or irritation? Sometimes, when she searched for the right word, I would throw one in as filler and, if it bugged her, she didn't let it show. "Speaking of food—if we make the eats ourselves, it shouldn't cost much," I said.

"Oh, I have some dynamite hors d'oeuvres we can make. And let's have a punch bowl. Not everybody does that and everyone will be taking public transit."

"Right," I agreed. "We go nuts with orange and black crêpe paper. People wear costumes. Music for dancing. They'll never know it's a better-late-than-never party."

We agreed: it sounded sure fire.

On Saturday, we prepped the security desk with a list of the persons expected that night and left our phone numbers.

We had come up with whacky prizes for the categories we planned to make up as we went along, depending on who came and what the costumes inspired.

First to arrive were Rhonda and Henry.

Beth met the door in her Little Red Riding Hood cape and apron, and I stood close behind her in my Dracula cape, wax teeth protruding from my red lips, and mimicked biting her in the neck as she opened it. She shivered and freed herself. "Thank God, you're just in time to save me," she said to them.

"Alright!" Henry said. "Looks like my kinda party." He was dressed as Al Capone in a broad-brim hat.

"Hey, you guys," Beth said and hugged Rhonda. "You make the perfect gun moll."

"Come in and see how the young and sleepless live," I said.

"Oh, yeah, Dracula and his female friends burned the midnight oil, didn't they?" Henry said.

"Only on Halloween," I said. "But a certain night owl can sleep an extra half-hour, since she lives closer to work."

The floodlit skyscrapers drew Rhonda like a moth to a candle and she stepped over to the windows. "Come over here, Henry. My God, the view is spectacular. Is that Millennium Park over there?"

"Yep and it's all included in the rent," Beth said and pointed out other landmarks through our still-uncurtained windows while I got everybody some punch.

We clicked our cups with our first joint guests since we had moved in together and said, "Cheers." I turned to Beth and said, "Cheers, roomie." She responded with, "Cheers, Josh," and I wondered if that said less or more than "roomie."

Then Beth asked them how security went.

"Well," Henry said, "at first I thought the big guy with the uniform and gun was just in costume. I think our get-ups freaked him because it looked like he was going to fingerprint us and call the real cops. But he finally found your list on a clipboard and checked us off." Henry took an appreciative swig of the rum punch and said, "Man this is good. Hope you have lots."

"The hardest part was finding our way to the right elevator," Rhonda said. "It took about ten minutes to get over to the ones marked for your tower. I just about phoned you for a rescue."

"Geez," I said, "I didn't realize it was that big a challenge. We'll see if anyone else manages to run the gauntlet."

I checked my watch and wondered if anyone I invited was going to show.

Corinne, Beth's girl friend from work, arrived next. I was hoping it might be Thea, Piper, or Chandra. I had invited them all.

I knew Corinne and Beth talked on the phone, and I had seen her on Beth's Facebook page. She could have been Beth's sister—about the same age with curly, reddish-blonde hair. She was from Milwaukee and came dressed as an Oktoberfest waitress, dirndl and all.

To my relief, next to arrive was Ian with Margaret. He was Robin Hood to her Maid Marion. "Fabulous that you got tonight off," I said and we shook hands.

"Hey, Margaret, I'm really glad you came." She looked at me with captivating blue eyes, and I gave her a *bisou* on the cheek.

"Great costume," she said to me.

"I've always wondered what it's like to live up in one of these towers," Ian said. "Does it sway when the wind blows?"

"Not that I can tell. I want you both to meet my flat mate Beth and her coworker, Corinne. And this is Rhonda and Henry. They are the ones who made this whole thing possible—us moving up in the world, I mean."

Beth gave me a dirty look and Rhonda raised an eyebrow.

Henry said, "What he's talking about is, I moved in with Rhonda and Beth moved out to sort of make room."

"Oh," said Margaret. "That did stir the pot. Where is your place?"

"In Lakeview," Rhonda said.

"I got sick of the commute downtown," Beth said, "so give me some credit."

"Well, if you hang on in Lakeview a while longer," Margaret said, "I think it will come around with the next upturn."

"Real estate is Margaret's game," Ian said. "She had a pretty good run the last few years. Before the bust. And she was smart enough to see it coming."

Marion gave Robin a peck on the cheek and one of his buns a squeeze.

Henry muttered, "That means rents will climb."

"Everyone get more punch," I said. "And the goodies are on those trays over there."

"Yeah," Henry said, and went for another glass. "I had no idea I would get this high on Halloween."

"Just watch yourself, friend," Rhonda said.

"Let's start with a game," Beth said. "It's 'Guess the Animal' and goes like this: You wear a piece of masking tape on your forehead, with the name of a kind of animal on it. Then go around and ask each person a 'yes' or 'no' question to help identify what you are. Like, 'Can I fly?' 'Am I a herbivore?' and so on."

My phone rang. It was Piper and she was sobbing.

"Excuse me for a second," I said to everyone and stepped down the hall to get away from the music.

"I can't make it tonight, Josh. I was on the way and got rear-ended on the Eisenhower. My car was probably totaled. I think I bumped my head. And now I'm waiting at the emergency room at Rush-Presbyterian Hospital."

"Wow, is there anything I can do?" I asked. "I can come right down there."

"I should be alright. Just a little shaken up."

"Promise me this. That you'll call me as soon as someone sees you, and I'll come get you."

I returned to the party and Beth finished up by stepping over and taping an animal's name to my forehead. "The winner picks the next game—either Two Truths and a Lie or Wooden Spoons," she said.

Margaret was the first to guess and Henry, who was pretty soused and finally gave up, was last.

An hour later, we were seated in a circle ready to start Two Truths and A Lie when the phone rang again. It was Piper. She sounded calmer and said, "Josh, the doctor wants to talk to you."

"Yes, hello? This is Dr. Gupta. Your friend has a concussion and we can release her; but she should have someone wake her every two hours during the next eight hours to be sure there are no complications. Can you manage to do that?"

Without hesitation, I said, "I'll be there to get her in thirty minutes. Please put her back on."

"Piper?"

"Yes."

"Don't worry. I'm grabbing a cab. Wait right there. I'll ring you when I get close. We can go to your place or come back here."

"You're not leaving before we have the Belly Dance Competition are you?" Beth asked, miffed.

"I really hate to bail folks but a friend I invited was in a car accident and needs some help. I gotta go. Thanks for coming. Maybe we can top this one with our next try. The witches and wizards are flying out there, so please stay and have fun."

"I may not get back tonight, Beth, but I'll call and leave a message when I can." She gave me a dark look and turned back to our guests as I walked out the door.

Downstairs, I got lucky and caught a westbound cab and, fifteen minutes later, stepped out at the door to Rush-Presbyterian Hospital. I found Piper in the ER waiting area. She sat slumped in her chair and had a bandage on her forehead. Across from her, a man holding a feverish, wailing child on his lap looked up expectantly as a harried nurse came in to tell him it would be a bit longer, since a gunshot wound had come in.

"Hi, Piper. Wow, this is one Halloween you'll remember."

"Yeah. It could be worse—I'm in better shape than my car, though. They gave me some painkillers and this pamphlet on what to do. I really appreciate you doing this, Josh. My roommate went home this weekend and, when the doctor asked who I knew that I could call, I said the party was my best hope. So thanks again."

"Hey, that's what friends are for. Let's see—are you ready to go?"

"Yeah."

"I don't think you'd get much rest at my place. The party is still going strong."

"Then let's go to mine. Besides, you haven't seen it yet."

"Right."

We took a cab to Bucktown where Piper shared a small apartment with another actress who waited tables. She had to steady herself on my arm as we climbed slowly up to the third floor.

It was after midnight by this time and she was totally blitzed. "You need to get some rest," I said. "Don't worry about me. I'll crash here on the sofa and wake you every two hours." I had a watch with an alarm I normally used to signal when it was time for a keyboard break.

She gave me an appreciative smile and went willingly. Soon it was quiet and I made myself as comfortable as I could on the sofa.

Up until now, our contact had mostly been fleeting: a quick conversation on the El, a distant image in my camera lens, a hurried encounter at the Elephant & Castle, and then my devoted stalking of her at every opportunity during the next months at rehearsals, on the phone and as part of her audience. The twenty-five bucks the two cab rides set me back seemed a small price to pay. After all, I was about to spend the night with Piper—albeit alone on her couch. I lay there and wondered if, instead of showing up as my date at our Halloween party, her accident would lead to a climax or a denouement.

I woke her several times during the night and then let her sleep while I headed back home to keep a deadline. The following morning I got a phone call from her.

"Josh, I just want to thank you for being such a good friend. I'm feeling much better now."

"That's great. Is there anything else you need?" I asked, hoping it might be some company until her roommate got back.

"No. But, thank you. It's just—I wanted you to be the first to know—I've decided to go home for now."

"Home. Like back to Iowa? With your parents?"

"Yeah. For now. I guess I'm worn out. And kinda discouraged."

I didn't know what to say and thought, *there goes another one.* Instead, I said, "I see what you mean. But, I'll miss you, you know."

"That's sweet. I think I just need a break. Not from you—but from all the rest of it."

She was taking the overnight Amtrak at 9 p.m. from Union Station and wondered if I could meet her at the station and help get her stuff from the cab to the train.

"Of course," I said.

After I waved her off at the station, I decided that sacrifice and devotion didn't hold the key to a woman's heart. So what was the answer? I might as well troll blogs and zines on the net to see what women want in men.

One source, based on scientific research on a speed dating operation in Germany, told me I didn't have knockout power—I lacked the wealth and position that drew highly-valued females. Playing the lottery was about the only way to compensate for that, and I didn't like the odds. And I still had no idea what divas and actresses wanted.

I turned the question on its head. What do I really want in a woman? I leaned back and let my mind wander ... someone to laugh at my dumb jokes? Someone to hang out with, and watch a Bears game now and then, take walks with. Do something crazy now and then? Someone to cook with, to hug? Back rubs? Sure, and to romp in the sack with. All of the above really. But I didn't seem to get past first base with the women I've met. The only person I've done much of any of those things with was Beth.

At six-thirty, I descended to earth to stretch my legs and join Ian at the Beer Bistro, a cozy bar on West Madison. The evening was balmy as rush-hour buses and cabs, horns blaring, sped past, and I was thankful not to be behind the wheel myself. It was two-dollar Angus burger night, and they came on a pretzel bun. The place even kept Ian's interest up with their changing selection of craft beers.

Unless the Blackhawks were melting the ice, the Bistro was usually quiet enough for conversation, and I wanted to tell Ian about how the curtain had come down on my Piper fairytale—and catch up on things with him. Since we met, he had never talked about family back in Dublin.

Three blocks west, I crossed the Kennedy Expressway and felt a rush as the ten lanes of raucous traffic below boosted my adrenaline and I dodged exiting vehicles spilling onto the overpass, a reminder of how perilous life in any lane could be.

Another six blocks and I would reach our safe haven tucked into a dingy, two-story brick building on Madison. But two blocks on, I saw a motionless figure propped against the free daily paper dispenser on the corner. Maybe he was reading the *Redeye* news headlines. I was about half a block away when he straightened up and lurched on along the sidewalk, weaving.

Wow, I thought, could he be coming from Beer Bistro? I hadn't seen anyone get that wasted there before, but I wasn't here when the Blackhawks took the Stanley Cup.

As the distance closed between us, he lost momentum and slowly collapsed onto the sidewalk about fifteen feet in front of me.

What the fuck? I thought and went up to him. He lay inert with his face on the cement as a puddle slowly spread from the bottle he had been carrying in a brown paper sack.

"Hey, partner, what do you need?" I said and walked around him. To my surprise, it was Queenie. Here on his home turf. He was face down, so no danger of his airway clogging.

"Hey Queenie," I shouted, "shall I call 911? C'mon, man. Talk to me."

He moaned and moved his arms ineffectually, remaining in the same position.

"Look, man, I can't leave you here like this. I'm going to call 911."

He muttered something unintelligible but still didn't budge.

I pulled out my phone and called in with a request for help for someone passed out on the sidewalk on the south side of West Madison between Peoria and Green. "His face is bleeding," I told them. They asked me to wait and promised to send an ambulance.

Meanwhile, Queenie managed to lift his head and retch whatever his stomach held onto the sidewalk along with enough bright red blood to scare me.

Christ, I thought. Here I gave him money to do this to himself. "Hang on OK? And we'll get you some help. Just lie there and take it easy."

His dull, bloodshot eyes looked at me but showed no sign of recognition.

Two more convulsions of retching followed while we waited. About ten minutes later, a police ambulance reached us and pulled over.

I told the EMTs what I knew, which wasn't more than they could already see, and thanked them for coming so quickly.

They packed Queenie onto a stretcher, connected an IV drip, and loaded him on board.

I watched them roll away and pulled out my cell phone to ring Ian.

"Look, old friend," I said, "Sorry I'm late, but I just spent half an hour getting an ambulance for somebody whose ulcer blew up. Lucky thing it happened in public," I said, "or he might have painted his pillow and never woken up."

"You're usually on time, but I knew you'd have a good story. You do get into the oddest run-ins. Are you part Irish?"

"I think spending time with you is rubbing off on me," I said and hurried the last few blocks. "Order me up a pint of the beer-of-the-month, and I'll be there before it hits the counter."

Ian was already on his second round, a domestic, by the time I arrived. He said, "We don't have ales like this at our place across town. In fact, you can't even come close in Dublin."

"I promise not to breathe a word to anyone," I said.

"That must be the part of you that is not Irish, or it would be all over town and turned into a legend within the week."

How wonderful the world is, I thought: here is an Irishman raving about an American craft beer and beer snobs I know won't settle for less than Guinness in the few bars where they swear it's handled properly.

"OK, then, let's get down to it. I spill the beans about the women I meet, but I always come away without knowing much about Margaret. A woman who looks like she must have a lot of experience to draw upon."

"Well, I know a good thing when I come across it, and I don't like to throw things out of kilter."

I liked to believe that Ian's choice of me as a friend meant the same thing. I know he wanted to meet here to relax and drink, away from the Celtic Isle. "I can't breathe deep there," he said, "and I'm always on—people wanting an understanding ear with a fresh Irish proverb thrown in. Here, no one knows what I do, and I can simply sit and sip my ale."

After a few minutes, he said, "Well I guess I do owe you—I could recite the names of your women from the last four months."

"You think I tell you everything?" I jested.

After a questioning look, he said, "Well, Margaret is someone special."

"How did you meet?"

"She came in with an older guy who could have been her father. Really distinguished looking. Everything he had was diamond-studded. Frankly, he seemed a little uncomfortable. She had been in a time or two before with one or two women and, of course, I noticed her."

"Say no more."

"That evening, they sat at the bar, and the guy had trouble finding something he wanted to drink—kept changing his mind. Finally, he ordered a dry martini on the rocks. While all of this was going on, she began asking me about what we had on tap and seemed to know her ales. I always appreciate that. I asked her if she had been to Dublin for field study; she surprised me and said, 'not only Dublin, but Galway, Cork, even Belfast'. Jeezus, do you know I haven't even been all over Ireland."

"How did that play with Mr. Undecided? Did he like his martini?"

"Hell, no. He spat it out and declared it was the worst thing he ever had served up under that name."

"Figures. You should have used a diamond-studded shaker and glass."

"I'm glad it happened. Margaret looked daggers at him and when he said, 'Let's go, I know somewhere you can get a good drink', she said, 'Charles, I think you will have to go alone. I am staying right here. I have no complaints'."

"He stared at her and just snorted; then he collected his things and walked."

"Is that how it started? I mean, did you two get something going that night?"

"Oh, come now, you won't hear the tale you're after from me—whether it's true or not. She apologized for Charles and told me, 'she just liked hearing me talk.'"

"Tell me Ian, do Irish women love hearing an American accent from men? If not, I think I'll take it up with the UN."

He smiled. "I can't say for sure. I think you best go back and do more field work."

My turn to smile. "Where should I start? Got any insider tips for me? How about your father? Why did he marry your mom when he was studying here?"

"She was a painter. She had sandy hair and freckles, and he hadn't been back to Ireland for quite a while. She even had an Irish name. She always told me she loved his Irish accent and his ability to spin a yarn."

"What kind of work did he do?"

"He's a computer programmer. He caught the wave in the Irish economy and went back and stayed. Mom was with us until I was ten."

"What do you mean?" I asked, realizing that death or divorce basically added up to the same thing for a child.

His voice took on a darker tone when he said, "She died of a heart attack. Right there in the kitchen."

"Oh, Jesus."

"She sent me to the store for parsnips and cream and, when I got back, there she was."

"Crap," I said.

"Well, we both took it really hard. Dad didn't go to work after that and stayed full drunk for the month."

"I stayed home to keep an eye on him. Together we got through it somehow."

I think now I had some inkling about Margaret's appeal for Ian as a way to fill a gap in his early years. I also understood why he hadn't brought it up before.

"Ever think of returning to Ireland?" I asked.

"It could come to that. My dad married a spirited, younger Irish woman who is causing him grief. Sometimes, I think about what it would be like to open a pub with him."

To change the subject, I asked, "What kind of work does Margaret do to be able to afford you?"

He smiled. "She's a head hunter. Works for a large search firm. Says it's all pretty high pressure, and what she likes about us is being able to completely unwind."

I bet that part was good but didn't pursue it. "You do have the luck of the Irish. Just standing there doing your job and in walks this fabulous woman and carries you away—like a lady Viking."

"Funny you should mention that. She's Danish. That is, her parents were. She was born over here, like me. When they worked in the States. They've long since returned to Copenhagen."

He returned his attention to his ale and said, "That pretty well sums it up, my friend. Now what mischief have you been up to? The last I know was Dracula rushing off to a damsel in distress—how did she react to the cape and fangs?"

I told him how the curtain had come down on my drama with Piper and that I had reclassified it as a farce.

A week later, I was walking south on Michigan Avenue to see an exhibit at the Art Institute and reached

Bennigan's Tavern at the corner of Adams. It had been closed for a while, and Beth had mentioned that it was open under new management.

Even though I had eaten already, I was curious enough to look in the window. What I saw stopped me short. Beth sat at a table just back from the window, leaning in close to a guy about her age. He wore casual business and I wondered if she was working.

I stepped out of the flow of foot traffic and stopped in a shadow where I could watch without being seen. She was laughing at something he just said, and I saw him smile appreciatively. They were having lunch and a beer.

I felt a stab of resentment about Mr. Smiley Face, like he was horning in on my turf. Was this my Henry? Should I just go in and chance to meet them, maybe ask to join them? Or was it something that would run its course—especially if I made a play to convert her from a roommate into something more important?

The regal lion sculptures over in front of the Art Institute looked across and I tried to draw courage from them. None came and a sinking feeling quashed any spark of initiative, so I abandoned my plan to visit the featured exhibit of World War One propaganda posters inside and headed west instead, to dodge my way back across town on sidewalks jammed with the noon lunch crowd.

By the time Beth got in, I was feeling resigned to having to make way for her Henry sooner rather than later. We had planned to cook together, but I didn't think I had it in me.

At six-thirty she hollered from the kitchen, "Hey Josh, did you forget? Tonight's our night. Get in here."

We had planned *Kartoffelpuffer mit Apfelmus* and *Rosenkohl mit Speck*, German dishes I had bragged about so long, she made me promise to show her how I did it. I pulled myself together and moved slowly into the kitchen. "I am not my best tonight," I said.

"Oh, but you promised," she said and pouted. "I can't believe I'm going to die without tasting your…whatever they were …potato pancakes and Brussel sprouts with bacon."

"The way I feel, they would probably kill you too."

"Tell me what's wrong then," she said, sounding more sympathetic.

"Uh, I don't know. It's just that I had a premonition today, that my future or maybe our future wasn't so bright."

She did a double take and said, "That's weird. What did you do, get your palm read?"

"To be honest, I happened to pass the Bennigan's that reopened and saw you having lunch with someone who looked like Henry."

"Like Henry! That's crazy. He doesn't look anything like Henry."

"OK, but that's the association that stuck in my mind."

"Why should it bum you out if I have lunch with my cousin Jared? He was in town and called me to have lunch."

It was my turn to do a double take, and a wave of relief flushed away my doldrums. It must have been written all over my face.

She said, "So you thought you were going to get the shaft without an elevator, huh? Look Josh, I do not do such things with my cousin. Are you afraid of getting turned out, or do you really care about—I mean like living here, with me?"

"It's just that there have been some moments when I felt like you cared about me, and they just passed by and nothing came of it," I said.

She shifted uncomfortably and took a deep breath. "Fair enough. It's true. I have thought that we were on the edge of something more than roommates ... but I got scared."

"Of what?"

"That going there could make it impossible to go back to where we were if it didn't work. What's more, I already told you. I got my fill of rejection in college."

I leaned forward and took her hand in mine. She left her hand there for a moment until tears came and tried to pull it away. But I held on and said, "Oh, no you don't."

"Thanks," she said. "That helps."

After dinner, we went to a movie and bought popcorn to share. The next morning, she walked me to the Amtrak train for Columbus before she headed to Wisconsin for Thanksgiving with her family.

I phoned Amy from the train when they announced how close we were to arriving in Columbus and she was parked outside waiting.

She had both Priscilla, her ten year old, and Peggy, her eight year old, in the middle seat of the SUV. I waved when I saw them and climbed in the front next to Amy.

"Well, brother, it's about time you came for a visit."

"Hi girls, Holy Smokes, you have grown! Hi Amy," I said. "It's great to see you again. Thanks for insisting."

"Well, since Mom found out she had breast cancer last spring, it felt like circle-the-wagons time."

"You're kidding," I said. "No one told me."

"We wrote you and the letter came back. I tried to call, but the phone was disconnected. It wasn't until you sent the postcard of the Chicago skyline that we knew where you had gone."

"I guess I haven't been very good about keeping up," I admitted.

We drove west and south to their suburb. She said, "You take after Dad. We are lucky to hear from him around Christmas. It's been three years since he went to Brazil, and he hasn't come back."

"Has it been that long? Any idea how he's doing down there?"

"Not really. His news is pretty sketchy. He's still doing the same work and likes it. Expects to stay a while."

Turning to the girls behind me, who had their noses buried in books, I said, "He's missing out on some good times with these young ladies. Whatcha reading?"

"Uh, I'm reading *The Little Polar Bear*," said the younger one.

"And I'm reading *The Magician's Elephant*," her sister said.

"I read a lot, too," Amy said. "Bernie travels a lot and, when I'm busy running the girls around, they are busy reading too."

"Any game players in the family?" I asked. "I remember you and I used to have marathon Monopoly bouts." I also remembered that Travis could spoil any game in five minutes with arguing and cheating and we never let him play with us—leaving us feeling both guilty and glad.

"I liked Sorry," Amy said, "because it always made you so mad when I sent you back to start over."

"You worked at getting my goat, didn't you? Well, it toughened me up. I can absorb the worst that women dish out now."

"We'll go into that later," she said.

"Well, I don't physically travel like Bernie," I said, "but I do get around a lot virtually. Jobs from all over the world." I thought of my encounter with Julia Bärlund but imagined that, under "love-life," Amy was talking about sustained contact with a single female that led to matrimony. That had been her experience at Ohio State where she dated Bernie for three years and then married upon graduation.

By this time we had pulled into the driveway and the girls headed in through the garage with their books. I called after them: "Hope you have bookmarks because Uncle Josh is going to give you a workout playing all the games your mom and I used to play. Maybe some sports while we're at it."

"OK," they said and scampered into the house.

To Amy, I said, "Remember, your bachelor brother knows some tricks in the kitchen, so I hope you take advantage of that in getting dinner put together for tomorrow."

"Awesome. Bernie is allergic to housework. He's in watching a football game. But he does know where the beer is and knows enough to share."

I set my small suitcase down in the office where the sofa bed was readied for me and went into the media room. Bernie was stretched out on a leather lounger that faced a TV bigger than anything I had been near outside of a sports bar.

"Bernie," I said, "how have you been?"

"Hi, Josh. On the road too damned much. I hope someone writes a biography of my family, so I can read it when I retire and find out everything I missed. How's life in the big city?"

"Stimulating. Now I live up on the 26th floor of an apartment tower, but I miss things down on the ground in my old neighborhood."

"I know what you mean. Familiar faces go a long ways toward making you feel at home. That's one reason I'm not anxious to run around when I get home—which of course is what Amy's ready for after being stuck in the house."

After the girls had honored me by allowing me to read that evening's chapter from their bed-time story and gone up to their room, the three of us sat around the kitchen table.

"So, how's the love life, Josh?" Amy asked. "You really are good with kids, you know."

I wondered if I had what it took to be a sustainable father—at least through their high school years. "Oh, I don't do too badly," I said. "Happy to report that there are no kids yet. I never have been the life of the party. But I do meet, or better said, see women that interest me. Sometimes we go out a few times, but nothing has really come of it."

"We can't all be lucky the first time, old man," Bernie said. "I walked into biology and sat down next to Amy and that was that."

Amy revised that version a bit but let the essentials stand.

"I did meet someone last spring and we have spent a lot of time together. In fact we moved in together— but as roommates. She has her life and I have mine."

"Nothing else there?" Amy asked.

"Sometimes I think there might be, but then it's gone again."

"Why not make a play for her," Bernie said, "and get it over with."

"That's just it. We have a six-month sublet together and sharing the rent works. I'm not anxious to upset the applecart."

"Six months isn't forever. Why not roll the dice before you renew and while you still have a chance to get out?"

"I guess, like most of the rest of the world, I'm afraid of rejection too."

The next day was a taste of family life I had never known as a child. Bernie drove over to get our mom, and we spent the day with only a few hectic moments—mostly relaxing with board games as family members moved in and out when they left to help get the meal put together—then happy times around the table with lots of laughter. I looked over at Mom and realized how different things had been for us back when we were still a family, wary of the next outburst.

I mentioned this to Amy that evening when we had a few minutes and she agreed. Life with Bernie was much more satisfying than the version she remembered seeing with Mom and Dad. We both knew what the difference was but still couldn't talk about it. Whiskey had damaged us all.

The next morning, Bernie invited me to stay on and go with them to his sister's for another round of turkey.

"I hate to be a drag," I said, "and thanks for the invitation, but I'm afraid I can't fit another feast day in and still make my deadline Monday morning."

"No problem," Bernie said. "It's going to get pretty wild. My other sister and her three kids are coming too and we almost have to eat in shifts."

"Actually, that sounds like a lot of fun. Maybe I'll get another chance another year. Please offer my apologies to your sister."

"You bet. Well, we're going to pull out of here in a half an hour."

"I'll get my bag. It's been great to reconnect with family."

"My feeling too," he said and headed out to the garage.

Just then, Mom came down the stairs. We had eaten a light breakfast and reminisced about some of the quirky turkey days we recalled from earlier. Amy remembered the one where the stuffing caught fire.

Mom recalled the three years in a row when the pop-up timer popped too early, delaying dinner by at least an hour to give it more oven time.

But I remembered the next year, and the last time Dad was home for a family Thanksgiving. To show he could get more involved with the family, he thought he would do something special. He had already had three whiskeys when he settled on smoking the turkey. He thought all was well when he saw smoke coming out of the barbeque and sat back down with glass in hand. But when he checked, the outer half inch or so was incinerated. He swore me to secrecy and carved off the blackened layer. The only way to camouflage the damage was drenching the turkey in barbeque sauce to take the edge off the charred taste. If anyone noticed, they didn't say so and any hopes for something different in the family went up in smoke as well.

The next year they separated, and Mom went to her brother's on Thanksgiving after that. I phoned her every few months and we always remembered each other's birthday.

I had a moment together with Mom in the garage, before Amy carried out the last of the things to take to the in-laws.

"Josh," Mom said, "are you alright up there in the city?"

"I'm fine Mom, I have friends," I said, stretching the truth.

"I worry about you without a real job. I mean just sitting in your apartment all day by yourself."

I had had similar thoughts myself, but now wasn't the time to admit it. Instead, I said, "Really, Mom, I'm fine. I like what I do. I'm good at it. And," exaggerating a bit, "while it's not great, it's a living."

"OK, honey. Don't think I don't appreciate the phone calls and birthday cards. And I am grateful that your father supports me, even though we live apart. Some women aren't that lucky with their men folk."

It was late Saturday afternoon when I got back to a Chicago now festooned in Christmas décor. Once back in our apartment, things seemed unusually quiet after the bustle at Amy and Bernie's. Beth wasn't due back until Sunday afternoon, and I realized how incomplete things seemed without her.

I had stretched out on my bed for a nap and woke when she came in half an hour later. My door was open and, when she paused, I said, "Welcome home."

"Didn't mean to wake you. When did you get back?"

"Yesterday. Got any war stories to tell?"

"A few. How about you?" she asked.

"Yeah, I don't think you've heard them all. Could you use a cup of tea?"

"That just might save my life," she said. "Let me dump my stuff and pee, and I'll join you."

We sat quietly at the kitchen table over tea, content to listen to the muffled sound of police or ambulance sirens rolling by far below. I broke the silence. "It's nice to have some company," I said.

"Yeah, I know what you mean," she said. "Freaky. Sitting here like old married folks."

"Yeah, it is."

"It's good to be back. My sis wore me out," she said.

"Tell me about it."

"Well, turkey day was nice and very tasty. Everyone was on good behavior, and my dad was happy to watch pro football on TV in the background while the women folk gabbed. Then my parents went home, and we crashed early. We cleaned the place up Friday morning. Then, Franny insisted I see the Milwaukee Art Museum so we went downtown and had dinner. It really is cool, lit up at night. It's their bean!"

"Tell me how long they've been together—Franny and Suzy?"

"Oh, about four years now. They met in New Buffalo when Suzy was driving through on her way back from a weekend in Traverse City, Michigan."

"Cool," I said. "So meeting the right one can be that easy."

"Yeah, isn't it something? Suzy stopped for lunch at the Stray Dog Café and Franny waited on her."

"What do you think? Are they a good match?"

"I think so. Four years is pretty good today. And they like the same things. They took me clubbing after dinner."

"How was that?"

"My ears are still ringing, and I've never been so hung over. My legs hurt from dancing."

"Bump into anyone interesting?" I asked, emphasizing the first word.

"Lots of people. Butt bumps, not head bumps. Much nicer," she smiled. "How were things in Columbus?"

"It was good to reconnect. Especially to see my nieces. They are eight and ten, and I taught them some nasty tricks at Monopoly."

"I see I don't know you at all. I'll bet you are funny when you try to be nasty," she said.

It felt good to talk like this, comfortable, with nothing to prove. Since an early winter storm was forecast for the following week, it seemed natural to make plans to ride out to a forest preserve with Corinne for some cross-country skiing.

By the time I went up to Evanston Saturday morning to check out a book at the University Library, arctic air had moved across Chicago. At the Davis Street El station, the pigeons were nestling under the heat lamps and occupying a sizable area which left paying customers to stand at the fringes, careful not to step on their fellow travelers. Like the commuters, the ruffled birds remained immobile and spaced to avoid squabbles.

As I braced against the wind and walked east towards campus, a stooped figure a half a block ahead of me in black pants and a splotched green hoodie moved unevenly. Something about him looked familiar and filled me with a mixture of dread and anticipation. He leaned against buildings as he lurched along the sidewalk, sometimes disappearing momentarily into doorways. At Einstein's bagel shop he collapsed onto a metal chair at an outdoor table and peered around. I crossed Sherman Avenue but paused at the traffic island, afraid of the truth. He cocked his head and turned in my direction as he repeatedly muttered something in a gravelly voice, his hands flapping at the wrist in inchoate gestures. Then, eyes alternately bemused and wild, he struggled to light a cigarette as his shaggy beard caught the wind and this gesture, which I had watched Travis execute thousands of times, betrayed his identity—he was not my brother. Shaken, I continued on to get my book.

When I returned to take the El back to Chicago and prepared to board, a young Black woman looking back at the intrepid pigeons whose ranks had swelled collided with me and we agreed on how well fed they looked.

"Just like the panhandlers," she said. "They show up like clockwork every day too."

I agreed, except I remembered I hadn't seen Queenie anywhere since the ambulance took him away.

"Don't get me wrong," she said. "I like animals. I'm a student and on my way to Lincoln Park Zoo to observe primates." We sat together and a gaggle of sorority girls on their way to the Northwestern Wildcat-University of Illinois football game at Wrigley Field followed us aboard. Their loud chatter filled the car and she said, "It's weird seeing them here. I just served them at Einstein Bagels near campus."

She described how she had started working for Einstein's in Hyde Park where she had grown up and now was at the store in Evanston where she was also a student.

I liked her spirit—something I could identify with. If she had been a few years older, like five or ten, I might have made a move on her but noticed that getting closer to Beth also dampened the sense of urgency I had been feeling to connect.

The coed hilarity grew in volume as we rolled along towards Wrigley Field. Just as we pulled into the Addison Street station at the ballpark, a girl with team mascot Willy the Wildcat's face perched atop her parka hood bent down with a shriek of laughter and Willy's leering face bid us farewell before they rose and jostled to leave the train and swell the throng of football fans.

That afternoon, Beth texted to suggest we meet at Gino's East after work. I was glad to accept. I had decided to suggest something like that myself. The walk north across the river into a brisk wind gave me time to think things over and the all-pervasive festive Christmas décor in the city was lost on me. What had guided my eye, time and again, was the phantasm about how exciting a woman who wore fishnet stockings or was striving for the limelight must be. Time and again, women with these traits found me lacking something essential. Or were they really like me and held back, playing it safe, then moved on when lightning didn't strike? In any case, it left item 4 on my list, *Find love*, wide open.

I had been roving around without a clear idea about what kind of person would best match my needs and had been so distracted that I overlooked what or who was right under my nose. In comparison to all the others, Beth was an island in the stream, safe and solid.

The result of Paula and now Piper marooning me was like the signal I recently got on my ever-slower computer to 'defragment hard disk' and reassemble all the components of the various files on my drive. Maybe my personal life would benefit from something similar, cut search time, speed up performance, and get me where I wanted to go.

I thought of this while I walked up Wells Street to meet Beth after she finished work. At Gino's East, I pushed through the door and stepped inside past the crazily decorated walls to find her.

"Hi, Josh. Over here," she called from a booth.

I waved and maneuvered between the tables to slide in opposite her.

"Well, here we are again," she said. "First Rosebud and now Gino's. We ought to start a food blog or something."

"Yeah, I'm glad you suggested this. I was about to ask you out. I hadn't gotten around to deep dish here yet."

We ordered a small deep dish pizza to share and had plenty of time to examine the goofy graffiti near our booth until the order came. Then I asked her about things at work. She told me that since she had gotten a new boss, she liked going to work in the morning. I had noticed that she seemed to get home later the last couple of months. Then she asked me how my work was coming and I filled her in on some of the jobs I had gotten out and reassured her I was still able to make the rent for now.

When our order came, I couldn't believe how flaky the crust was with the cheese and sauce top side, and we had no trouble putting it away.

"Wow," I said. "Great idea to come here."

She glanced away, then quickly met my eyes and said, "Somehow Chicago food seemed right for this talk."

"That sounds serious," I said. The status of our lease was still unsettled, but I hadn't figured that it would be tonight.

"Yeah," she said, "I need to tell you something."

"Oh, oh," I said.

"Well, better to be clear about where we stand than to let things drift."

"Ok," I said. "Let's get clear."

"Since our lease is up in three weeks, we need to take action—either renew or change the terms. Right?"

"Yup."

"OK. We agreed to give this arrangement six months and see where we came out."

"Right."

"Well, I'm glad we did this. It really helped me out and gave me some place to go. I couldn't have lived through another month of commuting."

I waited for more.

"You know you once said this wasn't really a sustainable option for you, money-wise? Well, I have to respect that. And I've been seeing someone I met at a training event in the summer, and it looks like we'll be taking a lease in the Towers together."

This left me with a bigger lump than the Chicago-style pie we had devoured. It was a struggle, but I had to accept it since I hadn't followed Ian and Bernie's advice when I had the chance.

"I know this may sound lame, Josh, but since we are friends, I'd really still like to go on the ski outing we had planned."

I figured it was better to face reality, so I nodded, and said, "Yeah. We really should. I'd like that."

The next day a winter storm rolled in with a cold snap that kept the city white into the weekend. From on high it was a calendar picture. Down below, the wind whipped snow in your face no matter which direction you walked making it more than invigorating.

Saturday morning added an additional snowfall of two inches. Corinne had a bad cold and begged off, but she lent us her car and we drove to the forest preserve near Dam 1 along the Des Plaines River. The leaden, gray sky held more snow, but for now the still, clear, air energized us as we stretched and reached for skis and boots.

I followed Beth across the meadow bordering the parking lot as she broke fresh tracks in the white expanse. Nothing but the swish, swish of skis thrusting through snow showing surface texture from wind the previous day could be heard.

Concentrating on balance and testing how far the remaining wax from last year allowed me to glide, I followed her red parka as it rose and fell rhythmically until she stopped at the woods and turned to wait.

I pulled up next to her and said, "You look like the real thing on skis. It must be the German stock from Wisconsin."

She smiled, releasing a plume of condensate into the still air.

"When was the last time you were out?" I asked.

"Cross-country you mean?"

"Yeah. I missed out altogether last winter. I was too lazy to go when I had the chance and then the weather shifted and it was too late. That happened to me during my year in Berlin, too."

"Well, I did manage to get out along the lakefront last winter a few times with Corinne, but nothing like her. She is really a fanatic."

"Good to know people like that. It keeps you going."

We moved on under the leaden sky. For the next hour, a monochrome scene of dark trunks against white snow unfolded before us as we skirted a black creek languidly flowing through the sparse woods. Wisps of snow wafted down from the trees when the air moved in the tree tops. It felt right to be here together, and I fought to keep the sense of finality at bay.

The sun had set and we were chilled to the bone by the time we got back to our place. Beth stopped at the kitchen and pulled out packets of mulled-wine spices her sister had given her at Thanksgiving. I took over and added them to a cheap bottle of red wine to simmer on the stove while she claimed the first shower.

I was stiff and anxious for my turn. When I stepped into the hall in my briefs to check on her progress, I froze. She had left her bedroom door partly open, and I caught sight of her stepping out of the shower with a towel around her head. She bent forward as she fluffed her long red tresses dry and then dropped the towel to the floor and they caught the light from above the mirror. Turning to examine herself, she began to dry her breasts and stomach with another towel, unaware of the audience in the darkened hallway.

I felt a tingling in nether regions and, despite the warmth spreading from my groin, began to shiver. I stepped back into my room and hollered, "Hey, Beth, let me know when the coast is clear. I'm freezing out here."

She called, "OK, just a sec. I'll be right out," and I heard her door shut.

Then I heard the door open again and looked out as she came down the hall in her fuzzy blue robe with her hair gathered in a matching blue tie. "That mulled wine smells great," she said.

"Could you check on it, please?" I asked. "I'm going to jump in the shower. I'll be right out. Oh, and let's turn up the heat."

Twelve minutes later, we sat on the couch sipping mugs of steaming mulled wine and munching pretzels with WXRT on the radio. The patterns of city lights stretching away into the winter night were generously sprinkled with reds and greens to announce the holidays.

I didn't have a robe but had gotten comfortable in cotton workout trousers and zipped into a hooded cotton top.

"Wow," I said, "that was a workout out today. I'm glad we went. But this is the real payoff."

We talked about memories of childhood and winter, recalling photos showing us on snowy afternoons with rosy cheeks and snow-clogged clothing.

Gluehwein, as it is known in Germany, best describes the effect of mulled wine on an empty stomach. After a third cup, we both lay back against the leather sofa, innards aglow, and eyes closed. When I opened mine, I noticed that Beth's robe gaped to reveal a blue lace bra I had never seen before. Once again, I felt a surge below and said to her, "It's really special to be here like this. Together. Especially since our time is ending."

She stirred and reached over with a warm hand. "I know," she said. I squeezed it and bumped over next to her.

When she didn't pull back or let go of my hand, I gently kissed her and felt the same feelings I had told Ian of from my dream of Thea.

But this time, Italian beef didn't play a role and it was not a dream. After hesitating, Beth returned my kiss with lips that were soft and yielding. We continued to explore each other's mouths for several minutes before I took her flushed face in my hands and felt the heat in her cheeks. When I started to draw back, she put her arms around my neck and pulled me against her. I obliged and slowly began to trace her contours through her robe, alert to signals that I should stop. None came and I continued. She pushed her hands up under my sweatshirt and caressed my chest. We continued holding and caressing each other with no further purpose than for warmth and pleasure.

After a time, the Gluehwein began to wear off, and she stirred and looked over from a nest of red hair. "Josh, I really wasn't expecting this. But I have no regrets."

"Nor was I," I said. "It was better that way."

I was hoping to escape holiday cheer the next night at the Beer Bistro when I met Ian for our session, but the bar keepers and servers wore Santa hats. Thankfully, we were spared the canned carols because the Hawks were squaring off against the St Louis Blues on the corner flat screen at the other end of the bar.

By nine-thirty the place had begun to fill up. This time he was late. I saw him in the mirror as he pushed through the door and waved and came down the bar to join me.

"How are you," I asked.

"I've seen better times," he admitted as he eased onto a stool.

Sensing a change in mood in my even-tempered friend, I paused before asking him, "What will it be tonight?"

"I think I'll have a Guinness," he said, which to me indicated he was reaching for comfort and reassurance.

"Well, it sounds like you may have some stories to tell. Do I get a rest?"

"I suppose so. You've always been straight up with me about your woes."

"So tell me."

"I've noticed that things are changing with Margaret."

"Is it something you see or something she says?" I asked.

"It's just that, what we do in bed no longer seems to be enough. I give it my best, but she seems restless."

"You once told me, 'there's nothing for the dumb dog'. Have you asked her what the matter is?"

"That's just it. She won't come right out with it. Me, I think she's met someone. Sometimes she doesn't turn up when she says she will. And then, there's been someone new calling, that she spends a lot of time talking to."

"What are you going to do?"

"'A windy day is not the day to be fixing your thatch'. I suppose I'll just wait and see. It's been eight months, since I moved in with her, and I never believed it was forever."

"You once told me, 'blow not on dead embers'."

"I'm not sure I'm ready for it to be over," he said. "I really like her."

I understood how he would miss those blue eyes. "Maybe we should just take a good plunge in the suds tonight and think of other things," I suggested.

"Do you have anything to tell me," he asked.

"I do," I said. "Beth tells me she has found her Henry."

"Oh my God. That takes the biscuit."

"Exactly. Just when I had started to see her with other eyes, she turns away and wants to go separate ways."

"Where would you live? Aren't you both on the lease?"

"Yeah, we both are. But our six months are up in two weeks. That's when we reshuffle the deck ... and I'm afraid I get dealt out of the next hand."

"That is serious, mate."

"Exactly. But hearing what you're telling me tonight sets me to thinking."

"What then?"

"Perhaps we belong together. Two mates can stand up to a stronger wind than a lonesome bugger on his own," I improvised.

"Not bad. That definitely calls for another round," he said but refrained from suggesting Car Bombs.

When the second round began to take effect, I said, "Well, that's not all I have to say: After I learned of my fate, I sat in my cell three days waiting for work to come in and was going stir crazy, so I headed over to cruise the Barnes & Noble Book Store to find something to read. Or, if I really got lucky, strike up a conversation with an interesting woman ... after all, the coffee bar is built-in so no need to go anywhere else to get down with someone."

"Any luck?"

"Promise not to laugh?"

"No."

"Well, I start browsing and checking out the women and in the background, I hear this folk-rock-jazz music and start to groove to the music. I looked around to see who else is moving and guess what?

"What?"

"Well, I see this really appealing woman just down the aisle from me starting to groove too. And I discover she is moving in synch with me. So, to be sure before making a move, I change my pattern from tapping my foot to nodding my head up and down and what do you think I see out of the corner of my eye?"

"I give up."

"Well she stops tapping her foot too and starts nodding her head—but from side to side. So I knew the score right away and left, feeling like I really had gained ground."

"How so?"

"Well, this new stealth method for detecting prospects saved me from a crash—after the experience with Beth, I don't relish more rejection. After all, you taught me that 'a good retreat is better than a bad stand'."

Ian laughed. He couldn't decide whether I was serious or not. And I didn't volunteer.

Discussion Questions For
Finding the Way Home

How do you think the title *Finding the Way Home* fits these stories?

Which of the stories appealed to you most? Why—was it a place you know or would like to visit, a character or setting, or the style of writing?

Which character appealed to you the most? The least? Have you known someone like one of the characters?

Should all stories end "happily" (is life like that?) or leave you wondering?

Was there a time in your life any of these stories brought to mind?

Have you found the references to each of the first eight stories in the final story, *Dumpster Days*?

How do you interpret the title *Dumpster Days*?

Your comments can be mailed to:
williamgeuss@gmail.com

CPSIA information can be obtained at www.ICGtesting.com
Printed in the USA
LVOW11s2210110416

483153LV00001B/16/P